Girls Before Swine

Joe Gaspe Fights Human Trafficking

Richard A. Minich

ISBN: 9780975872833
Library of Congress Control Number: 2007904241

All Esox Publications
P.O. Box 493
East Aurora, NY 14052
www.allesoxpublications.com

Artwork by:
Theresa Meegan – cover
Patricia A. Lanigan Eberle – portraiture
Theresa Meegan – pen and ink drawings and oyarons

Book Design by Janice Phelps Williams

To John Henning
Fisherman, Businessman, Quiet Man,

Rest in Peace

Acknowledgments

Thanks once again to my book designer Janice Phelps Williams. Her great work on design and editing gives me no need to look elsewhere for help. Thanks also to Mark V. Williams for his editorial input. Thanks to artists Pat Eberle, for her portraiture, and Theresa Meegan, for the cover, oyarons, and pen and ink drawings, who does her work despite my conspicuous meddling.

I received invaluable assistance from critical readers; Cheryl Morrisey, a hard worker who looks to help me and gets little reward, Rick Jackson, who represents my target audience and is always first to respond with helpful suggestions, and Margaret Rose, who keeps my sense of humor and pacing in line. I hope they had fun doing the reading.

Additional advice, and encouragement; including tips about fighting and actual fights, were provided by pre-readers, Chris Zeth and Cheryl Mediak. Thanks.

Ideas were extrapolated from, Tales of Treu as told by Mr. Toothy, and other hi-jinks from his checkered past, thanks to Jim Reynolds.

Thanks to my wife, Joan, and two children, Jackson and Holly, for support through some difficulties that occurred during the production of this novel.

Give not that which is holy unto the dogs,
neither cast ye pearls before swine,
lest they trample them under their feet,
and turn again and rend you.
Matthew 7:6

Joe Gaspe

Moxes X Snow

Marv Ankara

Radleigh Loonch

Cast of Characters

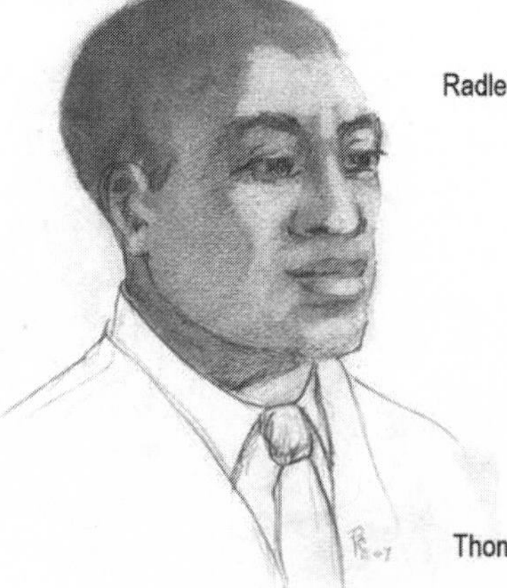

Thomas Andre

Preface

In *Fireships & Brimstone* we learned...

Assistant Special Agent in Charge Thomas Andre was a very important man in the FBI office in Pantherville. Everybody knew that. Few knew however, about his equally important work in the Special Projects Group (SPG) at the Department of Homeland Security. Circumventing the ultra jumbo meta-bureaucracy that was Homeland Security, the SPG carried out extra-legal intelligence gathering, connected the dots without absolute confirmation, leaped to timely conclusions, and did occasional wet work, all in the interest of protecting the country from real and imminent threats.

When one of Andre's assets, Derrick Chang, turned up murdered on the Oil Seep Indian Reservation, he needed to find the killer and replace his operative. Joe Gaspe, a musky fisherman with a sketchy background, became the new asset to fulfill both those needs.

Under Andre's direction, Joe formed an eclectic network of observers on the North Coast of the USA that included fishermen, charter captains, business people, and others who could feed him timely information about what was happening on and off the waterfront. An intern driver assigned by Andre, Radleigh Loonch, helped him. His regular fishing partner, Marv Ankara, and his super-capable Mohawk Indian cousin, Moses Snow, worked with him.

Together, using information garnered from Joe's network, and sparing Agent Andre the details, they foiled an attempt to blow-up the Friendship Bridge on a holiday weekend. A year later they were off to Ohio on a new adventure that would lead them on a raid and a running battle across four states.

Prologue
The Musky Straits

—November 26th—

The November wind howled across the Musky Straits with a cold-hearted fury that made the Pantherville region between New York and Ontario seem to be the coldest place on earth. The temperature was not all that low in the late fall, but a sustained thirty-mile-per-hour wind, with gusts to fifty gave one an all-over Popsicle headache. The warmth of body heat protected by layered clothing was whipped away by the rushing air. Joe Gaspe's exposed eyes and forehead screamed at him for mercy.

Joe and his partner Marv Ankara endured this weather because they knew that with the fading of the month of November their chances of catching a personal-best musky improved exponentially. Musky fishing is the coldest outdoor sport there is; colder than skiing or dog sledding where physical effort creates body heat; colder than ice fishing or duck hunting where the participant is sheltered from the wind. The only thing colder than riding around in an open boat in the winds of November for seven, eight, or ten hours is freezing to death, but no one has been able to prove that.

Joe and Marv had been trolling the area around Frog Creek debating with each other whether they should try running the gauntlet to the Upper Lake to continue their efforts. The area where the westerly winds roaring down the length of the lake were funneled into the Musky

Straits caused a wild, rough, dangerous cauldron of waves, wind, and combers known to locals as the gauntlet. This had to be traversed across the flow to reach the fish grounds of Pantherville Harbor. Geography worked against making the run. The wind had been blowing for three days. The waves in the Upper Lake, four- to six-footers, were choppy and confused. The wind gusts, up to fifty miles per hour, were scary. Small-craft warnings were out.

"The big fish are up in Pantherville Harbor, we've got to go," said Gaspe.

"Going over, we can use the wind at our back — coming back we'll be bucking both the rollers and the wind." Marv, unmarried and childless, was sometimes cautious on behalf of Joe who was married and had five daughters. They continued to troll with that unresolved issue sitting between them in the boat. The Boston Whaler had a windshield big enough to protect them both from direct-wind assault but they had no protection from the sides.

They had thought they were alone on the Straits when Marv stepped to the back of the boat to clear weeds from a tangled rod.

"Hey Joe! Look at this idiot."

Gaspe turned to see a boat, flying past out of Canada, with six people bundled up, some of whom were in life jackets, headed for the gauntlet.

"If they can do it, so can we. Bring in those lines." Joe throttled back to neutral. Marv at five foot ten and one hundred sixty pounds was more nimble than Joe who at six foot, two hundred and too many pounds could easily hold down his end of the seesaw. They each reeled in a musky-trolling rod and hooked up the lure. They positioned themselves behind the windshield and ramped up their speed, tucking into the wake left by the up-bound Coastliner. With every bit of winter clothing layered on and everything covered including his eyes and with a hood, ski cap, and a scarf wrapped around his head, Joe had never been colder. He could not imagine how those in the other boat stood it with no windscreen to break the freezing blast.

Joe's Whaler was gaining on the Coastliner when both boats passed Friendship Bridge and soon lost the protection provided by the shoulder of Canada. The wind screeched louder. The danger increased by an order of magnitude. In the Straits they opposed a current but, as the channel opened out into the lake, the combers started rolling in. Coming from the west, all the way down the length of the lake, those four- to six-foot waves pounded without end, and an occasional rogue wave came along that was eight- or ten- or twelve-feet high.

Joe, wearing sunglasses to protect his eyeballs from the wind, ripped them off when he saw what happened ahead of him. The pilot of the Coastliner had let his boat be broached-to by a wave. It took a thrusting hit from a harmonic double wave on the side. The boat, wallowing badly, lifted its side to the wind, was caught by a ferocious gust on her exposed bottom, and turned turtle. The passengers fell or slid to the downwind side and everyone was dumped into the Rainbow Channel.

"Jesus, Marv! They've been swamped! Call for help, then get the ring buoy, we've gotta save these people!" Joe speeded up toward those in the water. The water, warmer than the air, was dead-man cold at fifty degrees, and only some of the passengers had been wearing life jackets. Those ones had begun to float downstream, pushed by the current, and across the Straits, pushed by the waves breaking in from the lake. The ones without life vests were goners. Joe saw at once that he would have one pass to pick people up before the water got too shallow for him to maneuver in. He forgot the cold and zoomed his vision and thinking in on two people, in orange, clinging together.

"Coast Guard Pantherville, Coast Guard Pantherville, this is Dr. Dento (Marv identified the boat by its name and radio "handle") there is a boat overturned in the Rainbow Channel with six, repeat six, people in the water. We are moving to help. Request assistance!" Marv barked into the VHF on Channel Sixteen.

"Private vessel, Dr. Demo, please repeat."

Marv said it again exactly the same way. He was a good man in a crisis. He kept the main radio on Channel Sixteen to listen to the Coast Guard and turned the portable to Channel Nine where the musky fisherman would be listening.

Into the portable he said, "Any musky men near the head of the Rainbow Channel please assist. This is Dr. Dento attempting rescue of six people in the water. We cannot, repeat cannot, get them all in time. Anybody nearby?"

"Dento, quit breaking balls," Came one reply.

"This is no drill. People are gonna die out here!" Marv laid down the portable VHF radio and moved to the back corner with a rope and the ring buoy. He also had a boat hook at hand.

The Coast Guard in Pantherville Harbor acknowledged the emergency and stated that they had dispatched a boat. It would have to smash through the waves to come around the corner.

Joe slowed his motors and, judging the waves and current perfectly, sidled toward the two people, young women, clinging to each other in the water. He could see one other person floating and the overturned boat but saw no signs of the other three people. The other person floating was fifty yards away, attempting to swim, but weakening. Joe used his throttles, alternating between forward, neutral, and reverse to crab-walk the boat sideways right up to the two girls. Marv grabbed each of them by their lifejackets with the boat hook and pulled them to the gunwale. Both motors in neutral, Joe ran to the back and Marv and he hauled the women into the boat.

"Get them below and out of these clothes and wrapped in anything we have, blankets, rain suits, whatever." Joe returned to the throttles and looked up to see Johnny Lawrence, having come around the corner, bearing down on the remaining visible person.

"Johnny, this is Dento. You've got a bead on the one north of me. I'm going to check the boat." He maneuvered his craft in that direction.

"Coast Guard Pantherville, this is Dento, we have two people onboard from the water: we cannot bring them to you. It is too rough. Captain Johnny Lawrence is just now picking up a third person. All others are gone. Not visible at the scene. Please advise."

"Dr. Demo, this is Coast Guard Pantherville, our patrol craft is ten minutes from your position. Please wait for assistance."

"We have two women, very cold women, whom we are warming up as best we can. These girls are blue with cold. Cannot wait. We are next to the overturned vessel. It appears to have a dead guy tied to it. The other two passengers are gone."

"Dr. Demo, this is Coast Guard Pantherville, you are advised to hold your position."

Joe switched to Channel Nine, "Johnny, I see you've got another person. Can you warm him up?"

"Dento, this is a girl, she doesn't speak English and she needs to get out of the wind."

"Johnny, can you raft up with me and we'll get her in my cuddy?"

"Roger. My client will get her wrapped up while you and me bring our boats together and move her over."

Gaspe and Lawrence handled their boats better than they thought they could as they floated under the Friendship Bridge and got all three women into the Whaler's cuddy and bundled up all possible. Joe told the Coast Guard to dispatch ambulances to the Royal Marina gas dock, the closest place to take these women, and he and Johnny pegged their throttles for the seven-minute ride.

Marv came up from below as they turned toward the dock. "They are Russians, I think. They're going to be Okay, I rubbed them down with blankets, layered 'em with everything in the slop chest. They're huddled together for warmth right now. If I had to guess, I'd say they are strippers."

"Huh? How'd you figure that?"

"Well, no modesty about taking their clothes off, didn't care what I saw, tattooed, pierced, and shaved in all the right places."

"Here we are. Where's that ambulance?"

Chapter 1
Downtown Pantherville

—April 7th—

"You want me to what?" Joe Gaspe couldn't believe this assignment from his boss.

Thomas Andre, one of whose jobs is Special Projects for the Department of Homeland Security, touched the rim of his coffee cup with thumb and forefinger and traced the edge in a circle to the opposite side. They were sitting in one of the Greek restaurants where they conducted business. It was early spring and Joe, a carpenter by trade had been idle all winter, was eager for something to do. The noise of clashing crockery, yelling cooks and waitresses, and chattering customers was adequate cover for their confidential conversations. "It will be hard to explain if the newspapers ever get word of this, but it comes directly from the young women you rescued from the Rainbow Channel in November. As your friend, Marv surmised— "

"Partner," Joe corrected.

"As Marv surmised, the women were Russian immigrants, they were strippers, and they were being illegally transported into the United States from Ontario. There is a string of gentleman's clubs situated near airports in North America where we suspect the trafficking of human sex slaves is going on. Those women you rescued, though fearful of reprisals and addicted to powerful drugs — a combination of drugs we were previously not even aware existed — told us that the Sweet Cherries chain of clubs is operated by a Russian entrepreneur named Jimmy Maxwell. Many, but not all, of the young women are lured out of poverty in Russia with tales of a better life and subsequently kept in these clubs. We need you to confirm some of this information in Toronto, Ottawa, and Montreal."

"You want me to go to titty bars and find out what, exactly?"

"These women, most of whom will speak little English, will be dancers and we suspect prostitutes, and, if those you rescued were truthful, they will be branded. The area branded will be the web on the back of each girl's hand between thumb and forefinger. The brand will be a red star. You and your interns will confirm this information. Since this is Canada, I cannot send an official operative. But I can send you."

"I don't think Rad's gonna like this assignment." Joe spoke of Radleigh Loonch, a young woman who was his driver/intern/assistant with whom he'd worked during the time when he had been ineligible for a state driver's license.

"Ms. Loonch will not go with you. She will be undergoing special intensive training in Virginia during this period of time."

"Who's the intern?"

"We've assigned Gerhard Blog and Kyle Buckhalter to accompany you. You've worked with them previously. They are old enough to legally enter such establishments in Canada and their college terms have entered a final phase where internships count as course work."

"Those two? Yikes! I hope we don't have to do anything dangerous or subtle."

"If subtlety were required would you have been assigned?"

Joe, half Mohawk and half wild Irishman, had long ago gotten over the incongruity of the FBI Agent, superbly dressed and impeccable, meeting with a guy who looked like him. Joe wore a flannel shirt worn at the elbows, jeans, and his signature work boots. He looked as if he had combed his hair with an eggbeater.

He wasn't intimidated.

"Geez boss, that's an unprovoked shot across my bow."

"You will drive to the Toronto airport. Visit the club there. Find out if the dancers fit the pattern. Next day, drive to Ottawa. Visit the club. Determine the pattern. Next day, drive to Montreal."

"I get it. I get it. What about expenses?"

"Reasonable expenses have been estimated. Auto expenses, accommodations, and money enough to use in uncovering the information we need. No extraordinary expenses will be covered, if you take my meaning." Agent Andre handed Joe an envelope of Canadian currency.

Every action Andre took that involved Joe Gaspe was a risk. Though willing to take those risks (Andre had been questioned by many of his co-workers and a few of his trusted confidants) he had a brief moment of doubt but went ahead with his plan.

Joe was being paid a salary to observe the Musky Straits looking for suspicious activities. He was paid even during the winter months when nothing was happening. This was the best job he'd ever had. Hanging around with college boys would be a pain but it would all be over in four days. "When do I start?"

"Pick up your interns at Jackie B's next Thursday morning at nine." Andre looked into his cup at the cold contents, set it down, nodded to Joe and left the Greek Restaurant. Joe waved over the waitress and ordered a second Souvlaki.

Amelia Gaspe, stuck at home on a Friday night, was bathing her youngest sister when the call came in. Her mom and dad had gone out for their Friday Fish Fry, a remnant tradition from the days when the Catholic Church required meatless Fridays. The answering machine picked up on the first ring because her dad was dodging bill collectors. She thought that it was probably one of her dad's lame partners anyway, like that nitwit Marv. She knew it wasn't her boyfriend because she'd already told him the parents would be home too early for him to sneak in the back door. Her oldest sister would still be up and she'd tell everything.

Amelia finished up with Lucy, got her tucked into bed and went downstairs to play back the message. She opened the fridge and was getting out a juice box when she heard the message and froze, refrigerator door still open.

"Amy, are you there?" The voice was quiet, slow, and sleepy, but Amelia recognized it right away as Randi, her high school friend. Randi had run away from her drunken father's home. "No matter what, don't you run away. It's bad out here. Really bad. I don't even know where I am. I'm in trouble." As this speech went on, it slowed down more, grew quieter and more slurred. "Stay home where you're safe. Er…" There was the sound of a slap, a stifled scream, and the call disconnected.

Amelia played that message twice more when she was sure her younger sisters weren't listening.

When Joe Gaspe and his wife, Kate, came home it was late enough that all the younger girls were in their beds or asleep. Amelia played the answering machine tape for her parents and, after Kate went to check on the girls, played it again for her father. Joe broke out a beer, shook a cigarette from his pack and said, "Let's go onto the deck." He and his daughter sat in adjacent Adirondack chairs and ignored the chill of the spring night. When Joe finished his smoke he tossed the stub into the bushes, an act that would get him in trouble with Kate at a later date, and said, "Let's see what we can make of this message together."

He placed his hand lightly on his daughter's wrist, looked at the sky for a visible star, and said, "Uncle Mike says we can do this. We'll remember Randi as she was and…"

"Wait a minute, Dad," Amelia ran into the house and was back in a few moments with a bookmark from a wildlife rehab center. "Randi gave this to me. I'll hold it. Okay?" With the bookmark in her left hand, she laid her right arm on the chair and winkled it under Joe's left hand, turning the inside of her wrist up.

Upon closing his eyes, Joe felt lightness, almost a sense of weightlessness. From above he saw himself sitting with Amelia on the deck. He rose higher until his house, then his town, became too small to differentiate. He circled town once and was joined by a red-tailed hawk. He knew at once that this was Amy. After a lazy circle they took off to the west following the rising thermals coming from the pavement. They were able to glide with ease. In what seemed to be no time, they were over a large shopping mall parking lot, seeing everything, even though it was night. They circled the lighted lot. There, two over-sized men were hustling a young girl toward a vehicle.

The car door opened, the girl looked skyward, right into Joe's eyes. She tried to brace her legs against the car's frame to keep from being shoved inside, looked up again, opened her mouth in a scream that Joe could not hear. A man slapped her on the head and she was propelled inside the car.

Joe and Amy rose higher into the sky and began to circle up and up. They flew easily to the south and west for several minutes, passing above four large cities until they dropped down to a ribbon of highway heading southwest. Joe and his daughter were hawks, perched in a tree, watching sparse traffic flow by. The familiar bronze-colored auto raced past. He saw a girl's terrified face glance out the window at him as she struggled to keep a hood from being lowered over her face. The vehicle whipped past. Its slipstream ruffled their feathers and the hawks looked down the road at a sign that read "Cincinnati 66 miles." The two hawks rose into the clear night again, circled, and headed northeast.

Amelia opened her eyes, "That was Randi, did you see? Somebody snatched her at that mall! What can we do?"

"I saw. I don't know what we can do, if anything. Take that tape out of the machine and give it to me, I know a coupla guys over there in Pantherville who might know something."

"You saw the same things I saw?"

"Yes, Amy. I was right there with you. Now we must honor that dream, by remembering and acting upon it: at least that's what Uncle Mike tells me."

For the next few minutes, Amy related what she had seen to Joe, and he confirmed that he had seen the identical things. Amelia wasn't convinced that her dad didn't just say stuff to validate her. Joe, on the other hand, knew that they had shared a significant vision.

Chapter 2
Alexandria Bay Bridge

—April 17th—

In line to pass through customs at Alexandria Bay, Joe wondered if Marv would believe him if he said he was sick of looking at dancing naked women. He'd just completed a tour of strip clubs near the airports in Toronto, Ottawa, and Montreal, and he was tired. The trip, with college seniors Ger Blog and Kyle Buchalter, had gotten tedious. Joe, in his early forties, found the young men to be empty-headed. Joe had no illusions about being an intellectual giant himself; however, he was saddened by the dullness of these two who were supposed to be exceptional students.

Their assignment called for them to visit only one chain of strip joints, those that were situated at airports and called Sweet Cherries. It had been like roping an elephant to keep the interns from visiting every club at each airport, and by Montreal they had convinced him to visit every one. The expense money Agent Andre had given Joe had been limited, and, at the Montreal end of the trip, it made sense to spend it all. The Sweet Cherries Club was seedy, the girls were underfed, and the bouncers looked murderous. The other clubs, with prettier girls, better atmosphere, and a more upscale clientele, were semi-successful in creating the illusion of class.

As a father of five daughters, Joe Gaspe's moral strictures overpowered his male libido, and he felt seamy and dirty about the whole thing. They moved up in line at the customs booth. Four cars remained in front of them.

It had played out just as Andre had suggested it would: seamy joints, skinny dancers, non-English speakers, and not Francophones either. They were mostly, but not all, Russian girls, obviously drugged, and starved They were tattooed on the web between thumb and forefinger, a red five-pointed star on the left hand and a Chinese symbol on the right hand.

Marv looked up from his Budweiser, a beer he considered second rate, and did a double take when he saw the next dancer. She looked familiar, too young, and like most of them in this strip joint, malnourished. Marv loved to drive and was peacock proud of his stamina behind the wheel. Driving for hours, as he'd done to visit his girlfriend's family in Cincinnati, was nothing to him. He and his girlfriend were staying with her brother across the Ohio River in Kentucky. While the ladies were driving around looking at horse farms, the men were topping off an afternoon of gambling with a different kind of sight seeing. As usual, these bars were clustered around the airport. They thrived on the myth that a hard-charging businessman needed a lap-dance or two to get over the stress of his deal making.

With Cincinnati being one of the more prudish cities in the country, the strip bars were in Kentucky where the airport fit into the surrounding hills. Marv's prospective brother-in-law also lived in Kentucky. He had suggested a stop at Sweet Cherries, their third club, before heading home. Marv had enjoyed the view until he was abruptly disturbed by the sight of this young thing. She looked like someone he'd seen before, but the beery state of his mind didn't allow him to pin down who and where. The girl also had a listless haunted look, danced in a desultory manner, and picked up the pace when a painted old lady near the end of the bar, wearing a poodle's hairdo, barked at her. The command caused her to put a little more energy in her gyrations but only for a moment. Shortly, her dancing became listless and unexciting again.

Marv and Brian Hesketh left for the night with Marv still trying to sort out where he'd seen that girl. Strippers were overly familiar with customers as part of their shtick, but this little lady had seemed to be trying to send a message to Marv from across the dance floor. He just couldn't place her.

"That's the most crummy of the joints. Russian girls they say. Easiest place to score, I hear. What's the matter, buddy?" Brian was keeping up his half of the conversation.

"Nothing. I'm okay. Just thought I saw something."

"I hope you saw a lot," Brian said this with a hearty laugh.

Later that night, when he was rummaging for a Tums in his kit bag, it came to Marv where he had seen that dancer. She was a friend of Joe's daughter back in Muskedaigua. He'd sat with her on Joe's back deck one evening. What was she doing stripping in Kentucky?

The night he returned from Canada, Joe met his daughter at the front door.

"Amy, we've got to get down to see Uncle Mike one of these weekends. I know, I work most Saturdays and fish most Sundays, but you need to talk to him about some of these things you're seeing in dreams. Me, too."

"Don't you need to tell him that you're coming? Make an appointment?"

"He'll know when we're coming. The question is, will we?" Joe and his daughter went their separate ways. Children went through a phase when parents were a combination of nuisance, embarrassment, and automatic teller machine. Parents knew that this would change; sons and daughters thought, "no way."

Spirit Guides

Chapter 3
Muskedaigua

—May 7th—

Joe was involved in the strip-joint surveillance project for Andre, and he couldn't believe how his mind and emotions were betraying him. Any man would consider this an ideal job, wouldn't he? First, he traveled through Canada checking out these Sweet Cherries Clubs, now he was to be sent south to hit the bars in Pittsburgh, Cleveland, Washington, Charlotte, and Atlanta. All the while, expenses paid, he just had to look for a certain set of tattoos on the hands of strippers. Sure, he had had to go into Canada with two dorky interns, but in the south he could travel with Marv, his partner. And he would be allowed to stop off for some southern musky fishing with his buddies in various locales. Yet his dreams troubled him. And to top it all off, he had begun to feel embarrassed in these joints, a sensation that had started to overtake him in Canada. Maybe, with Marv along it would stop bothering him.

Sleep had snuck up on Joe Gaspe. He was sitting at a bar watching faceless female bodies rotate their hips while bad rock music thumped in the vibrating air. Marv was next to him grinning and leering but on the other side of him a raven perched on the bar and occasionally knifed his shoulder with its hatchet-like beak. Joe would register the pain, look at the raven, and see it twist its head and point over its shoulder. Back there in the dark he would see a dim outline of a girl with a recognizable face. One he couldn't quite place. After the third whack by the raven, Joe reached to rub his shoulder and saw that it was Randi, Amy's former best friend, looking at him with fear and trembling in her expression. Each time he concentrated on her she faded away and the gyrating female forms returned to the foreground. Marv leaned close and said, "You'll never guess what I've got to tell you."

Joe awoke with a sense of dread but also a conviction that he had to do something. He wasn't at all sure what he had to do. Joe never talked to Marv or any Muskedaigua friends about his visions in dreams and the astonishing things that happened afterward.

Moses X Snow was a combination of a traditional Mohawk and a successful businessman. He was not a gambling millionaire. He was just successful enough to make a living and help out a few of his nephews with jobs. Mo brokered live bait throughout Quebec, Ontario, and New York. Mo was tall with a long torso and short, sturdy legs. He sported a traditional Mohawk hairdo, sometimes allowed to grow long, though at present it was buzzed to a length of one inch all the way down. He had an antique copper complexion and was old enough to have a few wrinkles, adding character to his face. To strangers he presented the face of a stoic warrior. To those who knew him he was a trickster. Mo was one of the few who honored the traditions of his people with his spiritual ways. He also felt an unusual closeness to his cousin Joe Gaspe. He and Joe had been reunited, years after their days on the barricades at Oka, before they helped foil an attack on the Friendship Bridge.

Joe Gaspe and Mo inhabited dream states together. Mo's dreambody relied on the heron as its dream travel guide. For several months, at intervals, Mo's dream heron had been standing beside a marsh, gazing at a pure white egret. The white bird had been tempted to fly with him but reluctant. It was so this night.

Mo lifted into the air and took his leave of the egret, longing for it to join him, but resigned to be on his way. By circling ever upward Mo could see ahead, over the horizon. He headed southwest. He recognized the land as that of one of the tribes known as a little brother of the Iroquois, the

Shawnees. He saw a settlement in the forest, backed up against big tulip trees, as the Shawnee liked to live.

Several groups of young men were running and dodging in sport. Mo slowly circled lower and saw Radleigh Loonch, Joe Gaspe's partner, observing the men playing. Two Shawnee teams were playing basketball against other non-Indian teams. He saw himself on the Shawnee team and his vision zoomed to see Rad concentrating on a fish-belly-white player leading an Indian team to victory after victory.

Mo knew since he'd dreamt it, it would come to pass.

Since her dad had encouraged Amy to daydream and also to share her sleep time dreams, she did not resist or consider the sensations weird. She felt a tingling excitement when she began to slide into the dreamscape of a vision.

She saw herself as a young girl of ten in a light summer dress. She stood at a swimming place that her family had occasionally visited. Her mother, busy with other children, called to her to be careful. But, someone else beckoned her into the water from the other bank, and she saw it was Lucyneda, her grandmother, her Aksotha in the Mohawk language. Without hesitation, she dove in and swam toward Grandmother. Lucyneda met her under water and they took powerful strokes together into an underwater cave. Amy thought she should be taking a breath, heard her air escape through her nose, felt her ears pop. She began to panic and tried to pull away from Aksotha. But Amy was not able to surface, Lucyneda pulled her into an opening in the cliff. Swimming along in an underwater cave, she bumped against the enclosing rock above her. She swam, pulling hard for many strokes. Lungs screeching and burning, she rose up through the water, thinking she would hit solid rock. Instead she surfaced into a large room, roofed with rock but mercifully full of air. She could breathe. Aksotha beckoned her onto the shore to sit beside her. The room was filled with women and girls. Most of the older women sat in a large circle, gray hair hanging loose. Several were conversing quietly. Several others, young or mature, but not the old, slept in awkward positions snoring fitfully and sonorously.

Amy glanced at the faces; some were welcoming, some seemed contemptuous, some were merely curious. Grandmother smiled, held a finger to her lips and inclined her head toward her left. There, an ancient man sat with a wolf skin about his shoulders. The wolf head perched crookedly on his head. He grinned a one-toothed grin through a face of antique bronze wrinkles. He looked directly at Amy.

"Daughter, you are sent to us today to renew the dreaming. You see before you the line of healing dreamers that have made the Flint People an enduring people. From Island Woman," he spread an arm to his right, "who came to us from our enemy and made us into a great people with her guidance, her healing and her dreams, through all the other clan mothers who were dreamers, we have come this day to you. You must be trained to lead your people." The old man paused in his oration. Politely, no one spoke. Amy was amazed to see several women still snoring and insensible. The man noticed her gaze.

"The sunrise people gave us the strong drink, and we have lost many dreamers and almost all of our warriors to the effects of rum. These dreamers are ones who never were. You must complete your training, listen to Lucyneda who didn't live long in the shadow world but will stay in your real world, your dreams, forever. Where your training takes you, you must follow, remember, and study the patterns. We have become a weak nation. Our warriors have dropped their minds to drink. They do not hunt. They do not make war. They stumble about in a crazed stupor." Amy was shocked by the vividness of a vision of Indian boys crowded around a can, huffing paint, arguing over who is next, surrounded by insensible passed-out boys, sitting in a junkyard of wrecked machinery and dead cars. When this image faded, and the old man in the wolf skin spoke again.

"Daughter. We ask you not to save the nation of the Flint People. We ask you not even to save the Wolf Clan. We ask you just to save the dreaming. Without the dreaming, we will be like the sunrise people, nothing."

Amy looked around at the faces of the old women. Most were smiling now. They brought small gifts to her and laid them on a skin in front of her: beads, ribbons, a Jew's harp, tobacco, a four-leafed clover. A large male lobo dashed through the assembled women without them seeming to react. The wolf looked at Amy, then was gone. Lucyneda laid her hand lightly an Amy's shoulder. Amy dreaded the swim back through the sea cave. Then she heard a voice. It was her father.

"Amy! Amy! Do you want a burger or a dog here? Or how about one of each?"

Chapter 4
Delano

—May 11th—

On his trip with the interns into Canada, Joe had been told to look at the hands of the dancers. What kind of man did Andre think he was? In a strip joint, with naked dancers and barely-covered hostesses, he had been told to examine hands. It had been relatively easy, though, to get dancers to drink with him and chat. He couldn't accomplish much by chatting with some of them, since they only spoke Russian. But if you got a dancer to sit with you, used a lost-puppy-dog expression, and asked her to hold your hand, you could see the marks in the web between thumb and forefinger. More often than not, the tattoos were there, the star on the left-hand web and the Chinese letter on the right-hand web.

Joe was in Delano looking for some information from John Smith, a skin artist in his network, about what that Chinese lettering might mean. The tattoo craze, popularized by rock stars and athletes, seemed to Joe to contain a lot of ink with Chinese letters spelling out who-knew-what messages. Joe loved to talk to John Smith, President of the New York State Skin Artists Organization. John was a man in his early thirties inked all over and an example of body modification gone extreme. He had a forked tongue and had built up what he conceived to be devil horns on his head. A dumpy dough ball that drew the attention of passers by, John personified the absurdity of the lengths to which free humans could go. Joe considered him a friend and a nut. During their discussions, Joe sat in wonderment at why people did this stuff to themselves. The Mohawks were not strangers to body art. Many warriors had been elaborately tattooed. The outlandishness of the current tattoo craze appealed to Joe who enjoyed the sense of unreality that reminded him of his dreams and visions.

"So, what does all this Chinese stuff mean? I see it on basketball players. Do they even know what it means?"

"We have a phrase guide with translations into the pictogram writing of Chinese, Korean, or Japanese. So, if you wanted a phrase going down your arm saying, 'I am Superman,' we could get it right." John was cleaning tools while he talked. He had no customers, though his partner/wife, Mary, was working on a young lady behind a curtain nearby.

"So, I sketched this symbol. Can you say what it means?"

John took a glance, hit a switch on his inkpot to reverse the flow and said, "Chinese. Let's look it up."

He picked up a loose-leaf binder and began thumbing through it. "I seem to remember some bikers liking that one. The Road Buzzards I think, hmmm. Hmmm. Hmmm. Here it is. I was right. See, right there."

He proffered the page to Joe who looked at the book and said, "That's it. What does it mean?"

John pulled the photo to him and said, "The Chinese language is very context dependant. The same word can be pronounced differently and have different meanings depending on how it is used. Says here, Property, House, Mine, indicating ownership. There you go."

"Property. Mine. I wonder. Let me ask you this: Is there any similarity between Russian letters and Chinese symbols?"

"None whatsoever, I get zero requests for Russian stuff. The guys in the city might, but not out here. The Chinese stuff is mysterious, those who don't know can't figure it out, you see. No. No similarity to Russian."

"Thanks John. Can you photocopy that picture and those words for me?"

"Why don't I just write it on your forearm. Paperless, you know? Special price for my good buddy."

"No thanks."

Joe waited while John made a copy, then took his leave with something to think about. Did Andre connect the Russians mobsters, who were moving all these white slaves, with the Chinese who regularly smuggled people, and who knows what all, into the US across the Musky Straits? Of course he did. But, could they do anything about that connection?

Agent Andre had not been satisfied with the information from the Canadian branches of Sweet Cherries. The intel had been fine but there was not enough of it. Andre needed to know more about these franchises located on the fringes of some airports in the US. He'd given Joe a list of additional clubs to visit, eliminated the interns from the program, and encouraged Joe to take his partner, Marv, on the trip south.

Joe saw this as a double opportunity. He could indulge in guilty pleasures observing the girls with Marv—no need to be under scrutiny by the interns—and the two of them could avail themselves of the musky fishing in Pennsylvania, Ohio, West Virginia, and North Carolina on the way down to their last stop at the airport in Atlanta. Joe loved his job.

On their way south they decided that any fishing to be done in Pennsylvania and Ohio would be done on the way back. For the trip down it would be all business. Strip club business, that is.

Joe and Marv met with Bill Blue from the Pittsburgh Muskie Club for a tour of the local hot spots. Some communities limited these kinds of watering holes to the vicinity of airports, indulging the self-satisfied fiction that businessmen need to relieve stress at strip bars. Andre had mentioned how one of his local pals might consider any and all clubs other than Sweet Cherries to be the better ones, but it was Joe's job to go to the Russian-owned bars. There he could talk to and inspect the dancers.

"Oh, yeah! I'll be inspecting them alright." Joe thought that remark was pretty cute.

Andre had consulted his notebook. "No lap dances, Joe, no special entertainments. You are to stay sober enough to find out what's going on. Your expenses will be paid for buying the girls their drinks and speaking to as many as seems reasonable. You are not to appear suspicious or as if you are investigating. Just window shop the wares and move on."

Joe still showed enthusiasm for this assignment but a subtle change had been taking place. He didn't understand quite what it was. When he'd gone to Toronto, Ottawa, and Montreal with the interns, Kyle and Gerhard, he had been the worldly older mentor, showing the kids the ropes. Their boorish behavior, as testosterone flooded away any good sense they had, had planted seeds in Joe's mind. He judged their behavior, thought of his own when with Marv and others, and felt a tiny nudge of shame. He'd always known that visiting these bars was shameful, but with enough alcohol a man can justify anything.

Since the trip through Canada, he saw these dancers as girls young enough to be his daughter. That trend would only get worse as each of his five daughters became women. Two conflicting cultures ripped at Joe's psyche. His Mohawk side was very casual, matter-of-fact and healthy about sex and procreation. From a young age the children in Iroquois families knew what Mom and Dad were doing and thought it normal. His Irish side, repressed and shamed by sex, needed prodigious amounts of drink and a dollop of rage to participate in lovemaking or even think about it.

In Pittsburgh, Bill Blue conducted the tour like a retailer showing the customer the best product while also giving the option of trying a lesser brand. The gentleman's club tour started at Diamonds, where the dancers were statuesque, pumped up, and all blonde. Marv had already fallen in love when Joe prodded Bill to move down the hill. (Everything in Pittsburgh is up or down a hill from everything else.)

"Are you kidding? Why are we leavin'? That babe was hot! She liked me, too." Marv was looking at Blue who hooked his thumb at Joe.

"Gotta move on. Got a job to do here. You can go back later if you want." Joe had been nursing his drinks while Marv had been pounding his. For a man of many appetites like Joe, holding back on the sauce was hard.

"Over here at Sunset there is a lot more diversity in dancers — white ones, black ones yellow ones, nut-brown ones…"

"At that last place they all looked like they came off Hugh Hefner's assembly line." Joe was both intrigued and creeped out.

"What in the world is wrong with that?" Marv was not yet fighting drunk but he was getting there.

They entered Sunset, and Joe noted right away the quality of the amenities had dropped a notch. All these bars were decorated in a ridiculous and tasteless manner, appealing to the fantasies of post-teen men of all ages, but as the prices dropped, the shabbiness increased. The cover charge at Sunset was one dollar less than at Diamonds, the booze was no longer top shelf, the girls more natural, less stunning. Joe sat down to try his charm on a dancer. After their stint of dancing the girls were required to schmooze customers in order to sell them booze and possibly other expensive services.

When Joe sat down at the bar all the girls were either dancing or chatting up customers. He laid a one hundred dollar bill on the bar, ordered drinks, and let his change ride. When the dancers changed, two going on stage and two coming off, the bartender caught the eye of one of those coming off stage and gestured with a nod of his head. Joe's bait caught a pretty Asian fish. The young lady sat next to Joe wearing a wrap that covered her but left very little to the imagination.

"Hey, big fella, you want to buy a girl a drink?" She leaned in close to Joe. Marv and Bill had moved around the horseshoe-shaped bar to get a better look at a raven-haired dancer.

Joe paid for her overpriced drink and had a pleasant chat with the girl. He had been in this dilemma in Diamonds a half hour ago. When he realized, right away, that this was not one of the dancers he was looking for, he had the unpleasant task of trying to get rid of her. He loved talking to a pretty girl, but, to do his job, he had to turn down extra services, nightly specials, and stop buying drinks. He could leave his bait on the bar and, as the girls went up to dance, check out a few more prospects. But he was pretty sure that none of the dancers at Sunset were the ones he was seeking. He wanted to move on to the Sweet Cherries strip joint but not be perceived as obviously slumming by Bill Blue. He could always handle Marv by just telling him what he needed to know.

Marv's fickle affections had moved from the blonde (built right up off the ground) at Diamonds to a black-haired, tattooed, slightly enhanced, stunner named Raven at Sunset. He was in love again. This night would be filled with fantasy and throbbing with vigor. Marv looked up at Joe, saw he wanted to go, swore and said, "Oh no. I was just about to score."

"Sure, Marv. C'mon, it's down the hill we go." Joe tugged on his upper arm. Marv looked at the dancer to plead with her, but her attention was already on another likely mark.

Blue said, "Sweet Cherries is the last place. It's a little cheaper. Russian girls. I hear they're the loosest of all. Can't be talking with them much though, only a few speak any English." They descended the hill, turned a corner and entered the door of a converted airplane hangar. A small neon sign above the door read, "Sweet Cherries."

There had been a large sign at the turn up the alley, announcing the club, but only the small neon over the steel fire door. The bouncer, a big man with a flat face who was as ugly as Frankenstein's monster, looked them over and waved them through. Inside, the bar was playing the same cheesy eighties tunes as the others, but this step down in class was a steep drop. The facilities were dirty; the tables and chairs mismatched and in need of repair. Only cheap booze was offered. The commodity for sale was sex with no illusion of sophistication or class. The joint was honest in that way, at least.

Joe noted right away that these girls were beyond slim; they were skinny. Ribs were showing all over. Some of them could've been striking beauties with their high Russian cheekbones, blonde hair, and long legs. But, if ever a place exemplified the motto that to be a Russian required suffering, it was this dump and those dancers in it.

The clientele here made no pretense of being businessmen. The customers alternated between sad-case degenerates and intoxicated men trying to show off to each other that they could be unmoved by the undulations of naked girls and women. They were not well dressed. They were not poised. Looking around, Joe was reminded of ground-dwelling animals; woodchucks, badgers, skunks, peeking out of their holes and looking around, ready for flight or fight. He went to the bar and withdrew a new hundred from his wallet. He bought a round of drinks, and Marv and Bill moved off to watch a dance, as arranged. It was while Joe was noting the high number of enforcers distributed around the building that a tall blonde sat beside him.

She didn't speak. Joe waved at the bartender indicating an order of drinks and turned to her. She smiled widely and said, "Hey, Joe," in heavily accented English. The mouth may have smiled but the eyes were desperate and woeful. Joe took the drinks and held hers where she had to reach across him to retrieve it.

He saw her right hand and it had the Chinese tattoo he was looking for. She moved the drink to her left hand, put her right arm around Joe's shoulder, and made a completely indecent proposal. Her left hand had a star tattoo on it and he noticed while trying to turn her down politely, that several beefy Russian fellows were watching closely.

"Not just now, I wanna see the show." Joe thought how pathetic that may have sounded, realized that she couldn't understand, and saw the bartender barely shake his head to her. "What's your name?"

"Olga, what's yours?"

"I thought you already knew me, I'm Joe."

Joe Gaspe had an iron stomach or thought he did. This usually was the case but his overconfidence caused him to eat things that a man of better judgment would have passed up. The night that he and Marv drove to Cleveland to meet Joe's friend Mack Spline and visit the Sweet Cherries franchise near the airport was a warm one. Marv didn't eat all of his chicken nuggets and they were left in the car. Later after the thirsty and hungry work at the strip club, Joe wolfed down the remaining nuggets with some hot sauce and chased the meal with a glass of whiskey. A few hours later the horrors woke Joe from a dream and he reached for the water glass beside the bed, gulped down the stale Wild Turkey, gagged and remembered the dream he'd been having.

The visit to the Sweet Cherries Club in Cleveland had been much like the others: underfed very young women, pathetic-loser customers, nasty brutish bouncers, and an obviously thriving sex business, upstairs in this case. Joe's dream had been brought on by stale chicken.

Joe was sitting at the bar with Mack Spline on one side and a pretty dancer on the other. The dancer had jet-black hair, dyed from brown and her oval face was pretty and not needing more than the slightest touch of make-up. Then the face began to change before him, the chin receded, the cheeks changed to jowls, the hairline became a widow's peak. Her perfect eyebrows came together as a snarled unibrow. Age crawled onto her eyes and mouth with a few, then many, wrinkles. Joe was seeing the woman fade at the edges, and when he glanced full-face straight-on he saw his wife, but without Kate's well-preserved distinguished look. Rather it was a hard, bitter, frowning face, an exaggeration of the face she wore in fights with Joe. Joe's gaze circled back to the edges and he first saw Kate's honey brown silky hair, then circling the edges counter-clockwise he saw that wifely face change and become darker and lumpy and mottled. When his vision returned to the hair it was his own coarse Chia-head hair that he saw. A dark untamable mat of bristles appeared on top of the face, now morphed into that of his youngest daughter, her youthful beauty rasped away by the hard life of a sex worker. She looked into his eyes, accusatory, fiery, a guilt-inducing stare that made Joe feel the pain of betraying a trust. It was this vision of his daughter grown evil, mean, and low that had brought Joe back from his dream.

Chapter 5
Reynoldsburg

—May 26th—

"I can't believe the stuff you can buy here," Marv said as they stood in front of the monstrous bucket of the Big Muskie, which is all that remains of what was once the world's largest shovel, since retired. He and Joe were in southeastern Ohio at the Reynoldsburg Tradin' Days Festival, Memorial Day Edition.

"Uh, Marv, you're standing in a shovel getting your picture taken. What's so great about that?"

"But what a shovel! Look at the size of this thing! And, just think buying knives and guns, and talkin' knives and guns with everybody, what's not to like?"

"Okay, hold still." Joe clicked off a few photos. "I'm having fun too. Let me get in the shovel bucket for a few shots." Joe changed places with Marv and decided to pose with an Arkansas Toothpick in each hand. These twenty-inch combinations of a throwing knife and a sword are fearsome-looking weapons, often seen in the early Civil War-era photographs posed by Confederate soldiers. Joe and Marv had each bought a huge one — so big it had to be carried in a sheath that was worn like a backpack. Joe had also picked up a modest thirteen-inch example for his cousin Mo. Mo's had a sheath that was worn like a shoulder holster. Mo had asked Joe to look for a Toothpick that he planned to use as a general hunting and camping knife.

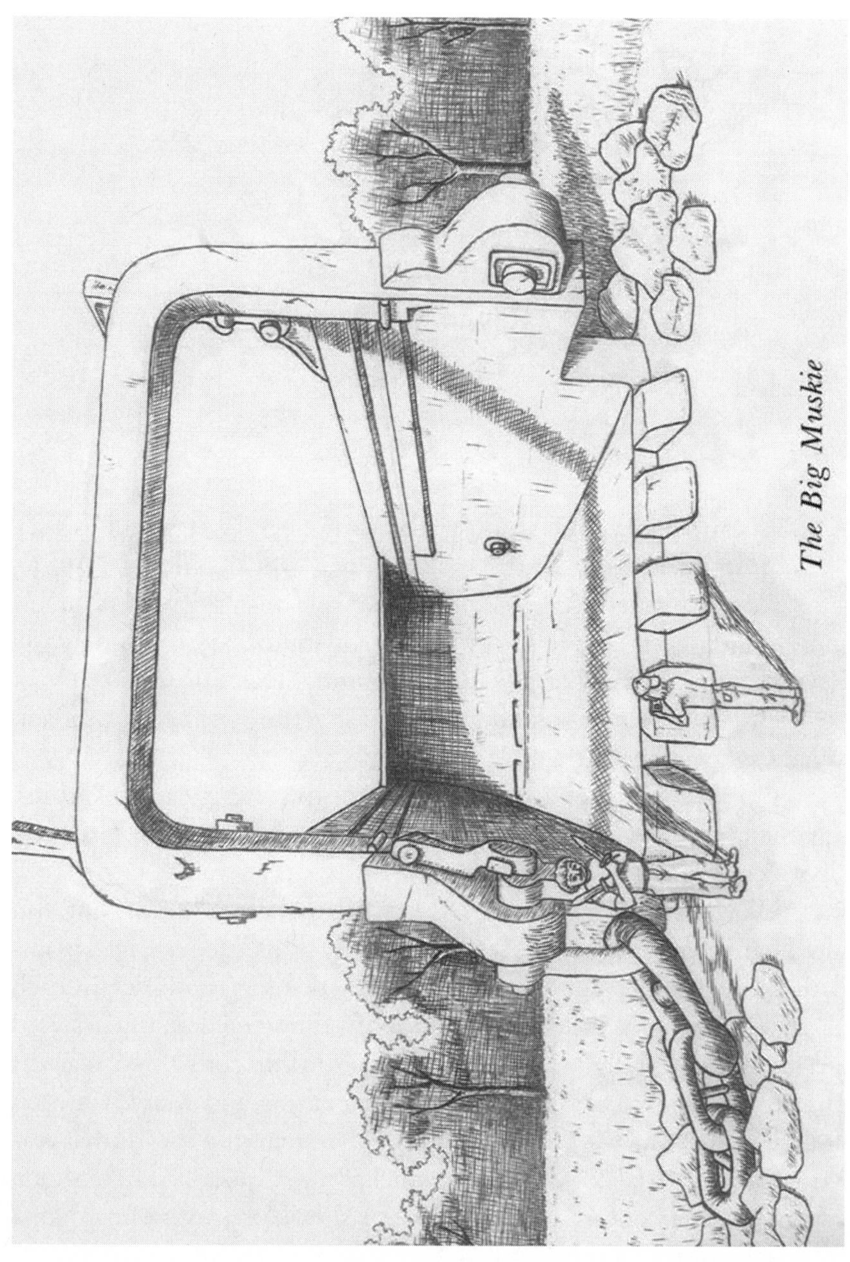

The Big Muskie

A man came up behind Marv and said, "Those are pretty bladey, where'd you get 'em?"

"Uh, we brought them to trade."

Marv and Joe had told Sperling Duncan, who was nicknamed Spunkin, that they would keep quiet about where they got such knives. With a twenty-inch blade, the knives were custom made. They were classified as swords and as such could not, legally, have a honed edge. Meant for display only, swords, other than historical artifacts, with sharpened edges were one of several semi-illegal things available at the Reynoldsburg show.

They had found Sperling Duncan's metalworking booth on recommendation of Melvin Loonch from the Straits Musky Club. Loonch had ordered the long custom Toothpicks on the phone and told his old Ohio friend Spunkin to expect a visit from Joe and Marv. Melvin had also asked Spunkin to recommend a vendor for some handguns. After Marv and Joe examined the knives and sculptures and picked up a cypress knee head knocker for Mo, Spunkin had directed them to Miller Lafe's display of long guns for sale or trade. By asking for non-standard items, Marv was approved and ushered behind the trailer. There he was shown a display of handguns from which he made his choices. Joe stayed out front, dickering over the trade of a bb gun for a pellet gun. Next, he spent fifteen minutes discussing paint ball guns with Lafe's assistant.

When Marv came back out front Joe saw he had purchased four handguns, a Glock Nine for Joe, a Smith & Wesson pistol and a Smith & Wesson revolver for himself, and a .41-caliber derringer for Radleigh to join the three Arkansas Toothpicks in the war bag. Marv wanted two different pistols, while Joe reluctantly got one to pacify his partner.

Miller Lafe had directed them to a booth where a young man, blinded in a childhood gun accident, made custom leather products. Melvin Loonch had come through by recommending him as well, and Marv was able to purchase seven holsters from the booth. They got ordinary belt-clip holsters for the pistols, a special bra holster for Rad's derringer, two back sheaths for the big swords, and a shoulder holster for Mo's knife.

Now, taking pictures at the Big Muskie, Marv had all his gear in a Rochester Americans Hockey bag at his feet. He and Joe had begun to draw a crowd at the shovel bucket. People at shows behave like schooling fish, any busy booth draws a crowd of onlookers, and an empty booth or display is ignored as if it isn't there. With Joe mugging an intimidating pose, gawkers were piling up near the Big Muskie.

They would be okay carrying the hockey bag into the south, but the guns and knives, with the exception of Mo's knife, would be left at Mack Spline's farm in Ohio. Bringing unregistered handguns into New York, while simple to do, was a felony.

Chapter 6
New River

—May 28th—

"This has got to be a trout stream, you knucklehead. Look at the way that water's rushing." Marv was just standing there, not even trying to cast his line.

"Hey, that hillbilly up the road said that this is the New River, didn't he? Just give it a try. Maybe if we walk upstream a little farther there will be a pool or two we can find a big musky in." Joe didn't even look at Marv. He'd seen that glare before. "There sure is a lot of fast water here."

Joe was positive that he'd heard that the New River in West Virginia was top-notch, cold water, southern musky fishery, but there was something nagging at the edge of his memory.

April showers may well bring May flowers, but, in the northern half of the United States, June is the rainiest month. Evidence of recent flood activity proved that the rains didn't know May from June. They'd walked along a streamside trail of sucking gelatinous mud that would claim a boot from a man's foot if it weren't tightly laced. Now, at a spot where they could find a rock to stand on, Marv stared across the water at the last flood's apparent high-water mark. Twenty feet up a sycamore tree were many plastic bags, one of which had burst its fill of dirty diapers. Caught among the sticks and leaves and trash was a child's plastic riding toy. Its pink wheels were incongruous amid the dirty browns, grays, and tans.

Marv succeeded in being pigheaded long enough that Joe gave in and the attempt to fish the greatest wild river of the east was abandoned. It wasn't until they were on I-64, headed toward the Sweet Cherries Club outside Washington, that the nagging memory of Joe's peeked out and he remembered that it was the New River in Virginia in winter that was the good musky fishery.

Standing in the store lobby of the Country Store Restaurant, Radleigh Loonch had a chance to think. She was always early wherever she went, and Joe Gaspe was usually late, and often frantic, wherever he went. They'd been scheduled to meet at seven and Joe was late again, so she started looking over the books on CD offered by the chain and thought about how her life had taken this unexpected turn. If only her mother and grandmother could see her now. The girl who got a job with Customs and Border Patrol because she could speak fluent Spanish was now in training, including weapons training, to move into the job of an FBI Special Agent. Tall, attractive, and turned out in inexpensive yet tasteful clothes, Rad looked the archetype of a college-educated woman. She had always been protected in a solidly middle-class life in the nicer neighborhoods, and now she was dealing with murderous terrorists, criminals, and the over-the-edge counter-terrorists who pursued them.

Agent Thomas Andre had picked her for his brand of Special Projects because she combined an attitude of assertiveness, and the ability to break down an idea and examine its essence, that was very rare in young people coming from the universities. With the exception of the practical disciplines, like engineering and computers, colleges were chaotic indoctrination factories. The faculties, nauseatingly timid and doctrinaire, only pursued excellence in the direction of being more leftist and more bizarre than each other. The graduates turned out in the liberal arts and social sciences were intellectually stunted and wrapped up in their feelings. The number one feeling inculcated into these grads was an overarching attitude of resentment toward all those who were able to achieve anything in the hard, cold, and dirty world.

Rad turned the rack and looked at more audio books. She'd had no idea that life could be as quick and deadly as it was turning out to be. Soon, in three days, she would be issued a service weapon and designated for assignment to an FBI office somewhere in the US. She thought that Andre would want her back, but no one at the training academy had confirmed that.

Rad thought about that day's exchange between the instructor and one trainee who seemed ill-suited to the task. This man, Danny, felt strongly that guns were an anachronism and that the fibbies could nab the miscreants that they pursued with computer work and financial research. Danny had insisted that only a coward would carry a firearm.

Rad could hear the instructor now: "Guns are not for play. If you put it in your hand you must be prepared to kill someone, and you must understand that you could die. So, yes, you should be fearful of using it, because an innocent person could be killed. You must be cautious, cool, and discreet enough to understand when there is a reason to use the gun and when there is not."

As she eyed the titles on the rack, Rad realized that she used her assertive persona as a tool to move ahead through life. While she understood the reasons for using her firearm, she was not at all sure she'd be able to handle a shooting situation if and when it came. During her adventures with Joe Gaspe she'd seen the safe and secure dissolve into horror in an instant. She had seen the elemental savagery of Moses Snow that had saved Joe from death. Seeing Mo dispatch a thug with his own baseball bat had shown her a different kind of understanding of the world, one more feral and violent, less ill equipped than her own. Rad was beginning to understand how to face trouble. She wondered if she could perform.

She heard Joe and Marv before she saw them, "Might as well have something to eat, a lot of food sounds right to me." Joe headed for the hostess station to get a table. Rad walked up and gave Joe a hug then turned to Marv and shook hands. "How are you guys doing?"

"Ms. Loonch you look as fine as frog hair — what have you been doing with yourself?" Though they had worked together the previous fall, Joe and Rad had not been in contact over the winter, and he had not seen her since she had dropped the cigarette habit and taken up training for long-distance races. While unable to eliminate her inherited swayback and small potbelly, her training had slimmed down her upper arms, face, and neck and perfected her already shapely legs. Rad was five ten and entering that mid-twenties period when women attain their peak of physical beauty. Joe was openly admiring in his gaze. Marv, who always seemed to be jealous of Joe's attentions and a little envious of Rad, was stone faced.

"Joe, what are you guys doing in the Capitol area? You don't look bad, either of you."

They were shown to a table before Joe seriously addressed the question of why he and Marv had come to the D.C. area. "You won't believe our assignment. Good old Thomas Andre has sent us on a tour of strip clubs in selected cities. He's got a theory that we're trying to prove true or false. We're paid just to go and meet the girls and check out the setup at these joints. We go from here to Charlotte and Atlanta and then we drive back to Pantherville. He's also given us enough time to do some fishing with selected friends of mine in several regions of the country."

"There's no musky fishing south of here is there? Or are you going for another species?" Rad had barely glanced at the menu.

"My sources tell me that there are tar heel muskies and even some in the higher elevations of Georgia, but we fished the New River today. We don't have any contacts south of here, so we'll probably not go after muskies again until we're in Ohio on the way back. We are seeing a lot though." Joe chortled and Marv looked up and laughed at his jest.

The waitress arrived and took their orders. She rolled her eyes when Rad ordered three portions of fried okra as her side dishes to go with chicken fried steak.

During dinner Joe explained about the previous November's rescue of the young women in the Musky Straits and how that had helped Andre start to uncover the human trafficking centered in the chain of strip clubs run by a Russian gang. He also invited Rad to come along to the local club, though he expected her to decline from embarrassment.

Ever the contrarian, Rad accepted the invitation. Joe and Marv were going to be her ride back to the hotel where the fibbies were putting her up. She considered new experiences, even distasteful ones, to be a test of her ability to handle her job as well as any man would.

As they drove toward Ronald Reagan airport, Joe probed tentatively, "So, you are going to be a brown shoe soon?" He tilted the emphasis to imply a question.

"I don't trust cops, they always want to make me a project. But I've never had any dealings with the feds." Marv piped up from the back seat.

Joe looked into the rear view mirror and said, "Uh buddy, I work for the federal law enforcement bunch now. Have been for a year or so."

"Yeah, but I grew up with you. I remember when you owed money to the Italians and product to the Jamaicans. That was a hot time. You remember, Joe?"

"Rad doesn't need to hear about our history. Do you?"

"Actually, I'd be very interested." She had the needle in him and she was going to dig it in harder. Rad went on, however, to explain her change in status to Joe. She told him how she was to become an undercover FBI agent and a CBP agent as well.

"Are you saying that the fibbies suspect the Border Patrol of being penetrated by enemy agents?" Marv asked.

"I'm not saying anything of the sort." She left the subject alone but she and Joe exchanged looks across the front seat that said that they both thought the government was riddled with people pursuing agendas of their own.

In the parking lot of the strip club, Joe pulled under the glow of a streetlight. "Marv, show Rad her present and the other stuff we bought. And the knife for Mo too." Marv pulled the hockey bag up beside him and showed off the weapons within. Rad was astounded.

"You taking this stuff back to New York with you? These unpermitted handguns will get you in pretty deep if you're caught."

"We're going to leave them at Mack Spline's farm in Ohio, except for Mo's blade. I don't think swords are illegal, are they?" Joe's chest rumbled with his signature laugh. Marv beamed, toying with his two guns, a semi-automatic Smith & Wesson Model 910 and a Smith & Wesson Model 625 Mountain gun. It was a potent looking revolver. He had that dangerous, childlike look in his eyes that men never outgrow.

Later, after they'd been in the strip club for a few hours, Rad realized that going there had been a mistake. Rad had become more and more embarrassed in the bar, especially by the behavior of the girl who had originally been trying to get Joe's attention and money. She had flaunted herself and assumed that Rad was a lesbian. Joe, acting weirdly with Rad around, while able to fulfill his mission, was nervous and uncomfortable. Marv, meanwhile, went from being sulky about having Rad along to being so brazen around the girls that he'd gotten warned off by a bouncer. The bouncer, who had a face that looked like he had contacted a couple of windshields at high speed, showed unusual interest in all three and consulted his apparent boss with much nodding of heads, rubbing of noses, and hand gestures that suggested they thought Marv, Joe, and Rad were persons of special interest rather than their usual pathetic customers. The whole episode had been a let down. At night's end, Rad had been dropped off at her motel and had taken her gift of a hideaway gun with her. She was not worried about returning to her job with a secreted weapon. Everyone in law enforcement had one of those.

Men's public restrooms are often nasty and sometimes dangerous. Conversations with strangers are avoided if at all possible. Many men fear pick-up attempts by desperate homosexuals and are suspicious of any talk, friendly or otherwise. The restroom at a strip club, while an unlikely venue for a pick-up, might contain a pimp or a thug who wants to use the privacy for a mugging or assault. The toilets at the Sweet

Cherries in Charlotte were cleaner than most, but Joe didn't figure on having any conversations. He was hostile and suspicious when the man in the stall stepped out and moved to the urinal next to him. The unwritten rule, implicitly understood by all men is: when at the urinal, leave an intervening empty one between yourself and a stranger, if possible.

"How you?" the man said in a Carolina drawl. Joe looked over at him and furrowed his brows.

"You better watch some of those guys in there. They been watchin' you and your friend. I understand Russian and what they're saying don't set well with me."

Joe was undecided whether to ignore this or not. He continued to go about his business.

"They gonna give you a beat down if your friend doesn't back off from that blond dancer in the purple. I know this is weird, but I've heard them talkin' and I thought you might wanna know."

"How do you know it's me and Marv they're talking about?"

"They ain't many Yankees here tonight. They call you guys 'the idiot and the ugly one.' Said they been watching you since Washington city. They wonder why you check out all the girls but never make up to one. Your pal, they understand. You, they worry about."

"Well, Marv does want to get married everywhere we go. Only get married for a few hours, but when it's happening it feels like love."

"You could fool them if you lit a shuck right away."

"What's 'lit a shuck' mean? They going to shoot or beat us?"

"Take off for parts unknown, Texas maybe. It's a whipping they gonna give you, guns bring troopers around. You've got the mark on you, if you stay here, you won't make it to your car. You may not live out the night.

"My mother escaped from Russia in the days before Gorby, they pursued her some until my pa and his country boys discouraged them. I hate these ex-commie bully boys."

"You aren't just trying to get Marv's girlfriend for yourself are you?" They were both finished at the urinals and stood a few feet apart face to face.

"Anyone with money can get her any night of the week. You've got second sight. Look into the future. You'll see."

"How..." Joe spluttered.

"I too am the seventh son of a seventh son. Mark my words, or make your peace with our Lord." He stepped past Joe, went out the door and headed back to the bar.

"Curious," Joe said aloud to himself. He had been successful in gathering his information for Andre. He was getting heartily sick of strip clubs, even when the girls were friendly. Marv would be disappointed no matter when they left. They only had one more stop on the itinerary Agent Andre had set for them. After Atlanta they could head home with just a fishing stop or two. Joe left the restroom, snagged Marv, and they left the club.

Joe smiled but it hurt his eye socket to do so. He was thinking about the way he had hopped into his punches instead of using all the energy he could. Lured on by his enthusiasm, he hadn't put all the power of his strong legs and back behind each blow. He'd been doing all right until the Russian bruiser caught him full force with a combination to the heart, stunning him. Joe had staggered under the heart shot and then taken three hard ones to the gut. Lamentably, he was soft down there having lost his edge over the years. Once his wind was gone, he was done for. Marv — he smiled again and put his hand to his cheek because of the pain — had tried his best, taking down two guys with his trusty sap. They'd both been overpowered in the end by an overwhelming number of attackers.

Joe thought back to how it had started. He had seen the same bouncer in the last three Sweet Cherries Clubs he'd visited. He first noticed the big ugly in Washington when the man had rubbed up against Rad in a too-familiar way, all hands and thrusting pelvis. Joe thought he'd just been another jerk with bad manners and adolescent fantasies. When he showed up in Charlotte, right after Joe had parked himself at the bar and thrown down his one hundred dollar bill, Joe knew he'd seen him before. Their eyes met when he took the barstool beside Joe. His glare was brief but fearsome. The girls didn't come to sit by Joe after one glance at the big lug Joe had begun calling Ivan the Ape. It was Marv who had chatted up one of the ladies; friendly enough, but she spoke no English, and they had determined that the girls were inked in the usual way. Then Ivan the Ape came right at them in Atlanta, telling Joe he wasn't welcome and that he should leave. It grated on Joe to be told what to do even when, or maybe especially when, the advice helped. He turned away from Ivan, felt a hand roughly pull his shoulder, turned back, and dropped the ape with one jolting uppercut that combined the full power of his right arm from his twisting hips, and his thunderous thighs. The thug's head snapped back, and he was knocked out before he hit the floor. That was when the boxer was brought out to pummel Joe.

The Atlanta franchise was the cleanest and classiest that Joe had seen since Montreal. Atlanta was the boomtown of the New South, so it contained an upscale clientele, less shabby and worn down than that in Pittsburgh or Cleveland. The disturbance caused when Joe dropped Ivan the Ape, made several patrons get up and leave. No one with a hot career wants to be arrested in a police raid.

A sharply dressed bald man, obviously in charge, had preceded the boxer coming from the back room. All six enforcers had gathered around to chastise the troublemakers. Joe recalled seeing a man run up to the boss and listen, nod, pull on his ear and return to his position. He spoke quietly, "A beating before our police arrive. Don't kill them. The usual treatment would be too messy, considering who is watching."

The former Olympic boxer facing Joe knew how to fight and seemed to have the pure joy of combat endemic to Irish boys who grew up with lots of brothers. The fighter removed his shirt to reveal a massive chest and a pair of high-waisted pants pulled up over his kidneys. "Hey Joe! Let's go!" he said, in accented English.

"How'd you know my name?" Joe said as he slapped him backhand across the mouth. The boxer looked perplexed, obviously not understanding the language. He took the backhand slap across his lips, splitting the bottom one and releasing a trickle of blood. Joe's forehand slap was parried easily when the Russian sent a snapping right at Joe's face that missed as Joe leaned back and covered. Joe took a step back, breathed deeply three times, felt the fury rise in him, strong and hot.

All his life he'd had this rage, what he called his Irish, simmering below the surface, controlled only with effort. He'd always felt a great ecstasy when his captive fighter's soul was able to escape and the urge and the challenge ran wild. His mother had said he had the devil in him, and Joe often felt that seduction to be stronger than him. Now the battle was started and each man threw and parried, covered and bobbed, through three exchanges. No damage was done. A crowd of onlookers had gathered. Marv had Joe's back, but his head was on a swivel looking at potential attackers.

To Joe, there was no one in the world but his opponent. He entered his own realm of savage joy where all that he wanted was to outlast this adversary by throwing hard, brutal punches until he could go no more. His enthusiasm clouded his judgment and his being out of fighting trim caused him to forget his training.

Joe's boxing instructor had always yelled at him when he started hopping into his punches. Joe could hear the lecture now.

"You lose too much energy when you leave your feet. The opposing reaction from the ground, multiplied from your solid base through leverage and rotational energy, provided by your hips, increases your force factor, Joseph, producing a ratio of six or eight to one.

"You are a flail, a two-armed catapult. Your legs and hips, transferring the ground's reaction force into your back, arms, and wrist, multiply the force of your muscles. When your form is perfect you will prevail with maximum force. You must be perfect. Waste no energy. When you get excited and start hopping, you are using only muscle power and effectively using only half of that." Joe remembered the string tied around his ankles shoulder-width apart. "Shuffle Joe. When you hop you will only defeat a poser never a fighter.

Now, sitting in a jail cell, empty except for he and Marv, listening to Marv snore, Joe wondered about some things. When did he become a target of the Russians? Where was he now? This wasn't any county or city jail. It was too empty, too quiet, and too clean. It was clearly a jail because he was locked in, or was he? He had not tested the steel door. Neither Joe nor the Russian boxer had been casual about fighting. Joe recalled seeing a fight on a street corner in a Puerto Rican neighborhood. The battlers had stopped traffic as they whaled at each other, kicking and punching across the street and back. Each backed away from the other's attack so that the battle looked like a ballet with high kicks, spins, and flailing arms. What it didn't look like was a fistfight because the blows seldom hit even a glancing shot. Joe and the Russian each knew how to fight. You got inside the other and hammered, with powerful punches to the body and ripping uppercuts to the chin and face. Only a few overhand punches, landing on the sides and back of the head, are ever effective. They do more damage to your own hands than to the opponent. The head is harder than the wrist is strong. Inside work to the heart, belly, face, chin, and neck was what was needed to empty the other vessel of its will to fight. The only backing away to take place in this fight was in order to regroup and dive inside against the opponent to make his blows ineffectual.

Joe was not in the best of shape these days. He tired quickly in the fight, he felt like his arms were made of lead. Now he sat and looked through swollen eyes at his stiff and bruised knuckles, badly in need of an ice pack. He wished he'd had the thin leather gloves worn by the Russian, so good at cutting the opponent without tearing up the puncher's hands.

Despite the preparedness of the Russian, Joe had had the better of the contest because he was inside the other's reach for the first two thirds of the fight. Firmly planted on his base, able to punch from the ground up, he pounded his opponent. He popped him with a left and shouldered closer, combined two powerful rights and a left and felt the boxer sag. Though Joe had loved the fight and felt his opponent weakening, after about three minutes of solid heavy work, he needed to step back for a breather. He then summoned his will and charged forward on courage alone. It would be his last flurry. They came together and Joe drove the Russian back, slugging with a will. The boxer smiled at him, conceding Joe's lead, until the Russian delivered a hard left elbow to the chin, and a supercharged right ripped into Joe's diaphragm. His wind emptied with a whoosh, leaving him flatfooted and vulnerable. No longer able to lift his arms, even to parry, Joe couldn't counter his opponent's seven-punch combo to the face. He passed out in the middle of several awesome body shots coming up from the Russian's heels.

Joe didn't remember anything else. Since they were in jail, he assumed that he and Marv had been arrested.

Through slow movements, Joe had found a position where most parts of his body didn't scream in pain and he'd fallen asleep. When he awoke several hours had passed. Marv was awake looking at him with his head canted to the left. Smiling but in pain, he said, "You were giving better than you got for a few minutes, tough guy. Then you dropped your arms and became a punching bag. Anyway I stopped them from kicking your head and ribs in until the cops showed up. Then I surrendered."

"I'm not as young as I used to be. Too fat and too old. I lost my strength all of a sudden. You got any idea where we are? You see anyone?"

"We're in jail, dummy. Hey, where's our breakfast? You hungry, Joe?"

"Might as well eat." Joe sat up in bed and swung his legs to the floor. He was surprised that he did not have any soreness in his middle and his knees felt good. He stood, was woozy for only a second. *Hmm,* he thought, *No concussion.* And walked to the small five-by-seven window in the steel door. Looking out, he saw a uniformed guard about to open the door. Joe stepped back.

The door opened. A guard said, "You two come with me — no nonsense and you'll just be an ugly memory for me in mere moments."

They were ushered down the hall through a locked gate, past a guard's break room where Rush Limbaugh's voice was droning away on the radio, through another locked gate, and into a room of the type attorneys might use to interview their clients.

"Sit," The guard said, then he closed the door and left.

"I don't suppose they're gonna bring us breakfast?"

"Sure, Joe, catered from the nearest hotel." Marv's expression asked how Joe could be so stupid.

The door opened and two men, dressed in conservative suits wearing the brown shoes of FBI agents, entered with take-out coffees and a box of Krispy Kreme donuts. They left the food and drinks on the table, walked out, and did not close the door. Joe glanced at the open door, turned to the table, and opened the donut box.

Special Agent Thomas Andre walked through the door, which was pulled shut behind him by an unseen hand.

"Well, Joe, you've upset the local authorities this time."

Joe shoved a donut in his mouth so he wouldn't have to comment.

"This assignment is finished." Andre spoke only to Joe, Marv might as well have been invisible. "You are in a minimum security federal penitentiary. Your van is outside here and when our interview is done you are free to drive back to your home or wherever you want to go. I have no further assignments for you at present."

After swallowing, Joe spoke. "We never got to check out the girls here in Hotlanta, but they were there in Pittsburgh, Cleveland, Charlotte, and Washington. Just as you said, tattooed on both hands. Does that mean the Russians are running all these clubs and these girls are slaves? And why always at airports? Have they got an inside man?" Joe was coming around, stimulated by a little food and coffee.

"The ability to plant moles in our civil service bureaucracies is well known." Andre provided a rare explanation to Joe.

"How'd these Russkies know what we were up to? They knew we were coming to Hotlanta." He looked at Agent Andre then asked, "You don't have a leaker in your group, do you?"

Andre flashed a piercing-hot challenging glance at Joe, furrowed his brow and said, "Finish your food," from his briefcase Andre dropped two large envelopes onto the table. "Go home and call me one week from today with a report." Andre picked up his briefcase and left the room without closing the door.

"Did you see the look he gave you when you suggested there was a traitor in his office?"

"Yes, Marv, I saw."

Chapter 7
Downtown Pantherville

—June 9th—

Whenever Joe Gaspe gave a debriefing to Special Agent Thomas Andre it was a verbal accounting. While Joe might or might not refer to some notes, he had been told never to leave a paper trail. If one day some investigator came looking for the reasons the feds were paying for nebulous agents to do unlikely things, the trail needed to be cold. Joe liked it that way but understood that when that day came he'd be thrown under the bus before the Special Projects program would yield any gems to a reporter's or senate staffer's notebook.

Nevertheless he had to make a report and take a dressing-down from Andre about the debacle in Atlanta. Joe was recovered enough to have the self-satisfied feeling that he was helping to thwart evil endeavors, and that his efforts to combat the Russian gang, while creating trouble for himself, were useful.

"How did you manage to get in a fistfight so quickly?" Andre asked. They were sitting on a bench watching the water flow past on the Musky Straits. It was Wednesday afternoon, too late for the lunch crowd. They sat beside each other with enough space between them to accommodate another person.

"I've thought about that. I saw the bruiser that started it in Charlotte, and he may even have been there in Washington. Of course, I wasn't looking for him, I just remembered afterward. I think they must have been on to us after Cleveland. We weren't doing anything. I was chatting up girls, and Marv was falling in love. But that's typical, huh? I mean, somebody must have had other information to figure out we weren't just patrons."

"Did you forget my instructions to not make yourself obvious?"

"No. No, I didn't. We weren't doing anything out of the ordinary. But, when I sat down, the goon sat right next to me. And the $100 bill attracted no takers. That was unusual."

"Joe, I need you to take a few days off. Relax. Enjoy your family. I've got a few things to work on. I'll be in touch."

"Don't call us, we'll call you, huh?"

"Most things we work on in life are bigger than our part in it, Joe. Just be patient,." Andre said condescendingly while he glanced at his appointment book.

"If you know these guys are enslaving women, even if they are illegal immigrants themselves, why don't you stop it?"

Andre looked at Joe over the top of his reading glasses with a look that exaggerated the patience he was extending to his employee.

"Oh, I get it. You are after the big fish, not just the girls and the goons. Other things have to play out, right?" Joe's voice tailed off as he realized Andre was not going to comment further.

"I'll call you, Joe. If you need anything, you've got my number." Andre turned a page in his book.

Joe took his leave. As he walked to the car he said, "Perfect."

"Sweet Cherries!? Why you wanna go back there? The girls are skinny and foreign and not very friendly." Marv's potential brother-in-law, Brian Hesketh, liked the upscale clubs where all the girls were blond, bobbed, and busty. He called them the Swedish bikini team.

"I've got something I need to check out. Important stuff. Can't you get your mind out of your shorts for one evening?" Marv could act like a stuffed shirt, even to himself.

"Why would I want to do that?" Brian asked.

Marv had driven back to Covington in one of the marathon road trips he was known for. He shook his head at his interlocutor and turned into the parking lot. Sweet Cherries was in an ordinary looking building set off by itself behind some warehouses used by airfreight companies. Neon beer signs decorated the front windows. Being sober this time, Marv noticed that the one-story rear portion of the building was over one hundred yards long and the windows had been painted over with black paint.

Inside the club the afternoon clientele was sparse. Only two girls were around, one dancing and one schmoozing a man whose face was covered with moles, skin tabs, and wens. An uglier man was hard to imagine. Sitting at the bar with Hesketh, Marv ordered a beer and waited to see more dancers. It occurred to him that there were more cars in the lot than clients in the club by a wide margin, and he deduced that the long, low, blacked out, section held girls who were entertaining other customers.

They settled in for a long haul of bad music, indifferent dancing, and limited conversation. A girl emerged from a door in the rear that had a sign reading Private on it, and sidled up next to Hesketh. She appeared to have been summoned.

"Vould chu buy me a dhrink sailor?" She got her bartender's special, Brian and Marv got Buds. It was Marv who ponied up for the round. By observing the setup while trying to go unnoticed, Marv felt like a kid playing cops and robbers. He wasn't a heroic sort, and had never considered himself a guardian of society, but now he was in on the planning of a daring mission, and he felt a prickly sensation on his skin. He had an intensified awareness and saw things that would have normally gone unnoticed. An older, hard-looking, woman at the end of the bar monitored that Private door. Marv figured her to be the madam. A flat-faced, square headed, crew-cut wearing, Slavic bruiser stood silently nearby. The bartender quietly approached any customer who sat at the bar by himself for more than a few moments. Their conversations were very short. Occasionally a man would emerge from the back. Marv's glimpse back there revealed another goon and a scantily-clad dancer for a second. No one seemed to speak while back there until one time when an unmistakably Midwest accent was heard to say, "Lay off, Ivan, I'm going." That was followed by a discernable smacking sound.

Marv waited. He bought more rounds — over-priced tea for Brian's date and over-priced beer for the guys. After each girl danced twice and socialized while the others danced, a shift change took place. There in the third group was Joe's daughter's friend, Randi. When she finished her first set of dances Marv tried to get her to sit next to him. She began to walk toward his side of the bar and was stopped by a one-word utterance from the madam. Randi went and sat next to her at the end of the horseshoe-shaped bar. Marv observed how Randi and the other English speaker, the one with the midwestern accent, were kept away from the customers. He had to develop a plan. Going into the men's room he took out a dollar bill and wrote on it, "Joe and I will be coming for you. Be ready to travel."

Marv didn't think of himself as heroic, he'd had too many scrapes on the shady side of the law for that. He sustained his self-image only by convincing himself that he was better than he knew himself to be. But he was no coward and like many men he relished a challenge. Bravery included facing the kind of weather that brewed up on the Upper Lake, taking Joe's back in the fistfights of youth, or facing down both Italian and Jamaican gangsters in the same week. He was scared those times, but he gathered his strength, faced the situation, and went ahead. The swallowing of his fear, accompanied by an adrenaline blast, was what he was experiencing now.. He now had to find a way to get the dollar bill with the note on it to Randi without the, always suspicious, Russian goons catching on.

Marv stared into his beer and breathed deeply. He was not given to sudden passions, rather he was a man of simmering grudges. He thought about Randi and other captive girls, convinced himself that he and Joe were going to do something to get her out of that trap and began developing a plan. Being slow to anger, he was deliberate if not glacial, in his capacity to get over a grievance. He now had a grievance against these Russians. He let his methodical planning side consume him.

He wasn't free of doubts, since he didn't really know Randi and had no idea how she'd react. He didn't even know if she wanted to return to Muskedaigua. But he overcame his doubts with a feeling of exhilaration. He was going to do something right, important, exciting, and alive, something that would give his life meaning. He just had to convince Joe that it was the right thing to do.

Men in these bars often moved closer to the dancers to offer a bill for the privilege of a special shake or wiggle aimed in their direction. They had to be careful not to jostle each other in crowding to the dance platform. Physical contact with girls was not allowed and, pushing, elbowing, and cutting in front of other customers was also prohibited. That kind of physicality was likely to cause fistfights. During Randi's second dance set, Marv seized his opportunity to move up and extended his dollar bill with the note written on it. When she reached for it her eyes were plaintive and her expression showed a mixture of sadness, dread, and embarrassment. She knew this was a man who was from back home in Muskedaigua. Grabbing the bill as she danced, she felt resistance and looked into Marv's face. He gave a slight tug as he gave up the bill and said, "Read the note."

Randi continued her dance but, as the meaning of his words dawned on her, she gyrated back toward where Marv watched and nodded to him and moved her lips to silently say, "OK, I will."

In Muskedaigua, Amelia Gaspe had learned to accept the riot that was in her mind. Her father's explanation of why she dreamed so powerfully made no logical sense, yet it clarified what was happening. She was no longer scared by her ability to enter another person's dream and influence their dream state. Before starting the dreaming, she would meditate for a short while on that other person. Then, in the dream, she could move into the dream and affect it.

Randi DesChutes was her target. Amy spoke in Randi's dream and visited her dream worlds accompanied by The Old One, the man who wore the Wolf Clan mantle, to inform Randi what was to come. Joe hadn't told Amy that he was going on the rescue mission, but she knew, because she could enter her father's dream state as an observer. She knew where Joe was going and she was going to make Randi see her warnings.

Randi and Mayella, being the only speakers of American English in the stable, had become friends. They could only steal time together when their guard, Anatoli, was drunk. His taste for vodka was so strong that this was most of the time. They had started their friendship with girl talk, ignoring their horrific circumstances and living a brief fantasy that nothing was wrong. It was during one such session that they had made a pact to not swallow their required "medicine" in defiance of orders. There was both an upside and a downside to that action.

With a clear mind, they didn't feel all drugged out when in the dorm, but their performances became listless and that got them shoved around by the goons that enforced the rules. In addition, the disgusting nature of the things that they were forced to do and their longing for their previous life became more acute. During a period when they were both clear headed, they had a conversation.

"When I sleep, after skipping the pill, I have strange dreams but very real ones." Randi was whispering. Anatoli was drunk and snoring, but the other dancers might be listening and most would rat on the girls to gain some small favor from the bosses.

"What's it like?"

"I had a friend back home in high school, Amy Gaspe. She is talking to me though I can't see her. Instead I see a strange old man with a funny fur hat. He points up in the air and says things that sound like a dog growling. But what I hear is Amy's voice. It's really weird, ya know?"

"What does Amy say?"

"She says, 'Be ready, they will come for you.' "

"Who?"

"I don't know who, but I've had this dream a few times and it gets longer and clearer each time."

"Weird. I had a Louisiana Grandma who claimed that her dreams predicted events, family events. She was a daughter of a seventh son of a seventh son. She was right, too. A lot."

The one thing Radleigh Loonch was sure she'd learned in college was that while there was a correct answer to every question, that answer had nothing to do with being right. Thus, polite society assumed that a one hundred pound woman could work all day changing eighty-pound truck tires, and a typical man would happily nurture infant children that were not his own. The general nuttiness of this kind of knowledge made Rad uncritical in her analysis of things.

She found herself in a similar frame of mind on her drive to meet Otis the Artificer. She was with Joe and his behavior was unusual. He was the big-game hunter who, while eager to meet up with his intended quarry, was hoping that he did not see the lion at all. Men were weird. Trying to think about something else and get Joe out of his mood, she asked, "Does Agent Andre know what you're planning? Did you tell him?"

"I didn't tell him. I avoid details with him if at all possible. But, I'm sure he knows. With Andre, you gotta remember, he doesn't want to know a lot of the stuff that I do."

"Yeah. But you don't work for him officially, like I do."

"I think he knows a lot of things. Way more than he ever lets on. Besides what's the worst thing he can do? Fire you? You don't have to worry. You can get another job. Hell, a white woman can always get a job." Joe knew when there was an opportunity to push Rad's buttons.

Rad stared daggers at Joe for a second. Then, eyes back on the road, she said, "I suppose it's no coincidence that he gave me the same leave time that he did you."

Joe said, "Exactly." He switched gears and asked, "What kind of a guy is this Otis feller, anyway?"

Rad shook her head and thought, *Men!*

Rad had come through again, she had told Joe about the twelve-year-old full-sized Cadillac Fleetwood, in excellent condition that her father would sell to him cheaply. It was big enough for Joe and his offensive lineman's body and had a full back seat for piling in numerous offspring. Now it was going into the shop for a major refit. Rad and her father knew a man who could do anything with cars as long as it didn't involve computers. Rad called him Otis the Artificer, and he didn't balk at her request to put armored glass in the back window, mount four self-sealing puncture proof tires, and install Kevlar armored fabric inside the trunk and rear quarter panels.

Rad drove her Malibu down the long driveway and inside the fence that screened Otis' activities from his neighbors. Joe followed in the Cadillac. They pulled around to the back and left the keys in the Caddy. Rad opened the door to the shop and stepped inside, followed by Joe. Inside the darkened shop, blinking from the change from the bright sunlight outside, Rad checked things out. She began to notice right away that a subtle change had come over Joe. He was wary and not just because three large dogs came bounding up. The biggest dog was a Rottweiler with a huge head and shoulders. He barked once, recognized Rad, and began wagging his stub tail. The Rotty went to find his toy, a tennis ball. He was a boy dog always ready to play. The two mixed-breed shepherd females circled Joe; wary, sniffing, backing off, and barking.

"Blondie, Schottsie, It's okay, he's a friend." Rad looked over and noticed lights in the paint booth. "Otis is probably in the middle of a job, he won't mind if we wait." She pulled a beer from the six-pack and handed it to Joe, got one for herself and took the rest to the refrigerator, putting them inside.

She pulled up a stool, pointed to one for Joe and turned her attention to the bigger dog and his ball. The dog offered the tennis ball but wanted it pulled from his gripping jaws. Rad knew that he wouldn't give it up easily and then it would be all slobbery, so she scratched him behind the ear and waited for him to drop the ball. This caused the ball to bounce away and resulted in the dog chasing it around the shop for a while.

The shop was crowded with work in mid-project, mostly painting jobs but also mechanical work on stern drives for boats. Otis had explained his system to Rad once. Every job met snags before completion, when parts would have to be identified, ordered, and be picked up or delivered. To keep from being stymied while waiting, two other jobs were always set up. This pattern of moving from job to job, while using time efficiently, required three sets of expensive tools.

Rad was right at home in Otis's shop, comfortable with the dogs and oblivious to the vintage pinups around the walls. Joe looked around, sizing up Otis from the way he took care of his equipment. Suddenly the dogs became alert, ran outside to the fenced kennel through their dog door to bark at an approaching vehicle, and then back inside as the side door opened. A comely young lady with two armloads of packages greeted the dogs familiarly and asked, "Otis around?"

Just as Rad was about to answer, the door to the paint booth opened and Otis stepped through wearing the tight-fitting hood that kept paint out of his hair. He smiled at Rad and turned to the parts girl, taking an invoice to be signed and exchanging banal dialogue with her. She left after some baby talk to the dogs. Rad introduced Otis and Joe to each other, and they shook hands warily.

For the next half-hour Rad marveled at men and their behavior. She knew what to expect, but it was a study in anthropology nevertheless. Like dogs circling each other for scent, the men engaged in a testosterone-fueled thrust and parry. Otis showed off his gear, commented on his projects, and nervously spoke too much. Joe meanwhile, held back approval though saying all the right words, judging the worth of Otis' equipment, habits, and appearance. Both men were old enough to be Rad's father and were both friends of his. They were practical men of considerable skill in the manual arts. They were guys she really liked and may have set her cap for if they had been of her generation. Even so, Rad could study them and note the ritualized behavior analytically. It was the German in her.

"Let me show you what I'm working on in here." Otis opened the door to the paint room, and there were the parts to an antique refrigerator, freshly coated, taped off, laid out shiny and perfect. Joe and Otis had found the common ground with which they could become friends. Both were painters, though in different mediums, and they ratchet-jawed for fifteen minutes about epoxies, primers, clear coats, orifice sizes and other minutiae Rad didn't care to comprehend. The anthropology lesson over, she pulled out another beer and leafed through a copy of *Popular Mechanics* while the two men arrived at a common ground of respect that would allow the business at hand to proceed.

They all walked out to the Cadillac to talk about what was needed. Joe opened the trunk. "We need to have glass in the back window and the two rear passenger windows that will need to withstand bullets. We need armor in the trunk that will deflect multiple hits."

"Is there a war starting that I don't know about?" Otis asked as he peered under the cloth liner of the trunk.

"We're going to steal a girl who's being held as a white slave by some Russian Mafia types," Rad said.

"Wow, you take on big challenges don't you?" Otis looked at Rad when he said this, smiling with admiration.

Joe hesitated for several moments and answered, "This is a local Muskedaigua girl, held captive near Cincinnati, and we're gonna get her back." Otis nodded when he heard this.

"You want the front windows protected?"

Joe replied, "No. I think after Hoser gives us our tune-up we'll be able to outrun anything they've got."

"You should be able to smoke most everybody with that engine. Okay, I can get a ballistic polymer film that I will apply to the windows, and they will not be able to penetrate it with anything less than a bazooka. I hope I can get enough Kevlar to line the trunk and rear fenders to make them bulletproof. The military is buying a lot of that lately. I'll put the polymer film on the taillights too. Have you got a surefire plan to get away?"

"These Russians are urban gangsters, they don't know this country or understand Americans all that well. We're going to evade them and call for help from folks we know along the way. We'll be ready for a fight but avoid it if we can." Joe sounded confident. Rad wondered if he was.

Otis looked at Rad, "Are you ready for this?"

"Yes." Rad had no clue what she was getting into but her assertiveness had carried her this far and it was the horse she'd continue to ride. "But, I will need a lesson in evasive driving."

"I can do that," Otis smiled. "How soon do you need this? It will take about a week to get the materials."

"As soon after that as you can do it."

"I'll put a rush on the materials, and I'll do it the day they hit here. Say next Wednesday. I hate Russians and I've got two daughters myself."

"I've got five." Joe offered his hand to Otis and they shook. Rad gave Otis a chaste peck on the cheek and walked out to the Malibu.

"We're going to practice a little in this parking lot. I'll show you how to use the rocket motor in this Caddy." Otis got behind the wheel. They were in the huge parking lot of a Presbyterian church, empty as it was early evening. This church had an unusual congregation, not declining like so many old-line protestant sects. This mammoth and growing congregation was made up of Korean Americans. Rad recognized the squares of Korean pictograms from her brief foray into stamp collecting.

"I'm gonna show you how to get up and scoot with this Cadillac They put the Corvette engine in it that year. It's easy." With that Otis tromped on the gas pedal and pinned Rad back into the passenger's seat with the force of his acceleration. Within seconds they had covered the half-mile length of the church lot.

"How fast was that? Won't these people object to us racing around here?"

"Only eighty-two, I bet with a longer run we could top one hundred. They won't beef me. Not since I dug them out of that monster snowstorm a few years ago. I had the equipment then, and my son and I cleared fifty inches of snow in time for Sunday services." Otis stepped out and moved around to the passenger's side. "You try."

Rad sat in the driver's seat and looked to Otis for instruction.

"You won't break it. There's nothing to hit," he waved at an empty lot without even light poles to block the path. "Just tromp down hard and fast." She looked ahead. Looked at Otis. "Go ahead."

Rad put what she thought was appropriate pressure on the pedal. The Caddy sped up smoothly and moved off. At the far end of the lot she stopped.

"Too timid. You can reach that speed in six seconds instead of ten. You won't hurt the engine. Do it again."

Otis had said this while Rad was turning the car around for another run.

"Punch it!" Otis yelled. Without hesitation Rad rammed her foot down. The roaring Cadillac rocketed forward, smoking the tires and sliding the rear end right then left. Rad lay off the pedal. The smoke cleared. She looked at Otis.

"Okay, now do it again. But steer your way out of that. Those tires are turning too fast to grip well. Just steer and keep on chooglin'."

Rad backed up to the edge of the lot. The third time she had it licked. The Caddy stepped out like a racehorse at full gallop. Rad corrected for the side slippage. The tires smoked but the car left the cloud behind.

Otis yelled, "Whoo hoo!" He beamed like a new dad. After another half an hour Otis was satisfied. "No one will catch you on a straight track unless their car is very special. You're a quick study girl, but I'm warning you, on turns you will lose a lot of speed. This is a big car. Its ass end will slide, and you'll have to control the wheel. Steer opposite like you do on ice. A more nimble car will gain on you on curves but you'll dust 'em on straight-aways."

Chapter 8
On the Rez

—June 11th—

Driving the length of the Oil Seep Seneca Reservation allowed Mo to assess himself and the fate of the Iroquois in the twenty-first century. The discovery of oil on this tiny Rez of only 240 acres, was a complete accident. The land, ceded back to the tribe, was supposed to be worthless and much of it was too steep to even build a cabin on. But with an income from oil in the Berea deposits, it had become one of the most densely populated Reservations that had been set aside for the Real People. Coming from a culture that reveres hunting and fishing as a way to teach young men the proper path, the Iroquois don't take well to crowding.

The young men hanging around, a few hundred yards up the road from the gas pumps at the smoke shop, were a sickening example of the problem. Moses X Snow knew what they were doing. One of them had a beer can full of gasoline and they were all huffing the fumes. He could tell by the stuporous postures and stumbling, falling, reeling gaits of those on the fringe that they were completely wasted and would be so all day long. The youth of his nation had learned that you could walk up to a gas pump at one of the smoke shops, tilt the hose on the pump, and get eight to ten ounces of gas to flow into whatever container you

Uncle Mike

had. This would get everybody high until the liquid evaporated at which time that hose waited, filled with more gas every time someone made a purchase.

Cheaper than alcohol and much more stupefying, huffing took over in a land where most people had no money. As much as Mo knew what these young men and boys were doing, he also knew that they were careening into oblivion, in both this Shadow World and the Real World of dreaming that he visited regularly. People like them, representing those from great swaths of time, wandered in the dream world without faces, permanently sleep-walking through eternity. Mo had seen them. His heart ached for their plight, but he was hopeful that his people of the longhouse could find the strength to overcome this non-personness brought on first by alcohol, then by drugs, and now by anything from gasoline to whipping cream to Endust.

Mo drove his Jetta, that most non-Indian of cars, past assorted pick up trucks — fifteen year old beaters in the junk-strewn yards of the trailers and cottages of the poor folks of the Rez. Around a curve he came to an intersection of an oil well haul road on the left and across the street a driveway to the modern, landscaped, split-level house of one of the gambling or smoke shop millionaires. The cars of these tycoons of the extractive industries (extracting money from non-Indians through untaxed tobacco, fuel sales, and gambling) were new SUVs or Lexuses or Cadillacs. When he passed the tycoon's fancy house, the road he sought was next on the right.

He had come early for a meeting with his cousin Joe Gaspe at the hilltop house of the Seneca Sachem Joseph Buck Brant, known as Uncle Mike. He looked forward to dreaming with Uncle Mike and entering the Real World of the Iroquois. Mo occupied the Shadow World as two different people. He was a businessman with a successful bait brokerage across the northern border of New York and the southern border of Ontario. He employed a dozen people most of whom were relatives. He made enough money to be comfortable without being lured into a consumptive lifestyle. He was a man of note in the white man's world and a big man among his Mohawk kin. He also nurtured his Mohawk warrior side with his fishing and hunting exploits. He took short trips into the woods and onto the water where he lived as a man of the longhouse was supposed to live: vibrant, alive, in touch with the essential nature of the animals he hunted. It was while he skimmed through the reeds and rushes to fish along the weed edges of his native Ottawa and St. Lawrence Rivers that he refreshed his mind, body, and spirit in order to work in the business world. Looking across a great flat of cattails, with herons and egrets rising and working the bait while being harassed by dissenting red wing blackbirds, he lived most like a Mohawk and most like a man. The sun, setting or rising, turned the weeds to gold, the water to tarnished copper, and let Mo work his musky baits to best effect. He had caught a few huge muskies, including one he had released that he knew was of legendary size. The catch of a lifetime, and he didn't even get s photo. But, Mo knew that it had been a gift from Mother Earth that confirmed his worth as a hunter and a man.

Turning down the rough gravel road to Uncle Mike's hilltop home, he shivered as he anticipated dreaming with a Sachem and entering the Real World that kept the parts of him together and in harmony. There was terror in the world of Mohawk dreaming where one saw the faceless empty husks of people who had succumbed to drink or dissipations. They had no life in either the Real World or the Shadow World. He had been there and seen these poor, empty, bland, meat bags. He would see them again with Mike.

After he parked the Jetta and walked up the steep hill toward the cabin, the dream state began to take his body with a lightening in the shoulders and a fuzzy haze at the edges of his vision. Each step up the path into the clouds brought him into a more complete state of awareness. Mike's house rested high enough up the hills that rain clouds, being squeezed of their drizzle, were below Mo when he came to the open door. He walked past a steaming teakettle on the stove and joined the Sachem in his darkened smoking room. The only lights in the room were the red coals from the Sachem's pipe and the luminescent glow of his piercing vision. Mo was in the doorway when Uncle Mike spoke.

"Yes, you must go on the trip with your cousin." Mike removed the lit pipe from his teeth and gestured to a wooden chair. Mo sat.

Shrunken, wrinkled, nut-brown, the Sachem continued, "He needs your protection. He needs your intervention with our Shawnee brothers. He will need your skill as a warrior. You will find sacred things on the journey. And, Moses X Snow, you will come to a pass in your life because of this trip. A turning point you reach will make your life in the Shadow World better than it has been in many many seasons."

Mo wasn't bothered by the Sachem's answering of questions he had not yet asked. He was sure, that Uncle Mike had observed him, ever since he had taken the turn toward the Oil Seep Reservation. He reached into his pouch and brought out an old Meerschaum pipe he had gotten during his military service in Germany, loaded it with Uncle Mike's mixture of Kinnikinnick and Kentucky Burley and lit up.

"We will smoke and then we can dream on this problem of your cousin Joe's." The gray light of the slanting sun came through the window and lit a streak across a trade goods tomahawk pipe, two hundred years old, decorated with Raven, Hawk, and Heron feathers. Mo's transport into the Real World was nearly complete.

Mo saw the front of a large Elmwood trade canoe slipping through a brown slow-flowing river. There were more canoes to his left and following. These were carrying the manufactured goods of the English, the Sunrise People. They were heavily loaded with the products native people had come to need and crave, iron kettles, needles, glass beads, steel knives and tomahawks and the thing wanted most by the people the Senecas were going to trade with, guns. The Shawnees, little brothers of the Iroquois, wanted glass beads and paints, but mostly they wanted guns, powder, and shot. They had a few rusting ancient muskets but little ammunition and no way to repair their guns.

A tow-headed German youth from the settlements in the Mohawk valley was being brought to Chalagawtha to be a gunsmith in the Shawnee capitol. The Ohio Shawnees had had little positive exposure to white people, save for captives they had taken in their raids into Virginia and some women they had traded for. The tribe had come to no accommodation with the whites. However, their chiefs had realized that, as stone-aged people, they were at a disadvantage against their Cherokee adversaries to the south across the hunting grounds of Kane Tuck and to the north with the tribes beyond Lake Erie. The Seneca tradition was to hunt deep into Ohio and trade for furs to send back to Albany. The tribe had arranged for a trade in guns and to bring the gunsmith and trader to live among them.

The Seneca's freight canoes would return with furs, sacred tobacco, silver, and flint tools. The Shawnees lived on the greatest flint deposits in the Indian's world and had traded it for generations with the Senecas. Now, with the coming of English trade goods made from steel, flint was mainly used in ceremonial items and for children's weapons used in training young warriors.

Mo thought of all this as the canoe armada turned north from the Ohio, known as the Spaylaywetheepi to the Shawnees, onto the smaller, clearer, faster-flowing Scioto. Uncle Mike was a bird on his shoulder reminding Mo that in the Real World of dreams all time is present. Mo was seeing the history of his people as it had been in the Shadow World.

When the canoes reached the tall tulip trees where the Shawnees liked to locate their villages the little children came to look. As the canoe with Mo and the gunsmith came into view, the children ran away toward the village in terror. The German boy, Johann, had an unpronounceable last name that sounded like a man spitting out a fly that had flown down his throat. He was as white as a pearl. He turned and asked Mo, "Is it me the little ones fear?"

Mo said nothing. Looking past the gunsmith he had heard the word, in Shawnee, that grandmothers told around the fire — the descriptive word for Mohawks that meant, "He's coming to eat you."

The trading proceeded. Johann and his parts and tools and benches and molds were unloaded and set up in a wickiup a little apart from the main village. He was taken under the protection of a boy of his age named Chiksika who would teach him to converse in Shawnee. Johann had a gift for language and he also had shown he could learn to dream. He showed no fear of being left with these fierce warriors. He looked on it as a convenient adventure, because he needed to leave the proximity of the Dutch, having been accused, correctly, of stealing sheep from the Patroon.

The canoes would eventually head back to the Ohio and against the current toward the forks of the Ohio. The Senecas had their tobacco and their peltries and their flint to knap. And Mo had a special gift. He had been given an offering. He had with him a comely, young, white woman who had been captured far to the south. She sat in front of him, happy to belong to one man instead of being cuffed and beaten as a slave by all the widows in the Shawnee capitol. She was well turned with dainty hands and feet and had a rosy red cast to her cheeks. She headed into a new life as the companion of a great Mohawk warrior.

An old Shawnee woman stood on the shore and said to her son's wife, "It was good that you gave the Mohawk that lazy white girl, he can eat her instead of one of your daughters."

Mo smelled the strong sweet smell of native tobacco and looked up at Uncle Mike who smiled with his eyes. Mo looked questioningly at the sachem, who said, "Yes, you must help Joseph. You must introduce him to those Shawnee still in Ohio. You will have a white Indian to help you. You will do some hunting and will protect Joseph and his companions. You will get the gift of a woman from Maneto."

Mo nodded, "Joe expects trouble."

"There will be a great need for you to protect Joseph from his enemies. He will need your help. You won't look for trouble but it will find you. Joe saved your life at Oka, and you are obliged to protect him now."

Mo looked at the ceremonial calumet on the wall as the streak of light illuminating it disappeared.

Mo was deep in thought when Uncle Mike left the room to refill the coffee pot. It was a warrior's path he had chosen: to live in the white world as a businessman subject to the demands of time and distance that required, to be a tribal member on the reservation on the St. Lawrence River and to be true to his ancestors, and to participate in the dream path of a hunter. Three paths, that each would be all-consuming to one with less energy, were followed daily by Moses X Snow. It was this warrior's path that compelled him to take on the battles of his cousin Joe and live on the edge between the dream world and the seamy side of the white man's world.

Uncle Mike puffed his pipe, nodded, and poured coffee. He offered sugar to Mo, who declined, then ladled five spoonfuls of the white granules into his own cup.

"You have never been to the Ohio country before this dream. But now you will find friends in the Shawnee Nation of Ohio. You have seen the ancient ones trade with the Shawnees and the white woman captured on the Natchez trace that was given to your ancestors. The Shawnees were little brothers to the Senecas since the time we allowed them to come from the south and east into the Ohio country, our traditional hunting grounds. But they always feared the Mohawks because of the ancient terror visited upon them when they lived below Kentucky and warred with the Cherokees. The Shawnees fear and respect Senecas but they have nightmares about Mohawks.

"You know, nephew, you will dream each thing before it happens. You're journey will take less than half of a moon phase but will contain five important events. You have the gift of remembrance. You must honor your dreams as these events approach and you will come back to your land at Akwesasne with your life changed. I know you are able to enter the Real World. You must guard your warrior's soul when around white men. Even when the white men are good men, their ways can lure you to your death."

"It's her Big Boy and she knows I'm from back home." Marv and Joe were heading for the fish grounds, speeding along the interstate. Today they were going to do some casting along the Musky Straits. They were preparing to go on an adventure but a little musky fishing, before, during and after, was still in order. Joe was scheduled to meet Agent Andre at five. They'd have three hours to fish beforehand. Joe and Marv had a friendship that went way back, but it was fishing that kept them together as adults. Instead of drifting apart as adults do, with varied work, family, and social obligations and agendas, Joe and Marv hunted muskies together and found a sense of clarity and a relationship with the natural world that, while dangerous, arduous and difficult, helped them achieve harmony.

Joe was used to Marv's enthusiasm getting the better of him. He nodded and murmured, "Um hum."

"I know your man Andre will not approve this idea of mine — that we rescue Randi and get her away from that place. He's not going to give his approval but, if the thing happens, he'll be glad of it. He may not be capable of action because of his position, but we are. We can just dive in and make a difference. He'll be pleased. I have no doubt." Marv often considered himself a leader and maker of plans. Joe indulged this fantasy.

"Have you ever met Andre?"

"Yeah, that time he got us out of jail in Atlanta."

"And have you two spoken?"

"Er, No."

"He'll not stop us 'cause he won't know. When and if he finds out, make that when, 'cause he *will* find out, he'll be pissed and he'll probably fire me from my job." Joe looked straight at the highway. Marv turned from the road and glanced at him.

"But, I told this girl we'd come. Are you really so concerned about your job?" Marv was pleading a little now.

"We will go. We won't tell Andre. It will be my show. My plan. My orders."

"Sure Joe, you're the boss. Jeez."

Joe Gaspe went to visit Jackie B's Draft Beer and Live Bait in Pantherville. There were two people he usually found there that he needed to stay in contact with. Rudyard Loonch, Rad's uncle, worked there and he was an intellectual mentor to Joe as well as an intelligence asset who supplied key data for Joe's use in his work for Agent Andre. Joe was also likely to find Mel Dumke at the barroom. Dumke was a person of interest that Andre hoped Joe could keep tabs on. Dumke was unaware of Joe's law enforcement affiliations and tended to talk loudly and revealingly in front of him. Joe was convinced that Dumke had engineered several attempts on his life — though none could be proved — and he had come to revile Dumke as an odious and thoroughly evil person. Nevertheless, it was his plan to schmooze Dumke while seeking information. Joe needed to keep his job.

Joe came through the side door, a private entrance, and walked up to Ned Niawanda who stood beside Dumke at the bar.

"Ned, how you doing, friend?" Joe clapped him roughly on the shoulder. "Mel, old buddy, how they hangin'?" Joe looked in the eyes of Dumke who knew Joe as an enemy but did not know that Joe knew he knew. Dumke nodded with a smile.

"Mel was just telling me about his terrific sex life. As if I wanted to hear that," Niawanda chuckled and winked at Joe Gaspe. The room had three other men in it, two strangers deep in conversation at a far round table and Rudyard sitting at a table covered by several open books and notebooks. Joe smiled at him and held up one finger. Rudyard returned the smile, nodded, and went back to his research.

"Mel, tell Joe what you were telling me," Niawanda egged him on.

"I can get laid anytime I want now. Different young ones if I want 'em. And they can't back sass me 'cause they don't talk English." Dumke let out a hearty self-satisfied laugh.

"You're not with that Czeck woman anymore?" Joe remembered that name because it was the same as his Gypsy grandmother's name.

"Sure, I'm with her, but a man wants a little strange once in a while."

"Oh sure, I understand.' Joe waited.

"I know people, important people in Canada, and they get these young girls for me. Really young girls, sweet and tender. All I've got to do is a few errands for them sometimes. Mostly driving. I can just pull up and tell my guy Alex to fill 'er up and he asks how many. I drive around the corner for delivery. It is heavenly."

"You say they don't speak English. Are they Chinese or what?" Ned drew him out knowing people need little encouragement to talk about themselves, and men with young sex partners are unstoppable in their boasting.

"Yeah, I could get Chinese but I like the Russian girls. They're usually blonde and a lot more lively."

"Be careful they're not so lively as to slit your throat. Or that Lorraine doesn't find out and give you the John Bobbitt treatment." Joe poked Niawanda in the ribs after this jest.

"I knew Bobbitt, he's from around here. Anyway these girls are submissive, guaranteed. I'm living in Hog Heaven nowadays." Dumke beamed. "All I gotta do is drive some of these whores to different places and deliver. How hard can it be to drive to Cincinnati and back, superhighways all the way and paychecks like you wouldn't believe."

"Mel, I always knew that when you got it together you'd really have her whipped big time." Joe ladled on the BS with a trowel. Their eyes met and they held for a few seconds, neither knew what the other was thinking, but each understood the underlying hostility in the glance. Niawanda noted the electricity in the staring contest.

"I've gotta see my partner Rudyard, you guys take care." Joe stepped over to the table.

"Joe, I've got some information for you when we have more privacy. Andre told me what you've been looking into." Rudyard spoke quietly.

Dumke continued his high volume bragging until Ned Niawanda had to leave. Then he made his way out the door as well, pausing to give a long glance at Rudyard and Joe. They were talking, loudly enough to be overheard, about the controversy surrounding the world record musky. This controversy simmered continuously and occasionally boiled over. With Dumke gone, Joe spoke on a different topic.

"He's an ass. I wonder if he gets those girls he's always talking about?"

"Who knows? I always take comfort in the fact that, no matter what his outside circumstances, the slimy bastard inhabits the mind of Mel Dumke. I wouldn't wish that on anyone." Loonch changed the subject. "Agent Thomas tells me that you've been looking into these Russian gangsters and even had a run-in with some." Joe's eye still showed the slight green tint of a shiner. Rudyard pretended that he did not notice.

"Rudi, I'm going to tell you something that I don't want Andre to know. It's not official and it cannot be. Can I trust you?"

"If you don't want me to tell, I won't."

"Okay, 'cause I need your advice. I went on two trips for Andre to identify some people being smuggled into the US and Canada, for that matter. These are Russian girls and others, even local girls, being held as white slaves. They are drugged with some powerful cocktail — something way beyond what people take to get high, something that makes them docile, almost robots. They are dancers and whores at these strip joints, a chain called Sweet Cherries. The Russian mob owns these joints, they are adjacent to airports all over, Canada, the eastern and southern states, everywhere. I think there's a mole in the FAA that arranges for them to be at airports, sometimes even on airport property. But that's just a theory of mine.

"So I went up to Canada to check these places out and I went to Pittsburgh, Cleveland, the Carolinas, all the way to Atlanta. Atlanta, that's where I took a whipping — he was a former Russian boxer — gone soft but not soft enough. Anyway, these strip clubs always have mostly Russian girls, skinny ones; the clubs are always on the low end of the class scale." Joe paused.

"I wouldn't call any strip club classy, but I take your point." Loonch smiled.

"My point is, these girls are all slaves and they are marked. They have tattoos on the web between thumb and forefinger. On the left hand it's a red star. On the right hand it's a letter of the Chinese alphabet. My buddy, a tattoo artist named John Smith, tells me the letter means 'mine' or 'my property' in Chinese. Anyway, that's Andre's problem. Mine is this. Not all these girls are Russian. Some have been snatched, runaways and such. Marv was at one of these joints outside Cincinnati and he saw a local girl, a friend of Amy's, and she's being held there. She is a slave. I am going to get her and bring her back to Muskedaigua. Andre doesn't know that I'm going with Marv and your niece, Rad, and my cousin Mo, and we're going to snatch Randi DeSchutes and bring her home." Joe looked at Rudi. He was glad to get all that out. He had voiced his concerns about the mission but he planned to move forward.

Rudyard sat for a moment, then said, "Draw us two beers, I'm going to make a few notes." Joe stepped up to the bar and brought back two twenty-two-ounce Schooners. He had drained half of his before Loonch looked up from his notes.

"Joe, I admire your sand. I hate white slavery. They call it human trafficking these days. It is a scourge on our society. Here are some things you need to know." He had made a list. He read off his points.

"Russian mobsters are more dangerous than our Italian friends. As fierce as the Jamaicans, they are indescribably brutal. The old Soviet Union didn't reward many behaviors, but mindless brutality was one that it did. Even before the communists, Russia bred a tough, brutal, ignorant type of thug uncommon in the west. It is mildly interesting that another type of person rewarded, within limits, in the Soviet system was the genius. Engineering, mathematical, scientific, geniuses were nurtured. So, you most likely are taking on an enemy who is both brutal and highly intelligent.

"There's another thing about these creatures created by the Soviet system. Hard work — something guaranteed to lead to rewards in the USA — was a sucker's game in Russia. They never got anywhere by working hard. So when given relative economic freedom, large numbers of them gravitated to crime and exploitation. Mostly exploiting each other. The collapse of communism created legions of young girls, poor and desperate, which have been sold and resold into sex slavery around the world. These women and girls represent property and the mobsters will kill to protect their property.

"The drug cocktail is probably a combination of uppers — so they can dance — and downers so they can lay quietly. Roofies are a possibility too. But remember that genius thing. They may have, in fact probably have, invented something new — a designer drug." Loonch took a few swallows of beer. Joe looked more worried than he had when this started. He stepped to the bar for another Schooner for himself. Rudyard continued to make notes.

When Joe sat back down, Rudyard looked up from his notes, "It's not all bad, and the Russians are not without weaknesses. They are arrogant. They do not believe Americans have the stones to challenge them. You will surprise them. They are urban gangsters. You can use the countryside to your advantage. Rad's father knows people and places in southern Ohio. Talk to him. The typical Russian is not comfortable with initiative. Many cannot drive well. Most will not know what to do without being given orders. They have little understanding of the creative abilities and self-reliance of Americans, especially rural Americans. If you need help from any country people ask and you will get it. There are good people in America wherever you go."

Rudyard paused. "When confronted with one who intends to kill you, the best defense is to kill him first. Do not be swayed by compassion. Create confusion and frustration whenever you can. Keep in mind the fact that they have a genius or two on their side. The foot soldiers are thugs, the leaders are swine, but they are experienced at using people. Beware of the unexpected." Rudi took several swallows of beer and laid down his pen.

"One last thing, don't be surprised if the girl, Randi, doesn't want to go with you. There is no telling what drugs she is on or what effects they have created. Time will be on your side in that endeavor."

"Thanks, Rudi. I appreciate your info, as always."

"Sure. Take care of Rad, please."

"She takes pretty good care of herself. But we like her. We won't let anything happen to her."

Chapter 9
The Musky Straits

—June 12th—

Fishing the area of the Musky Straits where the river curved eastward into the Red Rock neighborhood always brought a painful memory to Joe Gaspe. The dull pain that shot through his right wrist and his throbbing right temple, reminded him of an incident that had happened when he first began musky fishing with Marv. The escapade ended with an embarrassing trip to Dr. Marie Bramton.

When Joe and Marv had moved from nighttime carp fishermen to pursuers of muskies they were under-prepared in terms of equipment. Their boat was a used twelve-foot skiff and they were using rods and reels that were old cast-offs thrown away by other musky fishermen who now had newer tackle. Neither Joe nor Marv were experienced with bait-casting reels. These level-wind reels, preferred for handling musky lures and the powerful strikes of pursuing predators, are difficult for a novice to cast: with backlashes, where the reel overruns the line and snarls causing a bird's nest; and dangerous back casts, where the giant lure, sporting multiple huge treble hooks, is brought back too far behind the angler and snags an unintended someone or something, common for beginners.

On the day in question, Marv was fishing from the front of the boat with Joe tending the trolling motor and fishing from the rear. Without warning, Joe heard a loud popping sound and got slammed in the side of the head. It felt like he had been hit by an errant shot from a nine millimeter in the hood. Then he heard Marv yelling, "Hey where's my lure? What happened to my lure?" Marv punctuated these yells with violent yanks of his fishing rod. He had been hasty in his effort to throw his lure back at a musky pursuing his previous cast and had put too much oomph into his back cast.

Joe reached up and grabbed the lure snagged into the right side of his head and neck and screamed at Marv, "Hey half-wit! Let loose! You've got me."

Marv looked over and saw one of the barbed treble hooks imbedded in Joe's temple and another at the end of a bloody furrow on the side of Joe's neck. He looked back quickly to see if the musky was still where he thought it would be. He was half ashamed that he was hurting his partner and half ticked-off that he'd lose his chance at a good fish. He moved closer to try to unhook Joe.

"Can you back these out or what?" Joe was mad. He was in some pain, though less now that Marv wasn't yanking on the line.

"Hold still, I can get this back hook out easily." He handed Joe a bandanna dipped in river water. "Here, hold this against your neck. The hook in your neck is out and it ain't bleedin' much. This one in your dome I'm gonna have to cut."

"I feel blood running down the side of my face. How bad is it?" Never one to have a lot of faith in Marv's judgment, Joe was trying not to worry.

"Head wounds bleed a lot, don't get hinky on me." Marv reached for his handy-dandy, made-in-China economy bolt cutters and positioned them to cut the hooks. Instead of trying to cut each individual treble hook, two points of which were impaling Joe, he took a bite on the main shank where all three trebles were welded into one, squeezed for all he was worth and, with a loud report, the bolt cutters exploded into five shards of inferior pot metal.

"What was that? What happened?" Joe's worry was not lessening.

"Calm down big boy. We won't be cutting those hooks today." Marv said this as he placed one handle of the bolt cutters in Joe's hand. "We'll have to remove the split ring from the hook and get the lure off your face.

Anyways, with the hook still in there, your head won't bleed so much."

"You're gonna leave the hook in my head? Can't you at least cut off the point?"

"No-can-do partner, no cutters left on board that will handle that big hook." Marv was opening the split ring and backing out the lure to avoid the barb.

Joe felt like he was having a board nailed to his head with Marv jerking and turning to remove the split ring. With the lure removed, Marv left the hook embedded in Joe's temple. Two barbed points were protruding, one close alongside the skin and one sticking out about three fourths of an inch.

"That's the best I can do, buddy. You wanna go to Dr. Marie?" Marv tried to seem repentant.

Joe thought about a trip to the doctor and said, "No, let's fish like we were going to. We'll see the doc when we go home."

As the day wore on into the afternoon, it got hot and muggy. Musky fishing, being labor intensive, requires many casts with heavy lures. Having taken an Aleve and being absorbed in the fishing, Joe suppressed the pain. Working hard, he began to perspire. While wiping the sweat from his forehead he took a swipe across his brow with his right hand and connected with the exposed barbed hook on his temple. As quickly as he could, he tried to pull his hand back. It was too late. The back of his hand was now hooked securely to his head and he looked like a soldier frozen in mid salute.

"Now we've gotta go to the doc." Joe was ticked off, not least of all because Marv had been complaining for hours that his favorite lure was ruined by contact with Joe's cranium.

Joe didn't remember much about the drive to the doctor, but his arm got sorely tired and he had to hold it up with his left hand to keep the weight from pulling down on the hook. This caused a man-killing headache. Finally he found a position where he could prop his elbow on the door's armrest. He had wondered, "What if Marv, who always pushes the speed limit, gets popped on the highway? Joe could hear the officer shouting at him, 'Put your hands where I can see 'em! Now!' "

Joe's profile with the police in Muskiedaigua, the State Police, the various other constabularies, and the RCMP in Canada had never been good. He looked enough like a Mexican/ mobster/ terrorist/ biker/ etc. to make all encounters with cops a pain in the ass.

His fears had been unfounded. Marv got Joe to Dr. Marie Bramton's clinic without further incident. After demanding that Marv leave the office, Dr. Marie lectured Joe while attending to removing the hooks.

Marv had good intentions and lots of enthusiasm, but he was a dangerous pain in the neck at times. Joe worried about Marv and his own ability to control his excesses during their upcoming road trip, as he prepared to meet with Agent Andre. He felt a considerable amount of confidence because his cousin, Mo Snow, would be along for the planned intervention. That's what Joe called it instead of a rescue. He had continued to grow more adept at keeping secrets and gaming people. He was gaming the bad guys, he was gaming his wife and family. He was about to work a game on Agent Thomas Andre.

"My wife's really on me about the situation that happened in Atlanta."

Andre looked Joe up and down, smiled at the memory of the embarrassments Joe had caused, remembered the big fight in Atlanta and thought, "All I'm doing is getting rid of a pain in the neck for two weeks. It'll be like a vacation."

"Your record's clean on that. It has been expunged." Andre's sentences were terse, his patience with Joe short.

"She doesn't like me fighting no more." Joe shook his head, shoulders slumped forward. He wasn't lying. "I need to be out of it for a couple weeks. She loves the steady money, good money, she'll let me come back to work. I just need some slack to get things arranged."

"Two weeks leave of absence? It's done. Stay in touch." Andre gave him just what he wanted. Joe took his victory and wondered at it, but not for long.

His waterfront chat with Andre had been completely unremarkable. That in itself was remarkable.

After they rendezvoused at Tony Gill's hunting camp on the mountainside, where they were going to get organized for the interdiction, Joe and Mo set out for John Smith's tattoo parlor in Delano. Joe needed to confirm some information about the tattoos on the hands of the strippers he'd seen. He had asked Smith to make some discreet inquiries among his peers. Joe, though already clear in his mind what was going on, wanted additional confirmation.

They entered the door of the tattoo parlor and both men flared their nostrils as they took in the smells of the studio. It was in an old wooden-frame building, rotty at the edges, which had contained multiple businesses over time. The damp smell of the building was combined with the odor of a hot skillet, an electrical ozone metal smell, overlaid with the faint tones of burning flesh. Mo wasn't bothered by these odors but noticed that Joe was turning up his nose. It was the sense of decay that bothered Mo. He'd spent most of his life in temporary structures, cabins and trailers that were abandoned or torn down when they got old. Now he lived in a modest frame house that was only seven years old. Mo found it imponderable that whites lived in rotting structures.

There was a waiting area with two rows of former theater seats for patrons soon to be inked. Joe went to the curtained work area and peeked behind. Mo sat and looked at the examples displayed on the walls, and perused the books on the central table, catalogs of designs that could be used to adorn the customers. Mo was seriously tattooed in the manner of Mohawks. He had a heroic-sized Great Blue Heron that went across his chest with the bird's eighteen-inch long fish-stabbing beak extending down his right arm to the elbow. He also had a tattoo of the head of his oyaron, the black bear, on his left shoulder and a small, stylized wolf, the symbol of his clan, on his left forearm. These symbols narrated who he was. He marveled at the confusing array of non-complementary splotches that whites and blacks, men and women, chose to cover their bodies with. Chinese lettering, dragons, sorceresses, insects, he didn't know what all, covered the bodies of people who, he guessed, felt they weren't unique enough or something. He deposited these thoughts into the pail of things about other races that he'd never be able to sort out.

Joe came and sat down beside Mo. He had no ink on him and cared little for the idea of paying someone for fancies that would fade with time. Joe was ever curious about the ideas of people, however, and on occasion he would do impromptu interviews on the symbolism of body art. Joe loved to observe humans and was convinced that if he could ascertain their motives, he would give them more credit than perhaps would be due. If asked the reason why they had a particular devil or chain or butterfly plastered on some part of their anatomy, any answer would most likely be disappointing. The silliness of people, which made Mo a little sad, was, to Joe, just a hoot to be enjoyed.

They sat for a few minutes across from a man with a snake coiling his throat and rearing its head behind his ear. His arms and the backs of his hands were covered with ink and his legs were similarly blanketed. Joe was wondering where the next design would go when John Smith walked into the waiting room. He turned first to his waiting customer.

"I'll just be a minute Dex. Then we'll finish up your work." He turned to Joe, glanced at Mo, nodded, then said, "Why don't we step into my office." Joe followed past the curtained work area. Mo stayed seated.

In the small office, barely large enough for the computer and printer it contained, John turned to Joe and said, "You shouldn't go anywhere near these people, Joe. They're dangerous, deadly even."

"I just wanna know what the symbols mean. I'm not gonna do anything." Joe said but didn't look into John's probing eyes.

"I was at a convention in Toronto. I asked a few artists about the symbols and I didn't get any responses until I talked with a fellow from Ottawa who said he used to partner with an artist who did some of that work. He said his partner was spirited out of the shop, with his portable equipment, by a pair of huge goons — one Asian and one Slavic looking. The fellow I talked to followed them on a hunch and the giants escorted his partner into a nail salon. Later, his partner wouldn't talk for the longest time. When he did, he said that he was being paid to ink the hands of a large number of young, mostly Russian, girls and women. He never came back to work after he told my friend that. His body was found downstream in the Ottawa River a week later. His hands had been removed. My friend decamped for another location in Canada but still felt unsafe. Russian and Chinese gangsters, the combination couldn't be worse. Be careful Joe."

Smith gave Joe an inquisitive stare, waiting for a reaction.

"What does the symbol mean?" Joe asked.

"The Chinese pictograph means, roughly, 'my property' and the red star indicates that particular girl has been leased to the Russians as a capital asset."

"Russian girls are sold to Russians by Chinese gangsters?"

"The Russians never have figured out how to make money as well as the Chinese. Selling gee-gaws and gimcracks to Americans has created a tremendous amount of surplus wealth in China. And, believe it or not, all that wealth is not in the hands of nice, honest people."

As Joe walked into the outer room, John admonished him, once more, to take care.

Father Justin arrived at the hunting camp unannounced. Driving a Mazda Miata, he pulled in too fast and sprayed gravel against the Cadillac. Marv, sitting on the porch drinking a beer said, "What the hell?" Then he felt a little sheepish as the father stepped out of the sports car. Father Justin looked at the Caddy, inspecting it for damage, then shrugged his shoulders and walked toward the cabin.

"Excuse me, a friend told me I might find Joe Gaspe here."

"He's not here now but due back soon. Went to get groceries, you know. Come on up on the porch and set down. Wanna beer?" Marv waved toward a porch swing to his left.

"No beer for me. You wouldn't have any Irish whiskey would you?"

Marv did a double take at that and said, "Er… no."

"Hi, Father," Rad came through the door and extended her hand to the cleric. She introduced Marv and suggested, "There's some fine bourbon here, but we're waiting for Joe and his cousin to bring some ice back."

"I'll drink it neat. I learned to like warm whiskey from the English. My mentor over there used to heat up a poker in the fire then quench it in a tumbler of Old Bushmills before he drank it."

"Eeeyuuh." Marv didn't like that idea. Rad went inside and returned with a water glass filled with bourbon.

"Thank you dear," said the reverend, "This will take the chill off." The night was warm, humid and mosquitoes hovered about. There was a twinkle in the good father's eye that intensified after he'd swallowed a glug of whiskey.

"I suppose you're wondering how I found you and why I'm here?" He said this to Radleigh Loonch, whom he had met the previous summer. "Uncle Mike came over for a seminar at the mountain, and he told me that he had dreamed of the danger you folks were going to be exposed to. I thought maybe I could offer spiritual assistance."

"Uncle Mike is worried about us? I wonder why." Radleigh was more worried about the trouble she could get into with her employers than what might happen in the planned rescue of Randi Deshutes. She thought that her role would just be convincing the girl to head for home. Young women didn't run away from home unless the situation was bad there.

"The Sachem sees danger in the Ohio country. The Iroquois have always relished the danger and adventure of the western lands. They consider that state their tribal hunting preserve. It sometimes seems like the past two hundred years have been just an interlude to Uncle Mike. His dreams tell him that your group will face danger three times in Ohio, and it will follow you back to our fair state."

"Fair state, unfair more like it!" Marv piped up. Both Father Justin and Rad looked at him with puzzled expressions.

Before another word was said, Mo's Jetta pulled into the turning area in front of the cabin.

Joe Gaspe stepped out of the car with enthusiasm and a broad smile when he saw Father Justin sitting on the porch. His handshake was crushing. He grabbed the older man's shoulder and enthusiastically introduced Mo and Marv to the priest. Rad handed him a beer, and she and Mo walked into the cabin to see about a cup of clear tea for the Mohawk.

"Whose hot car is that? Your's, Father?"

"A friend of the order allowed me to use it; drives like a dream I might add."

"I'll bet it's a great winter car, eh?" Joe laughed loudly at his own jest.

Father Justin straightened himself in his chair and prepared to speak. Mo came outside with his mug and leaned against a support post of the porch, while Rad stood in the doorway listening.

"Joseph," he began, seeing that Marv and Joe had the look of schoolboys expecting a lecture, "I admire a man of enthusiasm such as you. We all know that there are many, too many, jaded cynics and skeptics in our world today. However, Uncle Mike, being very concerned about the dangers you will soon face, has asked me to caution you and issue a warning to you. He has told me that he foresees three dangerous encounters — he called them battles — in the Ohio country. He has also said that even when you are out of Ohio you will not be out of danger. I have known this particular sachem to be right too often to laugh off his predictions as mere superstition."

"Thanks, Father," Joe began to talk and stopped as Father Justin held up his hand, palm outward.

"I understand your objective is to rescue one of life's unfortunate young ladies from an intolerable and abusive situation. I applaud you for that. Evil lurks in the world and evil must be opposed. I only wish for you to understand that you are putting four more good people in harm's way to attempt this. Care and thoughtfulness are required here." The priest took a serious slug of whiskey that drained his glass before he continued. Looking at Joe, Marv raised an eyebrow in surprise at the thirst of the good father. "If you would all be so kind as to bow your heads, I will offer my blessing that all will come through your upcoming episode with success and safety." The father blessed the four: one Protestant, one pagan, and two lapsed Catholics with a Latin prayer that none understood.

After the blessing, Joe said, "Stay for dinner Father. How about another nectar?" He reached for the priest's whiskey glass.

"No, no thank you. I must return to the Mount for our evening meal and prayers."

"Well, at least let me check out that vehicle you're driving." Joe and the priest walked to the Miata after goodbyes all around.

Rad stepped back inside the cabin, Mo took a seat on the porch swing, and Marv leaned back saying, "I don't trust priests. God's cops, you know." He looked conspiratorially at Mo who raised an eyebrow but made no comment.

At the car, Joe took Father Justin's hand again and said, "Thank you, Father, and be sure to thank Uncle Mike too. I'll let you know how it turns out." The cleric spun his tires when he peeled out down the gravel driveway. Standing there, Joe was sure that he heard a war whoop come from the automobile.

Joe was all for staying around southern New York for a couple of days. With work and business commitments, Rad and Mo had only one week to perform their task. Those two were anxious to start. Joe seemed reluctant to be off, and Rad had a suspicion that he was trying to build up his courage. At eight the next morning, Joe announced that he and Marv had to visit Lorne Doren's tackle shop at Chautauqua Lake in an attempt to settle a monetary dispute.

"That son of a pup owes me for painting a bunch of custom lures for him and he ignores my phone calls. Since I'm already down here, we're gonna visit him. Marv and I would like to fish the lake while we're here, but the season hasn't opened yet." He turned to Rad. "Mo has agreed to allow me to use his Jetta; will you two get the Caddy ready for the trip while we're gone?" He inclined his head toward Mo who sat at the table with the steam from his tea rising into his face. He had that faraway look in his eyes that was archetypal of the patient Indian.

"TEETH!" Joe wrote in all caps. He was using his headlamp in the dark, writing notes to honor his dream upon waking. It was dark and Marv snored on the narrow couch across the Great Room of Tony Gill's hunting camp. Joe had been snoring away in a sleeper sofa. He had been startled out of the dream when the moldering mounted musky head had fallen from the wall above and landed on him. He awoke to find his hand inside its jaws. The falling trophy had not woken Marv when it silently landed on Joe and his bedclothes.

He recalled the dream. A huge wave was breaking above him as he stood at the transom at the back of a boat that was not his own. The wave crested two feet away and the jaws of a musky, wide and deep, open and slashing, surged out at him, took a snap and receded as the wave broke. The next comber to come in repeated the scene, huge snapping teeth, surging in a near miss, and receding.

Joe heard a warning spoken in a gurgling watery voice with each lunge of the musky's head. What had the voice been saying?

He closed his eyes and remembered. The warning had come on three surges in a row. "Care, Joe, you take care. Three times you will be in danger. Three times you will nearly be bitten. Take care, Joe."

Chapter 10
Allegany County

—June 13th—

Marv drove out of the drive causing a slight change of expression in Mo.

"Joe always lets Marv drive. He says it keeps him from getting too fired up. I hope they aren't going to give the guy at the bait shop, Playing Hooky, a beat down. I have a feeling we'll be bending the law enough in Ohio without having any trouble with New York State." Rad said as she and Mo arranged the load in the capacious trunk of the Cadillac.

Mo smiled. "Do your employers know where you are or where you're going?"

"Joe's on a leave of absence. I think Andre is fed up with him after the set-to in Atlanta. I'm also on leave. Officially 'between assignments' until I move to the FBI office, as the CBP liaison officer, the first of the month. Andre may suspect something but only knows what he wants to know, sometimes. How about your business ventures? This seems like a bad time to be off on a mission."

"I have two nephews helping me and taking the scheduled shipments. They are good boys, sober, but nevertheless easily distracted."

"So you risk a lot to help crazy Joe, why?"

"All of our efforts will be required, for there is great danger. We will need the help of some allies of my tribe. I will meet someone who will become of great importance in my life as well."

"Oh, so you and Joe have been making detailed plans already?"

"No, but I have dreamed with the Seneca Sachem. I have seen what is to come. Your friend from the southern end of the Natchez trace, what is her name?"

"Natchez trace? What are you talking about?"

"You call it the Big Muddy, we call it the Missitheepi."

"Okay, you mean New Orleans?" Mo nodded once. "Are you talking about Olivia? My old roommate, Olivia Shanio?"

Mo said, "Ah," with a look of satisfaction on his face.

"Did I ever mention her to you? I don't remember doing so."

"A finely turned young woman, that. Beautiful in mind, body, and spirit." Mo looked satisfied with himself, then said, "I must gather a few items in the forest; I'll be back soon." He slipped away quietly as Rad tried to remember if she had ever mentioned Ollie to him. She was sure she hadn't, so how did he know?"

Playing Hooky was a small bait shop with a storefront occupying half of an older building at one of the crossroads near the lake's southern tip. Tiny minnows for Crappies and worms and larger minnows for Walleyes were in heavy demand on the Sunday that Joe and his enforcer, Marv, came to collect the two hundred and twenty dollars owed to Dr. Dento, rod builder and painter of lures.

"This was a custom job for you, Lorne. Special paint, time away from my regular work," Joe's voice was raised. "Work for people who actually *pay* me." This caused heads to turn in the line at the live bait counter being manned by Doren's wife, who was hustling to keep up with demand.

"I haven't had the money to pay you, Joe. You want the lures back?"

"Hell no, I don't want the lures. I see some considerable money coming in right over there. Gimme some of that." He inclined his head toward the brisk business being done this morning. Marv, meanwhile, was walking up and down the aisles, looking over various items of tackle. His plan was to take it out in trade if Doren didn't pony up the cash.

Joe had been carrying a pile of Doren's bumper stickers in his left hand that he had edited to say, "I got cheated at Playing Hooky" instead of the usual, "I got crabs at Playing Hooky." He slapped them against the counter while giving Doren his best death stare. Doren shifted from foot to foot and looked around at customers craning their necks his way. He babbled through his beard, "I gotta pay my wholesaler tomorrow, and we're on a cash basis with him. I'll just barely have enough after today."

Joe repeated himself pointing out again, how a year had passed since the lures had been delivered. Marv began piling fishing rods and sundry tackle items on the counter. "I figure about $450 retail ought to make it right, eh Joe?" Marv grinned.

"I want money! I can't feed my family with fishing rods." Joe was loud again. Mrs. Doren was moving faster than before, trying to keep the customers from being distracted. "What's this I hear about you selling out and heading for Florida? That true, Lorne?"

Everyone but Marv was at a loss as to what to do next. Lorne's wife was tempted to offer up the money, which she had in a secret cache. Lorne was scared that Joe might unleash his weighty fists and administer a beating. A beating he was willing to take for $220. Joe knew that if he got no satisfaction asking for or demanding his money, he'd have to walk. There was no legal way to get the funds. Judgments in small claims court are meaningless to the dishonest. Any action that brought the cops, would be costly and problematic for Joe.

Marv, on the other hand, thought a nice big pile of products could be exchanged for Lorne's debt and he had a pile stacked on the counter. On his third circuit through the store, he began to drop things in the aisles. He had his hands on an end-cap display, about to yank it over, when Joe yelled.

"Marv! That's enough! Don't do that!" Marv stared at him. Then, in response to Joe's stern look, his expression turned guilty, the way he had looked when his older sister caught him misbehaving as a child.

Turning back to Doren, Joe said, "What are we gonna do here, Lorne? You gonna pay me? Or am I gonna plaster these stickers on every car bumper and signpost for blocks around?"

Doren straightened his shoulders and said, "I can't pay you now, Joe. It will have to be some other time."

Marv had stepped to the counter and was preparing to carry out two St.Croix rods and a few tackle items. "If you remove items from the store without paying, I will call the police." He looked at Joe but he was speaking to Marv. "And I've already settled on the sale of the store, so your bumper stickers will only hurt my successor, a man you could possibly do business with." Doren was gaining courage as he began to understand that Joe had no viable alternative here.

"Okay, Lorne. You win this round. I'll be back in a week. Then we are going to go for a walk."

Doren's wife stepped up. "A week you say? We'll have most, if not all, your money then." Lorne looked at her surprised. "Won't we, Lorney?" He turned back to Joe and nodded.

"Okay Marv, let loose of that stuff and let's get out of here. Joe took his bumper stickers with him. The disappointed Marv followed him out the door. "Do you know which car is Doren's?" he asked Marv while handing him the pile of bumper stickers. Marv inclined his head toward a mini van. "I'm going over there to pick up some cigarettes," Joe pointed to a convenience store. "I'll be a few minutes."

Marv nodded his head and then got a mischievous look in his eye.

Mo and Rad were on the porch talking. Getting the Cadillac ready for the mission ahead had been simple and was accomplished quickly.

"One of my professors said that the stories about whole villages fleeing in terror at the sight of a few Mohawks were apocryphal." Rad worried about Mo's reaction to this.

"Apocryphal, does that mean it is bull?" Mo had been to university classes in Canada occasionally.

"Well, not exactly untrue but embellished a little to enhance the prestige of the Five Nations."

"Your professor lived in New England or Huronia in the late 1600s, did he?"

"Well, no."

"What is the conventional wisdom? If it walks like a duck and looks like a duck…?"

"Oh, you mean, 'Perception is reality,' that catch phrase?"

"Daughter, you are a woman of great wisdom. You are known to me as a woman who can see through the shallow agenda-driven beliefs of a professor here or there," Rad was about to interrupt but Mo raised his right hand, palm toward her, "My people still live on their lands after all these years, we live in houses. We Mohawks are more numerous now than we were three hundred years ago. We have engaged in diplomacy and politics with the English, the French, the Americans, and the Canadians. We are not children to be taken care of. We are not buried in the ground because we took on a superior enemy when we could not win. Of the many Indian tribes, few have been able to hold their own as we have. It was our understanding of the English and our finding a role for our leaders and warriors, that enabled us to survive the onslaught. Look to our brothers the Shawnees, brave warriors, but tied to the past, unable to adjust. They were driven until they were mostly dead and the remnants carted off to the Indian Nation, what you call Oklahoma.

"There were many wars in the native world before the manufactured goods of the white world changed life for the Real People. The Mohawks won many wars, but we had to adopt people from other tribes to stay strong and recover our losses. We brought in those people through conquest but also through adoption and confederation. Entire villages and tribes became people of the longhouse, because we welcomed them. Before the English became dominant we had so thoroughly defeated the Hurons that we owned their land and the Seneca tribe's population was more than half Huron.

"As your presidential politics clearly points out, a convenient myth — based on reality or otherwise — is an essential part of politics and, even more so, diplomacy." Mo dropped his hand and smiled at Rad.

"So, it *is* a myth." This was a statement but a doubtful one.

"Who can say what has happened? The other people of the Indian world believed we would kill them and steal their children. They believed we would eat the hearts of their warriors. Are there not those who believe that the USA could destroy them militarily? Does America need to prove that?"

"You don't mind talking about this I see."

"Not at all, daughter. The Mohawks' ability to avoid being swallowed by the Dutch, though we were injured and insulted, and our triangulation, as one of your former presidents called it, of the English, was what allowed us to hang on when larger tribes like the Delawares and Shawnees were displaced and annihilated. Many Eastern tribes have no one to carry on their traditions. They are gone. Perhaps if the professors at your universities didn't put so much emphasis on in making Indians victims, your understanding might be more complete." Mo was satisfied with his speech.

It was eleven in the morning when they got underway traveling on the interstate across Chautauqua Lake to head for Harold Weber's shop in western Pennsylvania. Joe was not pleased with the outcome at Playing Hooky, but hoped he could count on a small order from Weber. Marv was in a snit because he had been keyed up for vengeance and then held in check by Joe.

Rad and Mo had come to understand each other more by talking on the porch. Though Rad was unsure of when Mo was pulling her leg, she accepted his stoicism with a grain or two of salt.

It was quiet in the vehicle as they crossed the middle of the lake. The deep part to the north had walleye trollers braving a windy and brisk June day. The shallow southern end had crappie fishermen anchored hard up against the banks. Despite the foreboding clouds and chilly wind, anglers had to take their opportunities in northern climes. You'd sit home forever, awaiting those good-weather days. The dreary choppy lake and the silence in the car made Rad philosophical, made Mo wistful for his reedy Ottawa River cabin, and made Joe anxious about the trouble ahead. Meanwhile, Marv snorted and looked out the window. No one spoke.

As the hills rolled by, Rad dampened her irritation by trying to remember what she had said to Mo to make him know about her friend, Olivia. She still didn't credit the importance of the dreams of these people, Joe or Mo, and she scoffed at their prescient abilities.

It was three hours later when Joe was standing at the counter in Harold Weber's tackle shop talking to Weber's wife. Joe had miscalculated.

"Harold and Jack are over at Lake Arthur, fishing. Did he know you were coming?"

"I told him I'd be down but not when. I didn't know for sure. Tell you what, I'll leave these seven musky rods and my friend's books, three copies of each. And then I'll leave him a note. I'll be back for our fishing trip next Sunday or maybe Monday. He promised that he and Jack would show Marv and me how to fish the Kinzua." Joe left his wares on the counter and wrote on the back of an envelope. There was no packing slip, no invoice. A lot of musky tackle business was still done on a handshake and a man's word.

"Uh, he makes most of his own appointments and all of his fishing trips are arranged through him. I don't know about this. What did you say your name was?" She shifted her feet and looked at Joe.

"Dr. Dento, he'll remember me. Does he have a cell phone?" She shook her head. "Me neither," Joe said. "But I can get access to one, and I think Marv has Jack Richardson's number. I've gotta go. We are going to fish the evening bite in Cleveland." Mrs. Weber looked out the window past Joe and saw the effects of a brisk wind. She shook her head and turned out the light. The shop was closed on Sundays.

Left behind when Marv and Joe went on their mission, Rad asked Mo what he'd like to do for the afternoon in Cleveland.

"Let's go take a look at Progressive Field. It's supposed to be quite a ballpark."

“I’ll check and see if the Indians are playing today. Joe said we’d be heading south early this evening so I don’t think we can fit it in. I didn’t know you were a sports fan. I love baseball and hockey and football. What’s your favorite team?” When it came to sports Rad’s normally reticent conversation ran away from her.

“The Indians, of course.” Mo’s response left Rad wondering whether or not he was pulling her leg. “They are in New York playing the Yankees, finishing up a weekend series. We’ll go down there. I know how we can get in and tour the stadium.”

“Okay.” Rad was doubtful.

Arriving by cab, Mo went to the front office and asked the greeter, “May I please speak to George Gale? Tell him, ‘The Chief,’ Moses Snow is here.”

Chapter 11
Cleveland

—June 13th—

Sitting in the bleachers with Mo after a guided tour of the fantastic ballpark that combined old school appearance with absolutely modern amenities, Rad was again wondering about this man she knew and yet did not know.

"George Gale was my pitching coach with the Padres. Now he's in charge of stadium operations in his hometown. I was just a poor boy from the Rez when he took me under his wing. The man was good to me in a situation where I took a lot of ribbing and could have reacted badly. I didn't even have two pair of pants when I arrived there at nineteen years old."

"So. The name Indians doesn't bother you? Make you feel dehumanized?"

"I played for the Padres. Padres. Black-robed priests spread the smallpox, mumps, measles, and other diseases among our Onandagan and Caughnawaga brothers and sisters. Those things were worse than war as far as devastating the Iroquoian population. No, the Indians have always been my favorite team. I played in San Diego — too hot, too dry, never rains. I would have loved to play here. The old park was a mess. I wouldn't have cared. I'm a man of the north. I love a chilly morning, hunting in the fall, ice covering the swamps. I never got a chance to play here though."

This was the most Mo had ever revealed to Rad. "Does anybody else know all this?"

"Radleigh, until now there has been no one to tell."

Returning from Atlanta, Joe and Marv had left their warbag — a Rochester Americans hockey bag stuffed with weaponry and sundries — with Mack Spline, one of Joe's musky fishing friends. They had met Mack at the storage locker and persuaded him to take them out on Lake Erie to find a nest of muskies in the waters of Cleveland Harbor. Joe was convinced that they were there, Mack said the locals felt there was no way and Marv changed with the wind. The three stood outside the suburban complex where Mack stored his boat.

"Muskies bite well in a choppy sea. Let's try it if you get uncomfortable we can come in." Joe spoke incautiously, leaning forward while Marv nodded his head, looking at Mack.

"I'm already uncomfortable. It'll be rough out there." Mack leaned back, already wavering. Marv nodded his head at this, too.

"If we find the muskies there, and I know they will be there, eating the baitfish, we'll have a secret spot. Nobody will know about it for a while. The big mamalookas will be in there. Think of that Ohio boy."

"Maybe if we stay behind the breakwalls we can be out of the worst of it." Mack's resolve had crumbled.

Marv pumped his fist and said, "Yeah."

After two hours of rockin' and rollin' in three-to-five foot waves in a nineteen foot boat, Mack was uncomfortable, scared, and sick to his stomach. Marv had dropped down to the bottom of the boat and was lyng there trying to keep his stomach from turning inside out. Only Joe was fishing, driving the boat, and swiveling to watch rods. He spoke though neither passenger heard, "I just want one more crack at the nice drop off at the end of this wall." He was turning the boat to get the waves behind him. The long rollers out of the west pushed him forward reducing the side-to-side motion that had sickened the others, and enabled him to handle the situation more easily. Joe didn't want to admit that the three-to-five-foot waves had grown bigger during the short afternoon. The spume whipping off the wave tops and catching the boat's bow had grown so thick that his vision ahead was through a cloud of mist.

The wind whipped past his face. It was strong enough to blow away the water forming at the end of his runny nose. Though it was June and the sun shone, he was cold. Having just brought the boat across the wind, his one side had become soaked by the spray. He held back a shudder in order to project an image of himself as proud, imperturbable, and in charge.

To cover large areas of relatively open water in search of active fish, a trolling presentation; in this case with four different types of lures at four different depths was an efficient search technique. When active fish were encountered the fishermen could pound that area thoroughly from all directions.

The reason Joe wouldn't give in and head back to the boat launch was because he had had two rips on his inside deep rod, alerting him that fish were present and active. He knew, from documentary films, that active fish don't always attack lures with their mouths open as if to eat, sometimes they head-butt the lures, sometimes they slap them with their sides. These actions are believed to stun the bait for later consumption. Joe reasoned that these rips he'd had, where the drag allowed line to go out briefly, were from these hunting but not biting fish

Joe had loosened the drag on his reels. Too tight, and the stalking fish might not be caught or a biting fish or a snag might snap the rod. Too loose, and the reel could be spooled. One of the musky's favorite tactics is to charge the bait from behind and continue on at high speed toward the boat. This can cause slack in the line if the angler could not reel fast enough.

Joe had gained confidence. He was so involved in his fishing that he did not hear Marv moaning and rolling on the deck, nor did he glance at Mack staring green-faced between his knees. Joe felt the ancient lure of his Irish sea-rover side. His cheeks were flushed. His hands, though soaked in spray, were hot as stove lids. He looked back at the approaching waves, glanced at the working rod tips, turned back to guide the boat's track beside the wall's end. Grasping the steering wheel tightly to keep the wind, that was swirling past the bow, from turning the boat, he looked back to see the rod with the Believer slam into a curve three times before the clicker began to scream. A garbled yell came from his throat, "Fish on! Fish on! Mack, take the wheel, this is a good'n."

Joe hopped over the supine form of Marv, yanked the rod from its holder and struck hard, to drive the freshly sharpened hooks into the musky's bony mouth. Rearing back on the rod Joe almost toppled over when his violent movement coincided with a wave crest that propelled the boat onward. Mack had moved to the driver's seat with a moan and barely nodded when Joe yelled out instructions. "Slow her down all possible. Keep control of your direction. We don't wanna broach. Marv, reel in these lines. Start with this one," Joe pointed at the outside rod trolling 140 feet back on the same side as the one with the fish on it.

Joe's pulse hammered, he felt a heat on his cheeks like a fever. He held on as the fish pulled off a few feet of line. She was forty-five feet back, shaking her head back and forth. She remained deep, which told Joe she had some size to her. Small fish always came to the top to jump and shake the lure. Large muskies might come up, but sometimes stayed down and defied the angler's efforts to move them. The wind whipped droplets of water off the wave tops right into the back of the boat where Joe faced down the elements. He was taking the spray all over his front getting soaked through. He let out a whoop reveling in the moment. Marv stowed one rod and moved to the other side. Mack had slowed the boat too much and he had lost his ability to steer. He goosed the throttle too much and the boat lunged forward. He over-adjusted again and slowed down too much.

"She's coming in. Somebody has to be ready with the net."

Marv began getting defiant. "I gotta get these rods out of the way. One thing at a time, Big Boy." When Marv called Joe Big Boy, he was getting ticked off.

Joe had the feeling now, It was a big healthy fish. It was under his control. He was reeling like mad and grimacing as if he was in agony. His feet were planted. He looked down at the reel in his hands and then looked up in time to see a harmonic wave, ten-feet-high, looming above his head. The stern, where he stood, was below this wave as the bow rode up on the crest of the previous wave. His mind emptied and time slowed down.

Mack had eased the throttle too much. The boat, instead of climbing the crest of the wave, slid back down into the trough before the oncoming double sized crest. Joe looked up to see a giant musky head, leering at him through the crest with an eight-inch long lure dangling from in its mouth. Joe's line had slack in it, and he was convinced that the musky was going to slide into the boat and land at his feet, green, thrashing, and slashing, with bared teeth and multiple treble hooks flying around.

Then one of the worst things that could happen, did. They were pooped. The Triton took a wave containing hundreds of gallons of water right over the transom and Joe was standing in water up to his knees. Marv who had slipped on the deck was briefly under water on his hands and knees, before most of the water just washed out the back of the boat. The musky was ten feet back thrashing and plunging but still hooked.

"Give it some gas! I'll hold on." Mack poured the coal to the outboard and water sloshed throughout the boat. The bilge pump, whining like a crazy sewing machine, seemed about to explode. Mack saw an opportunity, and banked to port behind the breakwall. The waves were smaller there and though they were showered with spray when the combers broke over the top of the wall, the bilge pump began to catch up and Marv bailed like a maniac with the pee bucket.

After four minutes in the calmer water with Joe holding a tight line on the fish, he said, "Okay, Marv let's take this big girl." Marv had the giant treated musky net and moved seamlessly in front of Joe when he stepped backward and brought the fish into the net. The water was now below their ankles. Joe's shoes squeaked and sloshed when he moved forward with extra-long needle-nosed pliers to release the fish. It had a huge green head and looked viciously at Joe when he leaned over the rail to handle the unhooking procedure.

"Marv, hold that net!"

"I got it! I got it!"

"Whoa, she didn't like the looks of me!" Joe reared back as the big fish thrashed and threw most of the hooks into the net. She only had one in her mouth but Joe would have to reach past two large treble hooks to remove that one. He handed the long needle nosed pliers to Marv and said, "Give me the cutters."

Reaching into the net with Knipex bolt cutters and the fish just under the water's surface, he cut away all the hooks in the net, he inadvertently cut some fair sized chunks out of his net as he did so. Marv, leaning over the side said, "That might be a fifty-inch fish."

Joe stood up to straighten his back and see what he needed to do next. He eyed the fish and said, "Forty seven, but we'll get a measurement."

Just after he leaned in to go after the hook in the fish; it thrashed, and spun, sending the last treble hook flying past Joe's face, leaving the steel leader draped across his right ear. He stood back up and the musky, in the net without any lure, continued to give him the evil eye. Marv removed the line from around Joe's head and they had a chuckle together.

"Well, let's get a measurement and a few pictures." The boat was still pitching around so this wouldn't be an easy maneuver. Joe had the sixty-inch measuring stick in his hands and asked Mack, "Camera ready?"

"Camera is ready."

Joe reached for the fish's gills, to get a hold for pictures, when the powerful tail gave two slaps and the musky swam out right through the net. "What the hell, she's gone!" Joe pulled the net in and saw that he'd cut a huge hole in the mesh, eight inches or more in diameter."

Marv cursed. Mack stared. Joe let loose with a big belly laugh, repeated his laugh and said, "Now we've got a story to tell, or not, about the Cleveland Harbor." They had no pictures and no true measurement, but they had caught and released a fine fish. Marv joined in the laughter, high-fived Joe, and both men looked at Mack Spline, who had begun to get a sly grin on his face.

"Let's get this boat in before we are drownded." Mack headed her in, thinking about his discovery of untapped musky waters.

Chapter 12
Ohio

—June 13th—

Rad was driving down the full moon, comfortable in the big Cadillac. The huge lunar disc, slightly to the left of their route, shined in the clear summer sky like a chartreuse tennis ball. Joe was beaming over his big fish, but more so because his theory had been vindicated. Mo was quiet. The moonlight was affecting him, shining through the back window, bathing his strong features. He twitched occasionally, unable to fully control the nerve impulses coursing through him. Marv, having gotten over his bellyache, continually asked Joe for details of their plan for the next few days. Tonight the foursome would stay with the Shawnee band of Indians that Mo had contacted. Joe had said he and Marv would make a scout tomorrow of the place near Cincinnati where Randi was being held. Mo and Rad would remain in camp.

"We'll go look things over, develop a plan after we've scoped out the layout, determine the roles to be played by each of us, and drive back to the camp. Then on Tuesday or Wednesday we'll make it happen."

"Why let them see us? Why not just surprise 'em, give 'em no chance to prepare. Blitz 'em!" Marv wanted to be seen as a man of action.

"Because, if you want me and Mo in on this and Rad to help with the girl, then you'll do it my way. Russians are nuts for shootouts, they don't care who they kill. We're not gonna take it to them like it was the

OK corral. Got it?" Joe wasn't as annoyed with Marv as he sounded. Hard to convince though Marv usually was, he responded well to commands and rough treatment.

The Shawnee chief was gracious and welcoming when they arrived at the creek-side compound that sustained a remnant band of the tribe. The group had left Oklahoma to return to what they considered their ancestral home. He introduced his family, including his wife's mother who whispered a guttural syllable when she was presented to Mo, and his adopted son, called Johann Hatchett, a blond-haired blue-eyed boy who looked as German as his name but was a full-blooded Shawnee.

There was an isolated community of Mennonite farmers adjacent to the Shawnees on the broad fertile plain of the valley. A creek that fed the Scioto River formed the valley and at its upper end a three hundred-acre forest of big tulip and sycamore trees buttressed the remnant band of the Shawnee nation. The land, bartered to the band that had returned from Oklahoma, had been the property of the Mennonites. It was the kind of place Shawnees liked to settle. Deep woods with little brush except as a screen around the edges, the settlement contained a few dozen small-frame houses and trailers. The end of the property, nearest the Mennonites, was cleared of trees and occupied by playing fields, basketball courts, and a community building. The upper end of the Shawnee settlement, away from the religious group, had a smoke shop, grocery, and gas station called The Prophet's Trading Post. An untaxed Smoke Shop was illegal except on an official reservation — a status for which the Shawnees had applied — but political correctness meant the authorities looked the other way for the time being. The post was the main source of tribal income as non-Indians flocked there for untaxed gas and cigarettes and to play the tribal lottery that was another income bonanza for the Shawnees.

The highly disciplined, strict, and austere Mennonites lived in complete harmony with the rough-and-tumble Shawnee families in the self-contained valley. It was common for the Shawnees to attend religious services with the Mennonites and some intermarriage had taken place. Elders of both communities were on friendly and cooperative terms.

Later, after feasting and speeches in their honor, Joe and his friends were shown to a travel trailer and a nearby tent that they could use for their accommodations. Sitting before the campfire, Rad asked Mo what the grandmother's problem was.

"She was afraid of being eaten." Mo was bland in his expression when he said this.

"No, really, what was up?"

"In the 1700s the Shawnees were part of the Iroquois covenant chain because it was a way to procure guns and ammunition in those early days. But they never were very comfortable with us, especially the Mohawks. They felt that we were cannibals and their name for us means just that. For many generations grandmothers have scared their grandchildren by telling them to watch out for the Mohawks who would eat them."

Rad wanted to ask about Johann Hatchett and how she might get to know him but, after that bit about the grandmother, she was reluctant to ask.

Later, it was decided that Rad would use the tent, Joe and Marv would sleep in the trailer and Mo, at his request, would sleep in the open air between tent and trailer.

When he moved his pack from the Cadillac to the trailer, Rad watched Mo lay out his bed. He used a half-inch thick camping pad, a similar pad rolled tightly for a pillow and one thin cotton blanket. He arranged ceremonial items beside his position, donned a headlamp and stacked three books beside the bed. He looked up at Rad, "The pillow is because I have developed a white man's neck from my years in business."

"I'll bite, what's a white man's neck?"

"White men walk with their toes out like ducks. In order not to trip they look at their feet as they go. Mohawks walk and run with their toes pointed in and look at the sky. We don't get neck trouble unless we look down all the time like those white men cowed by their domineering bosses."

Rad didn't respond, unsure as to whether Mo was kidding. She asked, "Whatcha reading?"

Mo handed the books to Rad. On top was a well-thumbed copy of Jared Diamond's *Guns, Germs, and Steel.* "I spent a great part of my youth wishing I had read more. Not wanting to be forever regretful, I took up the challenge. Now I read three books at any given time."

Rad looked at the next work, *The Great Big Musky Book* by Eli Singer. "I collect books on musky fishing, but I collect them to read and pass on to any sons I might have, not to speculate that they may increase in value. I read one book that is good for me, one book that affects my business or sporting life, and one book for pleasure." Rad turned over the third book, a hard cover version of Robert Moss's *The Interpreter* and looked at the flyleaf. She had always wondered how anyone could read a book and not destroy the dust jacket. Mo obviously revered his books, which he gently removed from her hands.

"I decided that much of my life, as anyone's life, is spent in pursuits that are trivial and meaningless. Devoting twenty minutes per day to each of my books has made me wiser, more complete, and more satisfied with how my time is spent."

"What if you really get into reading one of the books? Don't you want to go on?"

"Daughter, you reveal your German nature in this. If I wish to continue or finish a book or chapter, I do so."

Chapter 13
Shawnee Nation (Ohio)

—June 14th—

Rad was enjoying the morning sun as she sat on the meager bleachers set up near the basketball court by the Ohio Shawnee Nation.

There was a Flag Day basketball tournament today, Monday morning, and she wanted to watch all the games, because Moses Snow was participating, as a guest, for one of the Shawnee teams. The tribe offered two teams, the Owls and the Ravens. Their competition in the tournament consisted of pick-up teams from area high schools and teams formed by bars, clubs, and firehouses from the surrounding towns.

Rad was eager to spend the morning, enjoying this male display. She'd pick a favorite team early and try to root it home as the winner. She enjoyed herself during the early games. Rad loved watching rough play that featured glistening bodies banging and slapping into each other. The referees, hired by the tribe, let boys be boys. They only called fouls that affected the game's outcome.

Most of all, Rad liked the physical poetry of the game. Two types of plays gave her a little chill up her spine and revved up her interest. She loved the fast break basket where a man made a lay up by himself after getting open up court. The better athletes were graceful animals as they leaped, raised one leg deftly, and banked the ball in for a score. Because there would be no highlight reel, these amateurs, shorter than college or professional players, were less consumed by the need to make a fancy dunk shot. Most still laid the ball up with grace and precision. The other play that turned Rad on was the long arcing outside shot. This game breaker gave the shorter, less intimidating men a chance to affect the outcome with a different sort of grace.

The asphalt surface of the court radiated the summer heat. Those players who went down hard in under-basket scrums came up with angry welts that turned to bloody strawberry marks as sweat rinsed away the black stains. The Shawnee section, behind which Rad occupied one half of the bleachers and three girls of high school age tittered away on the other half. It also had a doctor of sorts. He plastered medicinal tape over the bigger scrapes to reduce the amount of spraying blood. These fans segregated themselves, between the whites and blacks, about twenty of them, occupying the side of the court opposite Rad and the Shawnee girls. As the tournament developed, games would be played with neither of the Indian teams participating, yet no fans moved to watch from the Indian side.

The first game featured the Owl team of Shawnees, on which Mo was a substitute, being pummeled by a bar team that looked like a favorite to win it all. Rad watched with all her senses, enjoying the heat, smelling the hot asphalt, and ignoring the insistent squeaking of the men's sneakers. The team, from the bar, called the Tannery, easily outgunned the Shawnee's second string. This bar team contained a few obvious ringers, college players who didn't quite measure up. Mo was playing forward for the Owls and throwing elbows, to clear out under the basket, with such relish that several of the better Tannery players cried foul and appealed to the referee. Histrionics directed at the referee were a product of the television age just as much as fancy dunks. The refs got worn down over time and gave the complainers some calls, to the point that Mo was on the verge of fouling out when he got a rare scoring opportunity on a fast break.

Mo took the outlet pass on the right side of the court, managed two dribbles, and leaped for the lay-up just as a Tannery player used his superior speed to slide in front of Mo. Mo raised his left forearm to the defensive player's chin, and popped his elbow up, giving the collision a little mustard. The Tannery player's head snapped back. He flopped, as players do who are trying to draw a charging foul.

Mo was credited with the basket, was charged with a foul — deemed to have occurred after the shot — and he was disqualified from the game. The Shawnee Owl team, because it had no substitutes, had to play the last four minutes with only four players. The contest, already uneven, became a runaway.

While other preliminary games were taking place, Mo joined Rad in the bleachers. The Shawnee girls looked admiringly at Moses Snow's gleaming copper skin adorned with his stunning tribal tattoos, until he went and sat beside Radleigh Loonch. An older man, especially a Mohawk, would be seen as dangerous but desirable by Shawnee girls, but a shaft of ice entered their eyes as they saw him sit beside, but slightly apart from, a white girl.

"Your team was overmatched in that game," Rad continued to watch as a high school team took on one from a nearby fire hall. "Seems like they had some ringers playing for them."

"That was the tribe's second string formed to round out the tournament field. We get one more game at least. It takes two losses to be eliminated." Mo had an ironic smile on his face.

"You don't sound confident."

"I am sure that I will commit my fouls, the clear out," He stretched out his left armed straightened the elbow and gave Rad's right forearm, which she brought up to block, a light shove, "That's my best move." He grinned.

Rad dropped her arm. She'd felt her skin tingle having experienced the power in Mo Snow.

"Why is basketball so popular among Indians? 'Second only to lacrosse' my anthro teacher said."

Mo turned to look at Rad, winked so only she could see, glanced at the three Shawnee girls, who had little interest in the two white teams cruising through the second half of their game, then, in imitation of traditional Iroquois oratory, he spoke, deliberately raising his voice so the girls could hear as well as Rad.

"Lacrosse, as you call our game of Baggataway, is a game of tradition played by all men and boys of one village against all those of another. It is played from sunrise to sunset with no let-up for injury or even death. It is a test of courage, strength and stamina and was our only game before the white people came from the sunrise. It is war — our real favorite game — played among friends." Mo paused and faced west, toward the Indian girls, turned to the south toward the game, and then to the east and Rad. The Shawnee girls were silent, hanging on his words.

"Then the Sunrise People came with trader's rum and the Real People began to lose their minds and their land. Before this, Mohawk men would hunt, fish, make war, paint our bodies, and talk of war and hunting. We would dream. The rum made us drop our minds, we lost our dreaming. In the days before the Sunrise People, women did all the work. They grew the food, made the clothes, prepared the food, and raised the young ones. Other than coupling, warriors had no duties in the lodge. Then the white man came with his rum and his rules. They changed all that. They wanted men to work. Many warriors dropped their minds to the trader's rum. Most men and many women lost their dreaming. Now women expect men to work. We need money to live. The ideal world is gone."

Mo paused. Rad knew the speech was partly a put on, but she also knew it contained some truthful elements. She glanced at the Shawnee girls, awed by Moses Snow, who did not appear to see any irony at all.

Mo continued, "Now we cannot organize a village for Baggataway, we cannot get eleven men for lacrosse or football, we cannot organize nine for baseball. The best the Indians can do is to find five or so men for a basketball team."

After a polite period of silence, Rad said, "I thought it was because you guys are relatively tall, at least that is what I learned in anthropology. Short legs, slim hips, long, slender torsos."

"Radleigh, my daughter, you discuss me as a specimen. Are you not ashamed?"

"Hey, I'd change a lot about college if it was up to me. But, anyway, wasn't my school the lacrosse national champion year after year? Isn't that a tribute to the Six Nations?" Radleigh countered.

Mo made no further comment.

The warm morning lapsed into a hot afternoon. The humidity was giving Rad's skin a buttery softness. She donned her CBP ball cap and watched with pleasure as the Shawnee Raven team advanced steadily toward the title game. The team had two powerful athletic forwards who could shoot and a stiff center who could not be moved from under the basket. In addition they had Johann Hatchett, an outside shooter, nailing three pointers and able to go to his left on almost anyone.

Rad had been mildly disappointed to see Mo's team eliminated after one victory, but she was glad to have him return to the bleachers. He started to walk toward Rad, stopped, gave her a sly wink, and sat quite near the three Shawnee girls. He acted the stoic for them by staring straight ahead and ignoring their twittering and furtive glances at his muscled chest.

The Raven team was completing their last victory before the showdown with the team from the Tannery when Rad asked Mo, "That white boy with the cross-over dribble, Johann, the one I met last evening, is he a ringer? He seems to make them better."

"Radleigh, the Shawnee team, little brothers to the Mohawks, has only Real People on it. There are no white men on that team."

Rad looked at Mo, beetled her brows and looked at the boy now leading a fast break. He was athletic, though slim, his skin was so white as to be almost translucent, and he had blond hair that dropped a curly wisp plastered to his forehead by sweat. He did not have an Indian's body, hair, or skin. Rad looked back at Mo who grinned at her. Beyond him the three Shawnee girls were staring dagger eyes at Rad for daring to insult their tribal teammate and favorite player.

"Johann Hatchett, the man you speak of, is a full tribal Shawnee, a direct descendant of the famous war chief Blue Jacket. He is a dangerous man whom the tribe has saved from prison twice. Do not underestimate Johann Hatchett."

"Blue Jacket? He was actually a white boy, adopted into the tribe, who rose to be the famous war chief in the time when Ohio was being settled." Rad stated a fact.

" 'Conquered,' your teachers would say." Mo's remark got a right-on power salute from the Indian girls.

"Actually, I read about him in some books my father had. The TA's that taught the anthropology courses only emphasized the failures and enfeeblement of the Native Americans," Rad zinged back. The girls looked to Mo for another salvo.

Mo said, "Your self education does you credit, little sister."

"I'd like to talk with him later." Rad said this without looking at Mo.

"We are invited to a feast with his extended family, in fact," Mo winked again. The Shawnee girls didn't seem to know whether to be triumphant or chastened.

Hatchett led his team to triumph in the final game, as the front lines battled to a rough standstill under the baskets. Johann drained jumpers, shot after shot, until the Tannery team began to foul him repeatedly. Trying to wear him down physically proved to be a miscalculation, because he never missed a foul shot in the game. The Shawnee sideline bleachers filled up for the final game, and Rad joined in the cheering and glee at the Raven's victory.

There were a few hours before the ceremonial feast that would mark the conclusion of the Shawnee basketball tournament and the victory. Rad assumed that Joe and Marv had successfully completed their scouting and were on their way back. She hoped that Joe would develop a good plan for the rescue. She sat at a picnic table near the trailer they had been loaned, sipping her diet Coke, mentally reviewing what she might be able to do to alter Joe's plan. She had a nagging feeling that he would be too aggressive, too confrontational, and dangerous. Alternatively, Rad hadn't had much experience coming up with subtle, indirect ideas to rescue a kidnap victim from thugs. So she was in one of those thought loops that went nowhere.

The westering sun heated up the back of her neck and the humidity sent trickles of perspiration down her back as she watched Mo and waited for Joe's return. Mo was decorating the cypress knob war club that Joe had purchased at Reynoldsburg. It had been in the war bag stored at Mack Spline's storage locker. Rad watched as Mo flicked, sawed, sliced, and chipped at the haft of the club with his thirteen-inch long Arkansas Toothpick, also a gift from Joe. Radleigh was well aware of Mo Snow's power, strength, and capability for fierce violence. She also saw another side of Mo, a gentler, deft, almost loving aspect, as he carved totemic figures onto his weapon. Rad knew he often gathered herbs and leaves making medicine bundles. These were practical items to treat wounds and ailments. Carving stylized animals and spirits seemed, to her, to be just superstition, unworthy of someone she'd come to admire. She was trying to frame a polite anthropological question when Mo raised his head, looked at her, set aside his knife, and flexed his right hand several times, loosening up his stiff wrist.

"Johann will be at the feast tonight. He asked my permission to sit beside you during the meal. But I must warn you, daughter. He has some troubles in his past."

"What troubles?"

"He'll tell you about Boston and Virginia when he is ready. This— " he regrasped his club and shook off several wood chips, "—is a talisman against bad fortune. It does not protect me as a physical object, but as a ceremonial item it protects me against a sloppy mind and wandering concentration. Will I use it in our coming battles? It is possible. I will know after I have dreamed."

Rad was flustered. Mo knew just what she had been thinking. Speechless, she stood, walked around the table, and asked Mo, "May I see your designs?"

"Yes, daughter. But do not touch the object, just look as I turn it."

"Marv, calm down. We need a plan, And we need to think it through. And run it by Mo and Rad to refine it. We can't just go charging in there and attack. They'll shoot us all and dump us in the Ohio River without a care."

Joe was trying out all the features of the passenger's seat in the Cadillac. He increased his lumbar support, then he decreased it, he moved the seat up toward the windscreen, then back, he reclined into what he called his thinking position, then instantly moved the seat back upright. "This seat is so cool."

"It was her! You saw that! I gave my word. I'm going back there even if you won't." Marv was ready to pout.

"Yes. We have confirmed that it is Randi. Though I don't think she saw me, I recognized her. We also know that the club is isolated, guarded, and bristling with hard guys. Russian hard guys, mean as wolverines, tough as rhino hide, and without any scruples or worries about the reactions of US law enforcement agencies."

Joe was on a roll now, he rambled on while Marv drove the Cadillac. "We'll wait a day. Then, we won't be on their surveillance videos; they're changed every twenty-four hours. Besides being the slowest day of the week, Wednesday gives us time to get everything and everyone ready. Those bouncers will be on the alert if we show up tomorrow, not so much if it's Wednesday." Marv snorted when Joe said that, Joe ignored him and went on.

"They don't expect an organized raid. They are geared up to pound an isolated drunk or two or discourage an irate customer. With five of us acting according to plan they will be confused. Bruisers like these guys are good at lashing out with a lot of violence but don't offer much in terms of thinking on their feet or showing initiative." Joe paused.

"Would you quit with the seat? Every time I look over you're up or down or back or forward. Just light someplace, huh."

After a pause, Marv asked, "Five of us?"

"Yes we'll need some outside help. It will take all we've got inside the bar. I think I know someone." Thinking about Randi's situation and his own eldest daughter, Joe had been getting riled up. He had the devil riding him and knew that it would require a day to slow down enough for him to proceed in a methodical manner. He was germinating an idea that would get the gangsters off balance and perhaps keep them that way for the day following the rescue.

"If he don't wanna eat, I'll take his portion. More for me. Mmm Mmm." Joe let out a big belly laugh. Rad looked at him, annoyed.

"Listen girl, Mo needs to fast before he goes into action. He says that makes his dreaming more clear. Me, I'm the other kind of Indian, the kind who doesn't know where his next meal is coming from so he eats everything available. Mo would prefer if I fast, but I ain't gonna. He doesn't need everything to be his way." Joe laughed again. He could see that this aggravated Rad, the anthropologist, even more, so he grabbed a turkey leg and began gnawing on it.

Marv and Joe had arrived just in time for the feast honoring the Shawnee team's victory in the basketball tournament. They had been hustled right up to the head table, where guests were seated with the honoree's family. Also at the table was Johann Hatchett, hero of the tournament, and two Mennonite young ladies, introduced to Rad as Johann's sister-in-laws. At those words Rad's spirits took a decided drop. *Johann was married? Where was the wife? That b—* . Then Joe came up beside her and said, "Johann is young for a widower, huh?"

Rad was annoyed with Joe. Was she that obvious in her interest? But things settled down when everyone had their food. Johann sat next to Rad and asked her about herself. He didn't offer much about his background. After learning his wife was deceased, Rad didn't know what to say. Mo, sitting quietly, drinking tea, eating nothing, was present in body, but Rad believed he was absent in spirit.

That night Mo dreamed the dream of a fasting warrior. *He was uneasy with the running battle he saw ahead of them. It was the Mohawk way to lead the enemy into an unwise attack and draw him into a prepared and*

well-executed ambuscade. The Heron slowly winged its way above four battles, each dangerous and inconclusive. The first was an attack. The second was a defensive standoff. The third was a running battle of defense and escape. The fourth and most troubling looked, to Mo, like a last stand for Joe and Radleigh. The growl of nighttime thunder woke Mo, and he was uneasy because he saw that he would not even be present when his people were surrounded and outgunned. War conducted between Indians was rapid, violent, and deadly, but neither tribe could afford high numbers of lost warriors. Leaving many dead on the field and relentlessly coming on was the white man's way. Mo saw that this new enemy was more implacable than ever because they were completely unconcerned with the loss of their soldiers. Worried and resigned to tragedy, Mo would nevertheless go ahead.

Joe had a cast-iron stomach but this night he dreamed the dream of a man with the nighttime horrors of dyspepsia. He was sleeping in a trailer, reached around for a water glass, and found nothing. Awake, he began to remember his dream. *Joe's nose hurt and his jaw seemed out of whack as if it had come unhinged. His stomping by bouncers in Atlanta came back to him as he observed himself on the floor of a club being stomped and kicked until a man in a tailored suit put an end to the proceedings. Patrons walked around him exiting the bar with his body on the floor. Police eventually entered and he was frog marched to a cruiser and carted away. A voice had intruded into his dream. The police are always an after-the-fact group and as the song says, "The law was not meant to protect the man from out of town."*

"Take the situation in hand, Joe, if necessary, ask for forgiveness rather than permission." Joe let loose with a volcanic rolling belch that rumbled and rolled across the floor of the tent. Marv looked up from his bedroll said, "Wha — what?" rolled over, and went back to sleep. Joe smacked his lips together and drifted back to sleep.

In Muskedaigua, Amelia Gaspe was dreaming of her friend Randi. *Randi was lying on a dirty mattress, sobbing, and shaking, A strange man had just left her room and Igor (Iggie the Enforcer) shouted at her, "Shut up, clean up, and make the men happy. I don't want to hear any more complaints from customers about you acting like you are not enjoying yourself. Tell this man he is handsome, exciting, important, and most of all, big."*

"But, so many of them are smelly, it's disgusting."

"Here, you little twist," he said and grabbed her chin with a hairy gorilla-like hand strong as a vise. He dabbed some greasy substance on the first two fingers of his left hand and shoved them up her nose. She smelled only menthol after that. Another strange old man opened the door. Igor stepped aside, collected some bills, and left the room. Next morning, Amy awoke smelling menthol in her room.

Chapter 14
Shawnee Nation (Ohio)

—June 16th—

"We're gonna have a Council of War. Each of us will state his opinion of the plan. I'll give my view last. Then I'll decide what we are going to do. If, after you hear my plan, you want out, I'm sure you're welcome to stay here with our hosts until we are successful with Randi."

Radleigh Loonch spoke first and asked for a clarification or two. Moses Snow offered no modifications to Joe's plans. He stated, "This rescue will work. It will be dangerous and difficult, but it will work."

Marv nitpicked Joe's ideas, because he could, then acceded to the plan with ill grace and the statement, "I don't care, I'm easy."

Joe's opinions carried the discussion. He was convinced, and everyone else had been reassured, that if they carried the fight to the Russians in unusual ways, kept them off-balance, they could succeed. An enemy who was centered, firmly planted, and ready was difficult to defeat. An enemy who was skipping around, looking behind himself, one who had lost his center, would not be as formidable.

It was a Wednesday afternoon at Sweet Cherries and there were only five customers when Joe walked in and paid his cover charge. One girl was dancing at the pole. Another, wearing a see-through shift over her leopard-spotted costume, was cadging drinks from a lumpy salesman. The remaining customers were two pairs of down-at-the-heels older men watching the dancer. A madam, lavishly made-up and supported artificially in all the suspect places, sat at the bar talking to the bartender. There was a door to the left of the bar with a man in an ill-fitting suit and a buzz cut scowling beside it. The club was dark, the music was too loud, there was a distinct odor of rot, and the bouncer at the door was the only other employee in sight.

After Joe paid, he turned back and opened the door letting in a stream of bright daylight. Waiting outside were Marv, carrying two sacks of take-out fried chicken in his arms, Rad with another sack, and Mo in his stocking cap. These three trooped through the door and headed for a table. Joe impeded the bouncer, attempting to intervene and stop the gatecrashers. They did a two-part excuse me dance with Joe frustrating the bouncer's ability to block the other's entrance.

Things happened quickly after that. They had started causing a ruckus. Everyone looked at the table where Rad laid out the food. The harridan reached for a phone. The dancer at the pole stopped and stared. The bartender backed away. Rad calmly arranged a fried chicken supper and motioned for the girl hustling the old man to come over. Marv piped up loudly, "You girls looked awful hungry to me, c'mon over and get some fried chicken. We'll put some meat on you."

The bouncer headed for Marv and Joe allowed him to pass. Mo intervened to deliver a penetrating death-stare that momentarily stopped the Russian's advance, while Joe stepped quickly to the guarded door. Marv advanced to the left of the bouncer who, recovering his poise, took a roundhouse swing at Mo. He missed. Luring him on, Mo backed up a step, and Marv pulled the sap from his sleeve and laid it vigorously behind the ear of the bouncer who slid to the floor like dry sand.

Joe was at the door marked "Private." He asked the guard, "This way to the men's room?"

"Nyet." The sentry tried to block Joe's way, but he stepped into a short, wicked right uppercut to the guard's chin. This was a gunman, not a fighter, and he was stunned. Joe grabbed his jug ears and smacked his face with a rising knee. Still holding the man's ears, Joe pulled the bloody face up then smashed it viciously with his right knee. Since that punch contained the power of Joe's massive legs, strong back, and rotating hips, it was a knockout blow. He dropped the gunman and bull-rushed the door.

The customers were frozen, staring, the music played on. One man still held a dollar bill in his outstretched hand. The dancer Rad had been motioning to was apparently hungry, and she'd edged toward the food. The madam looked on with panic as Joe went through the door into the woman's domain. She glanced at the downed guard, looked at the bouncer down near the door, and shifted her gaze to another door on the opposite side of the bar. In the center of the room, Mo reached into his otter skin bag and assumed a relief pitcher's stance, looking over his left shoulder, hands at his waist. Marv moved off to Mo's left and calmly drew his handgun, a Smith & Wesson revolver, known as the Mountain Gun. The bartender dropped down, cowering behind the bar.

A locked door in a small vestibule had impeded Joe's progress. He kicked it under the lockset and it gave way. From off to his right, another gunman rushed up drawing from an inner holster. Joe recentered himself after his kick, drove into the Russian with a football block, quickly raised his head, and butted him in the face with the crown of his head. Then, just as quickly, with the guard pinned to the wall, Joe snapped his head back down, rebutting the face of his opponent. The guard slumped to the ground, nose and lips bloody and broken. "How did you like the Liverpool Kiss, Ivan?" Joe said. He turned and stepped around the broken door.

In the barroom, the far door opened and three men rushed through, armed and belligerent. The first one through the door stopped one of Mo's ceremonial throwing stones, coming at ninety-one miles per hour, with his forehead. He toppled like a falling tree. The second through the door was a giant. Marv's gunshot was low, taking the huge man just below the belt instead of eight inches above it. With a gush of blood and a stream of curses, he crumpled and dropped his weapon, his hand covering his groin. The third Russian had apparently watched plenty of television. He came through the door in a crouch, sweeping his automatic weapon from side to side. He took Mo's second throwing stone in the temple with a sickening crunch and sprayed bullets into the floor, falling unconscious.

In the back, Joe went down the hall, shouting and flinging doors open. "Randi! Randi DesChutes! Where are you? This is Joe Gaspe, Amy's dad. We're gonna go now!" The first door he opened revealed a room containing a man with a woman's panties on his head, bent over the lap of a girl who was spanking him with a boat shoe.

"Hey!" he said, "How about my privacy?"

"Shut-up," Joe's face was well bloodied and his expression brooked no argument. He turned to the girl, "You want out of here? We're taking any that wanna come along." She looked confused and scared but dropped the shoe and rolled her client off her lap. Joe returned to the hall. Several doors had opened and undressed women were looking out. He flung open the next door on his right. A slim woman, hardly more than a girl really, was sleeping twisted up in a dirty sheet. Joe stepped over to her and gently rolled her over by the shoulder. It was Randi, gaunt and drugged, but this was Amy's friend.

"Randi, Randi! This is Mr. Gaspe. Amy's dad. Get up! We gotta go! Now! You got any clothes?" He looked around the shabby room. A bed, a straight back wooden chair, a few clothes hooks that held a dancing costume, a flimsy robe and nothing else. He looked back at Randi and she screamed.

"Wha, what's going on? Mr. Gaspe? You're all bloody! Joe grabbed the sheet and wiped his face. It rubbed away some of the blood.

"Get your things, let's go. You got any clothes?"

"They take our clothes. They're in the closet in the hall."

Joe went to the hall. He heard no more shooting or shouting. He hollered, "Marv get in here! I need you! Now!"

Marv motioned for Mo to take his position behind the curve of the bar covering the door that the gunmen had come through. Mo took Marv's weapon and watched the man who'd been shot. He was the only one even slightly conscious. Those men he'd beaned with his throwing stones wouldn't get up soon, if ever.

Rad had explained the plan to the girl who'd been cadging drinks. She stuffed a chicken leg in her mouth and said, in accented English, "Mm-hmm, mm-hmm, I go."

Rad said, "Get your things and tell the others they can get out of here, now! Quickly!" Rad turned to the dancer, "You wanna go?"

The dancer looked at the madam, looked back at Rad, who was gathering up the food as she talked, and said, "Da."

The joint's customers just stared, looking longingly at the door. The salesman with the dollar in his hand had it snatched by the dancer as she dropped down from the stage and headed for the chicken. The madam glared death rays at her girls but did not move. She was to Mo's left. He held up his hand, raised one finger and pointed at her. He glanced at the bartender face down on the floor.

Rad said to the madam, "How about you? You want to go or stay?"

"Nyet, I vill remain."

Rad spoke to Mo, "We'll take the food. I'll retrieve your weapons."

Mo nodded, and Rad moved toward the doorway near where the bodies of three Russians were piled up.

Marv entered the hallway to see total confusion. Barely clad women walked up and down, arguing and jabbering in a language he assumed was Russian. Joe walked up to him leading Randi roughly by the upper arm. He barked at Marv, "See that Randi gets into the Caddy. Find out if any of these others want to get outta here. If they do, send them out to Johann at the van. If they don't, screw 'em. Er, let them stay, I mean." Marv was staring at women, mostly ill fed and mostly naked.

"Partner! Marv! We gotta move, Okay?" With a meaty paw, Joe shoved the pervert with the panties, who was trying to leave, back into the room he'd come from and slammed the door. "I'm gonna get that madam to show me where some clothes are for these girls." He swept his arm back in the direction of the crowded hallway and went through to the bar.

Mo had not moved. Rad had found one of his ceremonial throwing stones and was searching for the other. Joe walked up to the harridan and said, "Where are some clothes for these girls?"

"I vill not tell you."

Joe backhanded her across the mouth. The devil was up in him and he knew time was not an ally. A man who would normally never strike a woman, he had no patience with this evil harlot.

Joe grabbed her by the upper arm and dragged her through the two doors to the hallway. Marv had gotten the women organized. Taking Randi by the hand he was leading them in the opposite direction of that taken by Joe.

"Where's some clothes for these girls?" Joe asked again.

"I vill not talk to you." Joe raised his hand and was ready to strike her a second time when he heard Johann at the back door. He had been told to time the whole escapade and end it after fifteen minutes. "Guys, we have two minutes. Let's load the cars." Joe lowered his fist and shoved the madam away from him. A soft growl escaped from his throat. The girl who had been dancing slid past him with a pathetically small armload of possessions.

Rad spotted the other throwing stone beside the groaning Russian giant and reached for it. A huge paw rose up and grabbed her left shoulder. His grip hurt her dreadfully. Squeezing her shoulder, the Russian got to his feet with a scream of pain and fury. He had Rad between himself and Mo. He had lifted her official CBP issue sidearm, from the holster on her hip, as he stood. He threw her Sig Sauer across the room and put both hands around her neck to throttle her. He squeezed. Rad felt pain worse than she ever had before. The Russian was so furious and confident that he could snap her neck that he gave no credence to her ability to resist.

The Russian was leaning against the wall to stay on his feet. He had Rad's feet off the ground using her to protect himself from Mo's potential gunshot. He squeezed. Rad saw only red, then black intruding at the edges of her vision. The Russian didn't care if Mo shot him, he would kill this woman.

With what she thought was the last of her strength, Rad reached with her right hand to try prying his hands free and her hand brushed her hide out gun in its special holster attached to her bra strap. She drew the .41 caliber Derringer, clicked off the safety, reached over the top of her head, and, using alternate triggers, fired two quick shots, each driving into her assailant's mouth and through his head into the wall behind. One shot was into the grinning, then surprised, face and one into the dead face of the man. His hands went limp and Rad slipped down, choking and gasping, to the floor. She had been deafened by the sound of the gunshots.

Joe heard the shots, raced into the room, ran up to Rad and reached around her shoulders. He supported her and led her toward the outer door. Marv was outside with Randi leaning against him with her arm through the crook of his right elbow. Marv directed the dancers to the van. "Ladies, if you'll proceed to the van, we'll get you away from here."

Johann held open the door to the club. Joe brought Rad through, spluttering and coughing. Johann blanched, though he was so pale that it was hard to tell. "What happened? Is she Okay" he asked Joe.

"She had a close one but will be alright. Are we ready?"

"I fixed all the tires on all the cars in the lot." Johann held up his switchblade to show Joe. "That should give us a good start." He looked at Rad, who was leaning on Joe, trying to catch her eye. Then he and Joe both looked at the twelve other strippers being motioned to the van by the two Mennonite girls. Some seemed reluctant to trade what they perceived as one captor for another.

Hannah, the older of the two Mennonite sisters said, "Sprechen sie Deutsch?"

One of the Russian girls snapped her head around and said, "Ja," rather tentatively.

Hannah spoke rapid fire German that ended with the words, "Mach schnell." At the translation of that into Russian the dancers trooped into the van.

Joe said, "Johann, we're going to cut a trail. Mo will be out in a second. You know the plan." Johann looked into the door to the club as the last stripper came out with two buckets of chicken and followed the others to the van.

Inside the devastated bar, Mo stepped to the first of the two men he had beaned, pulled out his long razor-sharp knife, and slit the man's throat, flicked a quick circle around the crown of his head, grabbed hair, and popped off his scalp. He shoved the bloody mess into one section of his bag, stepped over and picked up his second throwing stone, and looked at the other Russian. He had a poorly shaped crew cut. Mo cut his throat, waved in disgust at his scalp, said, "Bah," and walked over to where Rad's Sig Sauer was on the floor. He picked it up and walked out. This had all been so violent, furious, and fast that the customers were still sitting where they'd been. They were looking around in shock. One said, "Let's get out of here," and they began to leave.

Mo strode to the Cadillac, handed Marv his gun and Rad's through the back window, stepped to the front passenger side window and looked at Rad, whose face had a blank stare. He reached in, took her Derringer and handed it to Joe who was leaning over to speak to him.

"Radleigh," Mo said and she snapped out of it for a second. He held out his hand palm up. "You now can learn the ways of power."

"What, since I killed someone?" She put the throwing stone in his hand. He dropped it into his pouch.

"I will see you on Friday at the place mentioned," Mo said to Joe. "We will talk then, daughter," he said to Rad. He walked over and closed the sliding door of the van on the gaggle of girls, stepped to the passenger door and entered.

Johann walked up to Rad's window and looked at her. His expression was one of worry. He tried to make eye contact, thought he did, worried that he didn't, sighed, and went to the van.

The Cadillac, with Joe at the wheel, turned right out of the lot and the van went left.

Chapter 15
A Hilltop in Kentucky

—June 16th—

Marv had arranged to get access to his girlfriend's brother's compound on top of a Kentucky mountain. The plan entailed lying low there for two nights and then meeting Mo Snow in Eastern Ohio. The church van, driven by Johann with twelve strippers, two Mennonite girls, and Mo inside, headed toward Columbus and the Mennonite settlement south of there that shared a boundary with the Shawnees. Joe drove into the Kentucky hills confident that they could evade immediate pursuit. Johann had shown initiative to puncture the tires of all the vehicles in the lot at Sweet Cherries. Marv was keyed up in the back seat and looking around, pumping his fist and saying, "Yes!" to himself. He had yet to react to the fact that the battle was over. He was geared up and the sudden letdown hadn't arrived to tell his body he could relieve the stress. He fidgeted, examined his gun — fired once — looked at Rad's Sig Sauer, which hadn't been fired, and got excited all over again. Randi sat, curled up, slammed into the corner of the back seat, staring straight ahead.

The only person, other than the bartender, left conscious in the strip joint was the Russian madam. Joe assumed that she would call her boss and that pursuit would follow quickly. He had a little time.

Conversations with Father Justin and others led Joe to believe that after thirty-six hours or so a drugged person, Randi, would start to come back to herself. Rad, meanwhile, was alternately staring out the window motionless or shaking all over and bobbing her head. He didn't know what to do about her. Randi had shrunk so far back into the corner of the back seat. Joe could not see her in the rearview mirror. Joe had bruised knuckles, bloody and turning blue. He thought about picking up a bag of ice. Then, at a stoplight, looking in the vanity mirror, he saw a smear of blood running diagonally across his forehead. He'd get ice at the house. By the time Joe had driven slowly up the switchback toward the hilltop where the driveway became a private road at the end, he had begun to relax.

Rad sat at the edge of the hillside, outside the limits of the antenna farm that Brian Hesketh had for his Ham radio obsession, and she could not stop sobbing and shaking. Her logical side, so often ascendant, and her recent FBI training thought, *What I did was what I had to do.* Her emotions, racked by recent experience, just washed away her logic in a flood of tears. She understood that her desire for non-violence in her life had no effect on the murderous or greedy impulses of others. Her training could not overcome her sheltered life when confronted with brutality. She had killed a killer — justified, but still a life-changing experience.

She wanted to call her best friend, Olivia Shanio, but she couldn't compose herself. She'd been told if she walked out to the bench on this promontory, with its view of the city across the Ohio River, her cell phone would work. She needed to talk to Olivia, who was living in New Orleans, because Rad couldn't get her thoughts out of a concentric loop. The angel on one shoulder debated the devil on the other.

I've killed a man!

He had you by the throat!

He was a living person.

I killed him.

He was choking you.

He probably had a wife, kids.

It was you or him.

Then she would sob, choke, have a shiver go up her spine, and the same thoughts would come back.

She wanted to talk to her friend just because Olivia would listen without judgment, understand Rad's feelings, and not try to tell her what to do. She needed to compose herself enough to punch the button on her speed dial.

Joe Gaspe strode up and sat beside her. He was a clumsy man, confused by his emotions, scared to express them, but he had his heart in the right place.

"Rad, I need your help."

She looked at him with red-rimmed eyes, squinted, and was about to yell at him when he spoke again.

"Randi is having some kind of withdrawal from whatever drug cocktail she was on. Marv's with her. She thinks he's a hero, but he doesn't have any idea what to do. She's shaking and sweating and puking and claims she's constipated but feels a desire to go. Marv's getting really antsy. Didn't you tell me that your friend Liv had helped detox some of her friends and even a family member?"

Rad nodded, handed her cell phone to Joe and said, "Speed dial number one."

Joe took the phone and said, "I'll get her on and then you talk to her about some ideas for Randi. I know you're upset but we need you now. I need to clean your weapon." He held up the Derringer, wrapped in its holster and he stepped away a few feet.

When the call was answered he said, "Olivia Shanio? This is Joe, I'm a friend of Radleigh Loonch, please hold for her. I must warn you she has had a traumatic experience. She's physically okay, but very upset. Here. She'll tell you about it."

Rad took the phone, "Ollie, it was horrible. I don't know what to think. My mind's all crazy." Rad let go and her tears flowed. The noises she made were unintelligible to Joe. Uncomfortable around crying women, he listened for a few seconds and took the gun back to the garage for a cleaning.

Rad related her feelings to her friend. The fact that she had killed a man didn't faze Olivia in the least. By being matter-of-fact in her statements, she convinced Rad that it was self-defense. She made Rad consider what kind of man this Russian gangster had been. But, most of all, she listened, she validated, she accepted Rad doing the deed, and she accepted Rad being upset at doing the deed. Eventually they moved to the subject of detoxing a person addicted to unknown, but powerful and interactive, combinations of drugs.

Half an hour later Rad walked back to the house. She said, "All right Joe, get me two oranges, brew a pot of tea, and bring them to the bathroom. I'm going to get Randi into a warm bath and try to concentrate her mind a little bit. When you've got the tea ready — on a tray with lemon, honey, and milk, bring it and the oranges to the door and knock. Don't be barging in. One of the things she needs is to regain her modesty."

Gaspe smiled. He was pleased to see that Rad seemed to be her old assertive self again.

Johann picked up Interstate 75, drove across the bridge to Ohio, and plugged a cassette into the van's player. "Cassettes are really old-school,"

Mo looked at him but didn't comment.

"Luckily one of my step dads had a few. This one's Stevie Ray Vaughn. That's the real blues."

"Speaking of old-time blues, I have met Robert Johnson," Mo said with an impassive face but a twinkling eye.

"You're not that old. Robert Johnson died back in the, like fifties, or something."

"No one is dead in the Real World. He and I have met in the dreaming. That man played real blues on the acoustic guitar. McKinley Morganfield, Chester Burnett, that's Muddy Waters and Howlin' Wolf, are also there, along with others."

Johann did not know what to counter with. Mo had perfected a bland manner and impassive face, which he used to especially good effect when he was squeezing someone's shoes.

They drove on in silence except for quiet conversation from the rear of the van, which was screened from the driver by a curtain. A few words of German would be spoken, then a translation into Russian would take place. There was a rustling of fabric as the rescued strippers changed into traditional modest Mennonite clothes. Though it wouldn't fool a cop since most of the strippers were elaborately made-up, to the observer driving by the vehicle looked like a church van on the way somewhere.

Johann, though beardless, could pass for Mennonite and Mo, wearing a close fitting stocking cap, had his Mohawk haircut covered. A voice peeped up from the back, "Hey, I'm from Nebraska. Don't any of you crazy people speak English?"

Johann drove at exactly the speed limit.

On Thursday Johann hitched the little antique Airstream trailer to the church van, and he and Mo left for the point in Southeastern Ohio where Mo would rendezvous with Joe and the others. The Russian girls had been taken in by the women of the Mennonite community and put to work. It was baking day. The roadside stand at the south edge of their compound and two other locations had to be supplied with well over one hundred homemade pies as well as numerous loaves of bread, cookies, and rolls for the weekend. The stern but just Mennonites were challenged by the behavior of the Russian women. None of them wanted to wake up pre-dawn. Few of them were willing to work and fewer still had any idea how to prepare pies or bake them in a wood-burning oven.

Igor Nesterenko, Iggie the Enforcer, stood outside his boss's suite in an old building in the German Village section of Columbus Ohio. He was worried. His face was a mess, he had a lump on his head and he knew his interaction with his boss, Jimmy Maxwell, wouldn't be pleasant. The little Jew-boy who worked directly for the boss had left his gadget filled closet and been ushered in to the suite fifteen minutes earlier. Iggie despised him but feared his techno-geek influence with the boss.

Jimmy Maxwell was the American name of Dimitri Maximov a Russian who could and did pass as an internet millionaire. He spoke with a slight British accent, dressed in tailored clothing, shaved his head, wore Italian shoes and listened to heavy metal music. The only giveaways that he wasn't who he seemed were that he played the music at a low volume not remembering that metal only worked when it was loud, and he had dead eyes that looked right through a person. An American millionaire, while ruthless and severe, would know how to fake friendliness and concern because that masquerade was a key part of how business was done in the United States. Jimmy Maxwell knew he had to work on that glad-handing style.

Igor was mad. He wanted a shot at the guy who took him down from behind. He was resigned, however, to doing what the boss wanted — that would be to retrieve the lost assets, the strippers — that had been taken from him. Judah was in there cuing up the electronic devices that would locate the girls. With this technology he could find them, all thirteen, even if they had scattered. Besides being the boss's little pet, Judah was an RF expert and he knew computers, and all other electronic gear, perfectly. Igor waited to be told where to go and how many girls he was to pick up. Maybe he'd run into the ugly little bastard who'd taken him down. Then he'd do some stuff to him. He was tasting sweet revenge when the door opened and the boss's new favorite gunman, Alexei, beckoned him into the inner office.

Igor wasn't unused to guns, he'd been a soldier in Afghanistan, but he liked to work with his fists. Hard as iron, they never failed him when it came to persuading people to see things the way the boss wanted. Mostly it was other Russian émigrés that he intimidated and, he had to admit, it was easy. Russian people understood fear and expected brutality and terror. A snarl and a raised hand, promising a few blows, usually shut them up or stopped them from proceeding in an unwise direction. Americans were different. Some were cowards and shrunk in fear, but they were unpredictable and there was always the possibility that any one of them might have a gun and know how to use it. Vitaly, Igor's best friend had lost a leg because of a shotgun blast from a little old lady landlord protecting her tenants. When on the prod, Igor Nesterenko preferred dealing with other Russians. Extorting money from overpaid professional hockey players was the boss's latest gold mine.

Jimmy said, "Sit down." Igor sat. Jimmy looked over his henchman walking behind him to see the lump behind his ear, and said, "You can redeem your error by retrieving my assets. Judah is going to show you some film and then we are going to go over the plan. It will be best if you say nothing."

The boss was back in front of Igor when the far wall was lit up by a projected image from the security camera inside the Kentucky Sweet Cherries club. Judah narrated, "We've retrieved a good image of the short ugly one with the dirty blond hair. Here he drops you with a blackjack," Igor touched his sore head. "The fat one and these other two never got close enough for the camera to pick up their faces. Three men and a woman and they are deadly. Three of our people are dead and three beaten like you. You were surprised I'm sure."

"I am sending Geno the cleaner to the club location. He will close it temporarily for repairs. The waste matter will be going downriver. Soon enough the facility will be redecorated. The staff will undergo a shake-up, by this time next week." He snapped his fingers. "Business as usual." Igor knew enough not to smile.

Judah turned off the projector. He turned to Igor. "We have a series of antennas conveniently located on cell phone towers throughout the state. I will be able to track the property and direct our recovery teams to retrieve them. Right now I have located twelve of thirteen signals and, luckily for you, they are all together. Here is the location." Judah handed him a three-by-five file card and a sheet of paper. The boss spoke again, "Assemble your team and go take this property back. Here is Judah's cell phone number. Call for further information when you are close by."

The boss spoke. "Redemption is a good thing, Igor. You know what to do. We have men ready to assist if the property splits up or when that last asset surfaces. I'll have another team ready. Meanwhile, I have someone working on finding the identity of your friend," Jimmy Maxwell touched his finger to his head behind the ear. "When I have my property back in good working order, perhaps you can pay the ugly one a visit." Igor looked up and saw that the gunman now held the door open. He was being dismissed.

The boss walked back into his private office and beckoned Judah to follow. They stepped into a small vestibule and waited while an air curtain was activated. Then they stepped through to a room that was kept at a constant eighty degrees in order to house Jimmy Maxwell's extensive collection of live moths and butterflies. He turned to Judah as they sat on the expensive outdoor furniture. Maxwell waved his arm. "My collection is not on a board with pins through them. It is here." Judah nodded. "You will find the thirteenth girl. You will enhance the images to identify my enemies. You have all my usual resources available to you." The boss demonstrated his menacing stare. "If anyone causes you difficulty, I want to know."

"Yes, boss." Judah stood up. As a moth as big as a woman's glove landed on his clean head, Jimmy Maxwell grinned and waved his hand to dismiss Judah.

The strippers, eleven Russians and a girl from Nebraska, had been quite a lot for the farmers of the Mennonite community to handle. Most conversations were still translated from German to Russian. Several of the girls were drug dependent and acted strangely. The Mennonite community relied on one cure for everything, work. It was Thursday, baking day, when the eastern sky turned from black to gray and it was time for all the women and girls to do the work required to stock three roadside stands and the main store.

During summer weekends, the sale of baked goods was the main source of income for their community. If these Russian girls were going to be there, they were going to work. Hannah Miller and three of the other young women rousted the Russians, speaking German and English to inform them of their duties. The strippers pitched in with varying degrees of ill grace but all were made to know that they had to help. It was late afternoon on Thursday when the pies and breads, cookies and turnovers that had been baked and wrapped were ready for market. Unaware that their respite from Sweet Cherries was to be short lived, the exhausted women dragged back to the dormitory-like bedroom where they were staying. They all ended up on beds, worn out, and snoring softly. Mayella Braunfels, the eighteen-year-old girl from Nebraska, did not sleep. She went to Hannah Miller and stood before her as Hannah totted up the accounts of what was available to sell.

"I'm leaving. I appreciate the help in getting me out of the club. But, this is not my life. I'm going home."

Hannah looked up at her, "As you wish. We were not expecting this," she reached her hand out palm up toward the dorm where, with the door ajar, soft snoring could be heard.

Mayella pulled on a pair of jeans and a baggy sweatshirt, tied her sneakers, and walked out of the compound, determined to hitchhike home and rejoin her family. This action was discouraged but the religious leaders would not stop her. She had nothing in common with the rootless European women and she wanted to be as far from her bad memories of Ohio as she could get.

She turned west and began trudging down the road. She looked back to stick out her thumb at each pick-up and SUV that passed. She snagged her first ride almost immediately.

At five o'clock the next afternoon the eleven Russian women were assembled, fed a nutritious, if starchy and bland supper, and divided up. The six judged the least lazy were sent in twos with one of the elders who would handle the money at the three outdoor stands. They would spend the night with a family near the stand in order to be ready early Friday morning. The five lazy ones would stay and clean the commercial kitchen from end to end. This job would take all day Friday and was a backbreaking routine of sweeping, washing, scrubbing, and rinsing.

Igor was talking on the cell phone with Judah in Columbus. He drove a Suburban and his caravan of three Volvo station wagons sat behind at a roadside rest south of Columbus on Route 23. It was seven-thirty. They had an hour and a half of daylight left.

"They are splitting up. There are now four groups of signals and one lone signal. Consult your GPS units and enter these numbers." Igor didn't like taking orders from the puny little Jew, but he held the key to cleaning up this mess. Igor entered the numbers into the units and instructed his captains where to go and how to take care of the situation.

With Judah waiting, Igor doled out one handheld GPS unit to each captain. "We want these whores back, undamaged; we want no complications with civilians. Get the women. Persuade whoever you have to. No guns. No deaths. Get the women and go to the warehouse and report in."

After they left for the three locations, Iggie got back on the phone with Judah

"Okay that is six. Where are the rest?" He waited while Judah told him about the five who were not moving and one other slowly moving west. The thirteenth signal was still unaccounted for. "I will get the five and call you about the sixth, the one on the move, before I return to the warehouse. Da." Iggie liked having the outcome in his hands.

The RF finders that Judah had supplied could home in on a signal when the object was within a quarter mile. Farther away than that, Judah had used a huge antenna network and relayed GPS coordinates to the retrieval cars. That transfer of information had taken all day Thursday and it was after eight thirty when the Suburban pulled up in front of the Mennonite community along the Scioto River. Igor turned to his two helpers. "Scare them, do not kill them, fists only. We're here to retrieve the boss's property and leave. Five minutes no more."

"How shall we do this?" one man asked Igor.

Brandishing the RF receiver, Igor Nesterenko said, "Once I find the building they're in I'll knock on the door. Whether they answer or not we're going in."

Peaceful, gentle, religious people are unprepared for the violence a brutal thug will use to pursue his ends. All three houses that held women taken from the Sweet Cherries club had their blue painted doors broken down and any men present were assaulted. Each bruiser had grabbed an elder, identifiable by his beard, and smashed his face with a gloved fist. The gloves made the punches bloodier and scarier to the witnesses. The strippers capitulated to their recapture. They were sheep returning to the barn. Each recapture team called Iggy, reported success, and was instructed to return to the warehouse in German Village.

Johann Hatchett was exhausted after his drive to drop Moses Snow off for his rendezvous in the strip mine pits. He planned to drop the church van off, leave the keys under the front seat, and walk through the Mennonite compound to the Shawnee chief's house where he slept. It wasn't late, but he'd been driving into the setting sun and squinting hard for the last hour or so. When he pulled into the gate before the main church building, he saw a black Chevy Suburban over at the dorm. Johann had a sinking feeling, and, before he could quite see what was happening, the doors were slamming on the truck. With the van's door open and the keys in his hand, he watched the vehicle start up and accelerate past him. He looked into the dead eyes of the driver and the sinking feeling was complete. He was sure that those rescued strippers were gone. Their freedom was at an end.

Johann double-timed it across the yard to the building and into the open door. There inside the door was the elder who was chaperone to the girl's sleeping quarters. He sat on the floor, his spectacles beside him, and he held a handkerchief to his bloody nose. The front of his shirt was sprayed and soaked with blood. Johann's sister-in-law Hannah had a bowl of water and a cloth in her hand. She looked at Johann and said, "The man said that these were the last one's to be recovered. They already picked up the ones sent out there to work at the roadside stands tomorrow."

"So, they got them all?"

"One young woman left earlier in the day; said she was going home to Nebraska." Johann heard this, walked back out the door, and said, loudly, "Damn!" He immediately felt guilty about swearing but he felt worse for those strippers, and knew he could do nothing for them.

Igor called Judah. One of his assistants drove while another kept the five women quiet. They were easy to control because these "lazy ones" weren't all that unhappy to escape from the Mennonites.

Igor reported that eleven missing assets had been recovered. He asked Judah, "What about the last two?"

"One has vanished as far as my RF signals have shown. The last is near you, about twenty-five miles west." Judah gave Igor the GPS coordinates, and Igor agreed to call back when they got closer.

The coordinates led to a roadside truck stop on Route 35. When Igor turned on his short-range RF finder, the unit pinged joyously and Igor and one assistant strode into the truck stop, zeroed in on the girl who panicked, and ran when she recognized Iggie the enforcer. She ran out the side door, leaving a trucker behind. He'd just returned from the men's room and was wondering what had been wrong with his pick-up line. Mayella ran straight into the bodyguard posted at the side door. She struggled in the dark until Igor walked up and instructed his man to shut her up and get her to the car. When the door opened she braced her legs and pushed back to prevent them from forcing her in. Iggie put his RF unit in his pocket and grabbed her upper body. He gave a full-strength twist and heard a sickening crack. The woman went limp.

"She's dead. You broke her neck."

Iggie shrugged, "Put her in the back. We'll find a place to get rid of her." Later that evening when they stopped for fuel, for which they paid cash, the girl from Nebraska was left in the dumpster behind the adjacent convenience store.

Chapter 16
Stoneburner, Ohio

—June 18th—

Johann Hatchett and Mo had backed the trailer camper off the north edge of the flat that comprised the shooting range, backed by a near-vertical spoil bank. The range was where everyone living in the area was free to shoot his or her weapons for practice and training. Johann had returned to the Shawnee Nation and left Mo to wait for Joe's group,

Squinting to locate a memorable landmark, Mo stopped and looked back downhill from where he'd come. In the wilderness any place may have a different aspect, which is the reason that seasoned hikers watch their back trail, to know how the country will look on their return journey. A slightly different view of terrain, under different conditions of light, makes a surprising difference in appearance. By looking back, he memorized how the return trail would look. Toes inward, in a loping gait, Mo could cover remarkable distances on known trails, but he was new to the area around the shooting range. He had carefully and thoroughly studied the surrounding terrain. When he searched the woods for food, supplies, and ceremonial items, he found all three. In one afternoon and night and two mornings he had found fish and game to spare. Seven nearby ponds held fish, two of which had no road access. He had taken turkey, squirrel, and rabbit and had five fine bass smoking by the trailer.

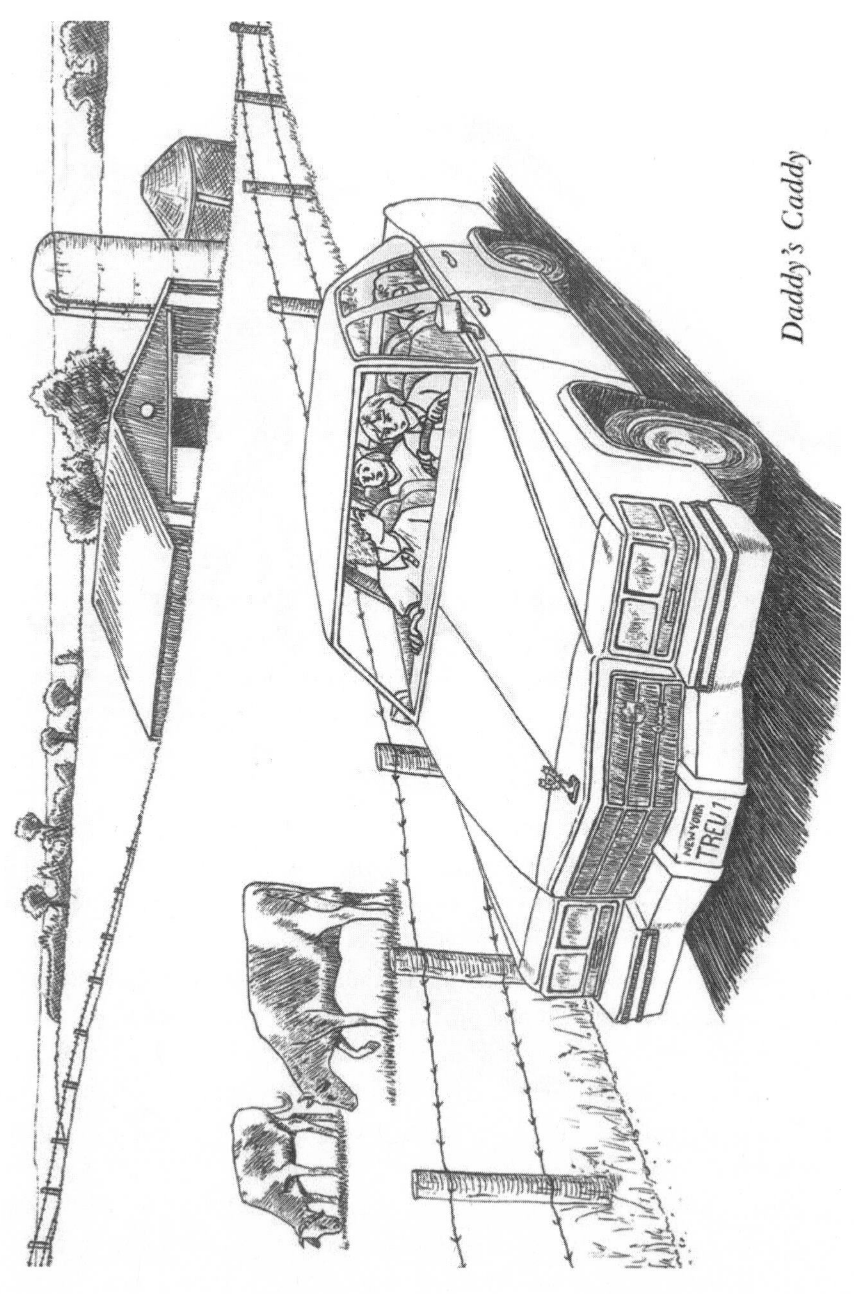

Daddy's Caddy

He was checking on connecting roads coming in behind the massive spoil bank that was the backstop for the shooting range. There were many such roads, several went nowhere, but Mo had found two that came close, and he thought the terrain indicated that there was another parallel trail just ahead. It could be another pond. There were many ponds around and only a few remained polluted.

At the camper, Mo had made a fire back under the trees. He used the hard locust wood that yielded a hot fire with low smoke, most of which was dissipated by the leaves above. What smoke there was, was was carried through a rack that held fish and meat for curing.

Mo's dreaming was not ever under his conscious control but it was usually focused on one subject or at most two. Having over-indulged in wild onions, ramps he called them, he went to sleep with a case of heartburn that caused him to wake often with loud rumbling belches. Each time he reentered his dream it was to observe a different activity.

Mo was practiced at using the first few moments of wakefulness to concentrate on what he had dreamed. Most men over thirty wake with such an overwhelming urge to urinate that they immediately forget their dreaming. Mo used that urge as a motivator. He willed himself to hold it until he had committed his dreaming to his conscious mind. His dreams of the previous night had a newsreel quality to them.

He had seen the recapture of the strippers held by the Mennonites and seen Johann's arrival, moments too late.

He had seen success in battle ahead for Joe's team. Three rearguard actions would happen without defeat. Each of these fights was dangerous and deadly, but ultimately they were successful.

He had also seen a vision of loveliness that would be his true-life partner. When a heron and an egret had conjoined, Mo had glimpsed his lover.

An owl had swooped through one fitful dream and warned him that a shipment from his bait business would be lost and destroyed.

Mo saw trouble ahead, both on the present rescue mission and with his business, which he was neglecting to help with Randi's rescue.

Mo's status as a warrior in his own estimation was central to his image of himself. His business was important to his well-being. His Mohawk dreaming and his warrior's life was who he was. He now saw the way ahead and was comfortable to wait for it to unfold.

Back on the road on Friday with Rad driving the Caddy, Joe was sure that they had lost any Russian pursuit. They'd waited two days on the hilltop. Randi had made some progress in her recovery and de-toxification, though she was still in very rough shape. She'd passed from painful constipation to excruciating diarrhea. She couldn't keep any food down except ice cream. She'd become very attached to Marv. She was scared of Joe, Amelia's father, and considered Rad to be the hated big nurse, resented but in charge. As they drove up the Interstate toward Columbus, Rad was behind the wheel, Joe was riding shotgun, Marv and Randi were in the back, and no one was saying much.

"Don't speed. We don't want to be asked any questions." Joe told this to Rad remembering the fuss that the local news programs had made about the riot at Sweet Cherries. A female reporter had interviewed a patron whose claims had been wild and unbelievable. Hearing about wild Indians, shootings, blood on the walls, fistfights, vanloads of women and girls; the newswoman allowed the doubt in her voice full play. Joe hoped that those in law enforcement had given that witness no credibility either. A spokesman for the club stated that they were closed for remodeling. He said nothing had happened.

Rad glanced over at Joe with a look that said, "Who's the driver here?" The radio played, the windows were open since everyone was a smoker. Nerves made them smoke more. A beautiful summer sun shone in their faces. The Friday morning traffic had thinned out.

An hour later, Rad said, "Joe there's a car gaining on us."

"Punch it. See if they try to keep up."

The Cadillac picked up speed easily, without vibration. In a few seconds Rad watched the digital readout pass 86 then 90; she leveled it out at 95.

"They speeded right up. They aren't cops or they'd already have lit us up." Marv was looking out the back window, slightly cloudy since Otis had installed an acrylic bulletproof layer.

"What do we do now?" Marv looked at Randi as he asked. She lolled her head around and started to shake.

Rad noted that a string of three semis were ahead in a convoy. She lifted the mike on the CB radio, changed the channel and said, "Break on 19 is there anybody there for Daddy's Caddy?"

"Go ahead Caddy, this is Leroy."

"I'm coming up on a Roadway truck two miles from the weigh station, and I need help."

"You've been smokin' them tires, Caddy, What's the trouble?"

"We are being pursued by a car full of Russian gangsters. We stole a kidnapped girl from them and they want her back. We need help to get away." Rad was passing the Roadway truck and pulling up beside a Yellow Freight.

"Say again, Caddy. Was that Rooshians?"

"Yes, they are behind us, they are well armed, and they want to capture a young girl."

"I copy, Caddy, anybody out there on nineteen?"

"This is Big Bear, I hate Russians,"

"Lamplighter here, glad to help, Caddy. Pull in between the Roadway and the Yellow. I'll just move over to the left here."

Rad tucked in between the two semis. Joe looked at her and smiled. The first truck in the convoy pulled to the left to block that lane and the Cadillac was now in a cocoon, surrounded and safe.

"This is Lamplighter, I've got a Volvo blocked for now. That's an ugly bunch in there."

"Lamplighter, this is Daddy's Caddy, I'm going to move into the B lane and pass Big Bear, smoke my tires again, and leave that Swedish meatball behind. Can you boys hold him up awhile?"

"The B lane? What the hell's the B Lane?"

"The shoulder, the berm. Let me get around there and then you stop them. You boys be careful, they probably have guns."

"Okay Caddy, you take the B lane, and we've got your back. This will be fun. Like a little checker game."

Rad pulled over to the right as the truck ahead, Big Bear, gave her enough room. She mashed the accelerator and with a cloud of smoke from her tires took off at full throttle.

"Whoo-eee! Look at that girl unwind. Lamplighter move up beside me and let that Volvo move between Leroy and me. When he tries to pass on the right I'll cut him off and if he tries to go left you cut him off. If he gets aggressive Leroy can give him a love tap. It won't take long for that Cadillac to outrun him. Those Volvos can't outrun our American engines. Big Bear out."

"Roger that Big Bear, Lamplighter out."

"I'm on board. Leroy out."

At the speed Rad was traveling, she was out of range of the trucker's CB radios very quickly.

The next day two state police cruisers were observed at the weigh station examining an abandoned Volvo with no plates. The car looked like an accordion having been folded multiple times from front and back. The vehicle identification number revealed it to be one missing from a dealership in New Jersey.

It was still daylight at 9:07 P.M. when Rad turned the Cadillac off at Wallace's carry out and looked at the hand-drawn map. "Six right turns denied, then take the seventh. Deny all left turns. Deny the next six rights, some of these roads are rough, then pull through a saddle, cross the shooting gallery and pull off in the middle of the three forks in front of you. The right fork leads to a few good fishing ponds. The left fork goes nowhere." These were Melvin Loonch's instructions at the bottom of a crude map.

"Do you suppose Mo will be here with the camper?" Rad asked.

"He'll be here." Joe pointed ahead and waved his hand in a gesture that meant, proceed. After passing a scrubby fenced pasture with a horse that was trying to find shade in one corner, they entered the strip pits.

The ground changed. It became more angular with the spoil bank hills having knife-edges at their tops and the drastic vertical contours shutting off the view in every direction. They drove along a wide gravel road, graded and level, but those roads that they were to deny left and right were dirt, not gravel, and sprinkled with water filled potholes some of which were wider than the track itself.

After they had passed a road on the left and one on the right, Marv said, "Pond on the left."

Joe said, "There's our second road to the right. Pull off, I want to look around." Rad eased the car to a wide spot and Joe got out. He smelled the air, looked ahead at a near-vertical spoil bank thirty-feet high. It was the color of coal but the consistency of shale. A few scraggly pines clung to its lower edge. The sides and top were bare and black. Joe crossed the gravel road. He used a game path to avoid stickers and slid down ten feet to the shore of a pond. As he came to a stop, a heron raised itself into the air with a few lazy beats of its wings and flew to the northwest. He looked into the water, slightly green at the edge with an algae bloom, and saw a long dark shadow dart away from the bank. His steps caused small slides of gravel as he crept along the shoreline. Several frogs splashed into the pond. He looked down the thirty-yard length of the pond, no more than ten yards wide at any spot, cattails and willow trees rimmed the edges. Joe returned to the car. Everyone was standing around stretching. Rad paced and smoked a cigarette. They were loosening the kinks from a long time in the car and the tension of their escape from the pursuing Russians.

"That pond is alive with fish and stuff, maybe things are less polluted than your dad remembers."

"Maybe," Rad said. "It's been a while."

"Nothing growing there," Marv said, as he inclined his head at the spoil bank in front of them.

They got back in the car, Joe said, "Let's find my cousin." And Rad pulled back onto the gravel road.

They moved along slowly, looking for their road. They observed the battle of natural renewal versus the wreckage of strip mining. The next pond they saw was rust red and edged by spoil banks, no weeds, no trees, and no birds. And, Joe guessed, no frogs or fish. Across the road a green field of tall hay, ready for cutting, came right down to the edge of the gravel. A lane led off to the left to two oil tanks and a gas pipeline valve behind a chain link fence. To the right there was a pile of shale, not black and oily but featureless except for rusty chunks of metal; wire rope, a piece of a dump body, partially buried rusted wheels and axles. The next bend brought a planted pine forest into view, neat rows and columns marching to a green hilltop. On the left a road led away where four antlerless deer stood, their heads pivoting like a chorus in a Greek tragedy as the Cadillac passed by.

It went on like that, moonscape and bucolic pasture, woodland and garbage pile, until they reached that seventh road to the right that they were seeking. This road was wide but had not been graded, so the wheel ruts on each side were filled with muddy water and showed evidence of cars driving around the biggest puddles on the edges. Rad proceeded slowly, maneuvering her way around any puddles that appeared big enough to need an exit ramp.

They passed through a necked down area where the trees reached right down to the road and came onto a narrow causeway between two ponds. On the right the pond was brilliant green, almost chartreuse, not the green of algae. On the left the water was black like Guinness Stout, not because of the darkening night. No birds, weeds, or trees, were on either side.

Through the next saddle, there was a riot of fertility as ducks and geese flew up from a pond on one side and crossed above them to a pond on the other side. A flock of turkeys ran and flew barely above the ground in the other direction. Marv pointed to deer watching from the side of one pond. A heron led the way down the haul road with its slowly beating wings. Rad wondered, "Was it the same bird they had seen before?"

The Caddy came to a gap in the hills just wide enough for their road. Each of these hills was covered with trees, though none was larger in diameter than a man's leg. As the car pulled through the gap, Joe recognized this as the shooting range. Since they were looking directly west, the setting sun glinted off the brass of thousands of spent shells littering the flat area. Ahead, Joe saw the front of the trailer. Johann had left the trailer here. Now, where was Mo?

Rad executed a three-point turn and backed in beside the trailer. "Head the horses for home," she said and Joe nodded in approval. Marv got out and walked toward the trailer behind which a six-man tent was set up. A fire was going and a smoking or drying rack was arrayed with meat and fish laid out on willow sticks. The smoke smelled of apple and mint.

Marv looked in the camper with Randi staying right by his side. Joe looked into the tent. Both were empty. Radleigh lifted the lid on a pot boiling on the fire.

"Throw in some tea and set it aside," Rad jumped as Mo said this. He seemed to have materialized from nowhere. "Open the cooler, I have black bass, wild mushrooms, and wild leeks. We will eat and then talk." Mo moved to help with the fixin's.

"Where did you come from? I didn't see you anywhere."

"I was nearby."

Joe Gaspe was thankful that Duncan and his boys had shown up, warning of the impending arrival of two carloads of Rooshians. They had driven up an alternate road through the pits and walked up to the camp, well armed and friendly.

Approaching Joe, as he stood beside the campfire having a cup of coffee, Sperling Duncan thrust out his right hand and said, "Howdy, Radleigh Loonch said I'd find you here."

Mo was ten feet from the fire, slowly grinding a rough patch off of a ceremonial throwing stone.

Duncan introduced himself as an old friend of Rad's father along with his son and son-in-law. Looking over the three, carrying weapons slung on their backs, weapons in duffel bags, weapons in hard cases and each wearing a loaded back pack, Joe and Mo Snow heard news that caused the hairs to raise on the back of Joe's neck.

"Two Volvos loaded with Rooshian bad guys are on their way here. They were at Wallace's carry out an hour ago. Peanut Wallace gave them some bad directions but they will find this place, eventually. Everyone around knows where the shooting range is. Radleigh came to my house after Peanut told her about them commies. She asked for help and told me where to find you. We didn't know how well armed you'd be so we brought a few of our weapons." Duncan waved at the arsenal being laid out: rifles, shotguns, handguns, crossbows, laser sights, rangefinders, it was a Christmas morning for the gun enthusiast. He was looking over Mo, who commanded attention, though he never spoke much. Marv and Randi had emerged from the trailer after the conversation started. Marv was rubbing sleep from his eyes while Randi, near the low point of her detox, was unsteady on her feet.

"We've got a few guns but are probably going to be outnumbered and we can't skedaddle 'cause Rad's got the car." Joe was looking around.

"We'll defend from behind that spoil bank." Duncan's left arm indicated the pile of oily shale mine waste that was used as a backstop for the shooting range. "Get what you want out of that trailer, that will lure them in close enough then we'll start the dance. We should have help, soon. I sent Rad over to the Eagles Lodge in town, they're having a dart tournament today. I told her to ask for Polo Braxton and any volunteers who want to mix it up with the Rooshians."

He smiled a broad denture packed grin, tapped his huge belly three times and said, "I've an idée we'll get plenty of help."

While they unloaded items from the trailer, Joe asked, "How do you know they're the Russians looking for us?"

"Volvos, nobody around drives a car like that. You can't get parts for it or fix it under a shade tree. Bad suits, too. No matter how much money these clowns have, they still look bad in their clothes. But the kicker was that Peanut saw a machine pistol sticking out of one guy's suit coat. Who wears suit coats in June on Saturday around here unless there's a funeral? Surly bastards, too. We speak to people around here. Course, I s'pose they didn't speak no English."

It took fifteen minutes to get the defensive positions set up. Then they had a strategy session. Sperling asked, "They after you to catch you or kill you?"

"They want Randi back, think she's their property. The rest of us they'd probably kill." Joe answered for his group.

"Then I'd just as leave start the dance with the first shots; seems to me we'd have an advantage then." Sperling's comment drew nods from his group. He looked at Randi who sat with her back to the trunk of a tree nodding off. "She on drugs or somethin'?"

"She was kidnapped from a mall in Pantherville, fed an extremely addictive drug cocktail, which she's just been off of for three and a half days. She was forced to strip and be a prostitute in Cincinnati. She was once my daughter's best friend. We snatched her back from the Russian strip joint and they've been pursuing us ever since. We need to get these bastards off our trail." As Joe explained this, all three men got angry.

"We'll fix 'em," said Duncan's son Crash.

"Amen brother," Snoot was stern, "We'll read to them from the Good Book and take our Old Testament lesson from Job, fourth chapter, eighth verse: 'They that plow iniquity and wickedness, they shall reap the same.' "

"My son-in-law takes after his wife's great granddad, a Free Methodist preacher." Sperling Duncan had a proud but ironic glint in his eye. The boys were wiping down their long guns with rags soaked in gun oil. The smell of gun oil reminded Mo of his dad preparing to hunt. The memory was pleasing to him.

"A nice looking girl. They won't get her back. They won't get out of these pits, either." Duncan was confident.

Mo was examining his latest hand-ground throwing stone. When he spoke, everyone paid attention. "When enemies fight Mohawks they must learn to fight like Mohawks or they will die. The one who attacks first always has an advantage. They will shoot up the trailer with their little toy guns, thinking we are inside. When they stop and start to look around I will start the real battle with this." He tossed the rock up and caught it. "Then we will put them down."

Duncan looked skeptically at the stone.

"Mo was a big league relief pitcher. He can throw those at ninety-seven miles per hour. He doesn't miss. He can have three in the air in ten seconds. I've seen him do it." Joe was proud of his cousin.

Sperling Duncan stared at Mo and made an imprecation to himself, words he hadn't said since his grandmother passed away.

Duncan shrugged his shoulders. Each man took his place in a rough semi-circle around the shooting range. Only Mo was not entrenched behind the pile, he was off to the side, amongst the trees unmoving and silent. Randi, never far from Marv, settled herself five-feet below his position.

The sound of cars coming down the road put them on alert. They heard the engines and the splashing through the puddles. The cars stopped at the entrance to the range where the driver was able to see the edge of the trailer and the smoke from the fire behind it. Mo had thrown a punky pine knot on the fire as he'd walked into the woods. It created a visible smoke cloud.

The Volvos revved up and sped into the clearing. All doors flew open and the gangsters baled out, firing their guns on full automatic. They shot the travel trailer to splinters with round after round. The tires were blown out, the windows and door shattered, the aluminum skin riddled with jagged holes. Abruptly, they stopped shooting. A big man with a machine pistol in his left hand and an electronic device in his right walked to the campfire and kicked the pine knot onto the roadway. Then Mo started the war.

Cut multiple times by a spray of gravel, Marv rolled and slid ten feet down the back of the spoil bank. His face was bloody, his sunglasses smashed, and he was angry to be out of the fight. Marv's injury energized Randi who'd been in a torpor, enduring the heat. She crawled over to Marv, said, "Ooh," and began mopping blood from his face with his handkerchief. Joe's team was entrenched, protected by the near-vertical backside of the pile of mine waste.

"Keep moving around, don't let 'em see you in the same place twice. They're pinned down. Keep up the pressure," Joe had instructed.

Marv ignored Joe's admonition. He stuck his head up in the same place once too often. The spray of bullets from the Russian's Uzi hit the slag just below the crest and peppered Marv's face with shards of shattered rock.

Joe's team had allies in the clash of cultures and technologies taking place near the shooting range. The low-technology side was the

American side using a variety of low-tech, yet deadly, weapons and frustrating the Russians with their fully-automatic weapons.

Mo Snow had started the ball with one of his spirit stones by taking down the closest gangster with a fastball to the temple that crumpled him like a soggy grocery bag. That man was not going be able to fight much after that but, when he rose to try getting behind the RV, Sperling Duncan's son, Crash, shot him through the neck with a crossbow bolt. He died. Duncan's son-in-law, Snoot, was firing a.56 caliber Spencer Carbine that sounded like a cannon going off with every round. Shooting a bullet as large around as a man's little finger, this weapon had smashed the knee of one of the gangsters. He'd left a blood trail as he crawled behind one of the Volvos.

Sperling Duncan, an expert marksman, had dropped the leader of the attackers with a lever action .22 by putting the first shot of the contest right between his eyes. That big man lay on his back staring into the sky with an Uzi in one hand and an RF detector that the team took to be a hand-held GPS, in the other.

Since that first flurry, the shooting had become desultory. The Russians were pinned down and the six defenders were moving around on the one hundred twenty-yard-long spoil bank. Joe was firing a .203 varmint gun and Marv had a brace of pistols more suited to noise than accuracy. The Russians had Uzis and AK-47s that sprayed masses of small caliber bullets, suitable for short range work but inaccurate at a distance.

No one was likely to be drawn by the noise and show up to interrupt this party since the area they were in was known as the local shooting range. The bottom of the spoil bank was littered with cans and bottles that had been shot up for target practice by the local folks.

Randi murmured soothing sounds as she picked bits of rock and a chunk of glass out of Marv's cheek. He wasn't badly hurt so he enjoyed the ministrations. Many of the rock fragments were too small to be removed but a threequarter inch chunk of glass from Marv's sunglasses spouted a gusher when removed from his cheek. Randi pressed a hankie against it and said, "This one will probably leave a scar."

"That's all right, I was ugly before."

"You're beautiful to me. If you hadn't seen me and led my rescue I'd still be being raped and drugged by those bastards." She inclined her head toward the Russians.

This was the first time Randi had come out of her drug induced haze long enough to even acknowledge that she had wanted to be rescued.

"Joe led this escapade, not me." Marv said this as he tenderly rubbed his hand up and down her upper arm.

Randi smiled. In a conspiratorial whisper she said, "Amelia's dad has always scared me a little. And I'm *so* embarrassed he saw me naked; I can't even look at him."

Boom! The echoing report from Snoot's Spencer was answered by a bambambambamabam from the Russians. "Joe's been down the river and under the bridge many times. He's certainly seen naked girls before. Heck, he's got five daughters."

"Yeah, but I'm not his wife. Okay?" She was getting peeved so Marv shut up and let her swab out his cuts. Except for the one from the glass, none of them were bad. He reloaded his six-shooter, a revolver he had for nostalgia and knocked the grit off his semi-automatic. Marv was itching to get back into the fight. He was a happy warrior in this battle but he didn't know why. He didn't think about it, either, unlike Joe, who spent considerable energy analyzing why he did crazy and dangerous things. Joe usually did the deed but fretted about it afterwards.

The hazy heat of Saturday morning began to make those on the black hill sweat profusely. The morning had the kind of prickly humidity that warned of thunderstorms to come. Mo moved along behind their ragged entrenchment going from the far left to the far right in order to talk with Joe.

"Cousin, we should move down for rest in the shade, one at a time. You're friend Spunkin says Radleigh will be bringing help." Below their position, there was a small clearing at the end of one of the strip mine roads, where Sperling Duncan's car was parked. Trees, surrounding a tiny pond, cooled the grassy area. Marv and Randi were already down there. The temperature there would be at least ten degrees cooler than on the oily black spoil bank.

"His name's Duncan. You're right. You relieve Crash and after a half hour he can relieve his brother-in-law. You and I will go last. It's our fight."

Mo nodded. "They are enjoying the fight — there is a hint of the Real People in these friends of yours." Mo winked and began sidling back along the bank with his bow and quiver on his back. Moving back to the southern end, he spoke to Duncan, and Snoot, and took Crash's position.

It was the booming report from Snoot's carbine that started off every new round of the dance. His slug would tear completely through the trailer and start the Russians AK-47s and Uzis blasting away, without aim, in response.

After an hour, no one but the Russians had taken a hit, except Marv who took the spray of rocks in the face. The gun battle had settled down to a stalemate. The only thing likely to change things would be Rad showing up with reinforcements or dark, whichever came first.

Sperling had sent Rad to the Eagles Club in nearby Stoneburner to talk to Polo Braxton about her problem. But she couldn't figure out how to get in. The front door restricted access as befitted a club that allowed gambling and smoking of tobacco products. It was only ten in the morning and no one manned the buzzer at the front door. Rad was trying to peer through a small window in the door when a man walking a dog stopped to admire her Cadillac. Looking it up and down and all around, he turned his attention to her. He said, "They ain't gonna open that door 'til after noon. Don't want the Bible thumpers to know they're drinkin' in there." He smiled at his joke.

"I need to speak to Polo Braxton. Is there a way to get his attention?" Rad was trying to be urgent yet not frantic.

"If you knew him you'd have his cell phone number, or he'd know you were coming." He held up his hand as Rad started to speak. "Since you don't appear to be no bill collector, why not go 'round back? That door's always unlocked for those who're thirsty of a Sattiday morning."

"Thanks, mister." Rad started down the alley.

"Nice car, do you wanna sell it?"

Rad declined his offer and went around the frame building to the back lot one level down. She gently opened the door and stepped into a dimly lit hallway. There were two sets of doors on each side as she went forward. Two were restrooms and two were marked private. The end of the hallway opened onto a large dining room/dance hall with a bar at one end. Two towheaded hulking backs presented at the bar. They were arguing over whose turn it was to play a gambling machine. They didn't turn around. Rad watched, fascinated and repelled, as one man shook salt into a fresh glass of beer.

"Excuse me, are either of you gentlemen Polo Braxton?" Sperling had forgotten to give Rad any description of the man she was looking for.

"Wa'll looka here, Gerald. A city girl." Rad couldn't help it, she looked at her outfit, scuffed trim jeans, Doc Martens, a Carhart barn coat over her Rush t-shirt, and a CBP ball cap. She let her hand rest on the coat so that the outline of her holstered Sig Sauer .380 auto was just barely visible.

"Don't mind Harold, ma'am. He ain't used to being called a gennelman. Polo's back in the storeroom, who should we say's callin'? Polo's a married man ya know." He chuckled.

"Tell him Radleigh Loonch, Melvin's daughter. Sperling Duncan told me I could find him here."

In a loud voice, the man shouted, "Hey Polo, you got a visitor you're gonna wanna see."

A voice from the back room said, "Okay Gerald, I'll be right there."

"You guys are twins, huh? Either of you around in the eighties when my dad, Melvin Loonch, worked around here?"

Now it was the twins' turn to look at themselves. Blond, red-faced, considerably overweight, dressed in t-shirts, jeans, and running shoes, the only difference was one had an NRA t-shirt and the other had a USMC t-shirt. Looking as if they had extra potatoes at every meal, they realized that turnabout was fair play and laughed. "Loonch, did he work at Cresscom? I think my big brother, Darrell knew him. Or was it Merrill? They both worked over there, back in the day."

Rad was trying to imagine big brothers to these hulking hayseeds when a trim man walked through the storeroom door. He came up short, obviously not expecting Rad, who had let her coat drop back over her automatic. She offered a firm handshake and taking Polo's elbow in her left hand gently steered him to a table a few feet away.

Polo Braxton, a ladies man in his own mind, overcame his confusion at once. He established eye contact and succeeded in making Rad believe that she was the most important woman in the world.

Rad explained about Randi, the rescue, and the inability to shake the Russians from their trail; Sperling's offer of help, and how she came to be asking Polo for reinforcements.

During that time another set of twins came into the bar. This pair was bigger than the first. A bartender, crisp and efficient, came from the back and said, "Darrell."

Darrell said, "Captain. The usual."

The bartender said, "Merrill."

Merrill said, "Captain. Set me up, too."

Then the twins greeted each other.

"Darrell, Merrill," said Gerald with a nod.

"Gerald, Harold," said Darrell with a nod.

"Merrill, Darrell," said Harold with a nod.

"Harold, Gerald," said Merrill with a nod.

"Twins run in the family," Polo told Rad. Then he asked the boys at the bar. "You boys got varmint rifles in your pick-ups?"

"Is the Pope Catholic?" asked Darrell. All four heads nodded.

"We're gonna hope God is on the side with the most artillery," Polo said. Rad inclined her head in a question. "Napoleon." Polo confirmed the quote.

Polo looked at Rad, nodded, and said, "This little lady is the daughter of a friend of mine, and she's got some Russian gangsters trying to kidnap another young lady and kill her and her friends. They are over in the pits and wonderin' if we could help."

"Rooshians, I hate Rooshians. Let's go!" All four heads nodded.

"Okay, here's what we'll do. Captain, you bring your Desert Eagle and come with me in the Explorer. You twins take your pickups, we'll stop at the last turn around the spoil bank before the shooting range and plan our next move. Miss Loonch, you follow us."

The captain asked, "What about the bar? Should I lock up?"

"Mary Lou will be along drectly. Leave her a note. Any money in the till?"

"Just enough to make change."

"Leave it."

Rad stepped out into the back lot with Polo and his posse. A huge thunderhead crossed in front of the sun as she watched the younger twins get into a beat-up Ford four-wheel drive pickup with a front bumper that consisted of a four by six wooden beam. Two rifles hung on a rack in the back window. The older twins jumped into a late model Ford pickup also featuring gun racks. Polo motioned for them to roll down their windows.

"You Hamner boys love a fight and you're gonna get one, but you keep it under your hat, no radio, no cell phones, no yellin' out the window. Word gets out and there won't be anything left for you to do. Got it?"

"Sure, Polo. You lead, we'll follow."

"Ms. Loonch, we know where we're going so you follow along behind, but not too close. We don't want folks to think there's a parade or nothing.'"

The caravan proceeded through town. From the fourth position, Rad observed both sets of twins mugging out the window at those they passed on the street. She didn't know what they said but an eerie and satisfied feeling came over her that she had unleashed the whirlwind.

The defensive line had been shifting along as the men each took a fifteen-minute stretch under the trees. Those on duty remained on the scorching black spoil bank. Mo had moved along the line with each relief. When his time came to rest, he removed something from his kit bag, and slipped into the trees. Joe noticed but wasn't worried. Mo moved to his own rhythms. For the last few hours the gun battle had alternated between long boring silences and, sporadic, rapid, deadly, exchanges. Only when a round from the Spencer was loosed at the trailer, behind which the Russkies sheltered, did they return fire and then only for a few seconds.

A .44-or .45-caliber bullet would penetrate into the trailer. The Spencer's .56-caliber slug tore completely through both sides and slammed out the backside making the Russians hug the dirt and jabber at each other.

Joe's people had deliberately not fired on the two Volvos that stood at an angle to each other, the trunks and doors open. Joe deduced that the trunks contained ammunition and water, and perhaps more guns, that were unavailable, but needed by the enemy.

Marv's face looked as if a blind man had shaved him with a straight razor. It was covered in nicks dabbed with tissue paper. His one bad cut had been patched by dabbing it with Super Glue and slapping on a piece of duct tape.

Snoot rose up and loosed a booming shot from his Spencer that smashed completely through the badly shot-up trailer. One of the Russians swore and reached around the vehicle to let go a wild blast of automatic fire at the pile of black shale.

"Nyet, nyet!" yelled another Russian, worried that they were wasting bullets. The one who'd fired looked at him like a petulant child intent on doing what he wanted. Then he shrugged and hunkered down. They were in a tough spot. Their leader was dead. They couldn't agree as to who was in charge. None of them considered the others to be more intelligent than a moron. Brutishness, a quality rewarded in the Soviet days and easily transferred to gang life, didn't serve one when forced to think for oneself. Their position was not as uncomfortable on the shale shingle of the shooting range as those on the spoil bank, but they were overdressed for the hot and humid Southeastern Ohio summer. They sweated, each thinking his own thoughts. Ominous thunderheads were rolling in from the west in steady ranks that drew closer together as the morning expired.

Polo peered around an oak tree. It was part of the second growth, replacing the original scrub pines and locusts planted thirty years ago, to reclaim the ruined land that had been strip-mined in the late sixties. He watched the reaction to the one round from the Spencer and turned back to his boys.

"Gerald and Harold, you take your rifles, slide up on that knob and start laying down a steady covering fire. Take plenty of ammo." Polo pointed to his right. "Darrell and Merrill, slip into the woods over there," He swept his arm to the left, "And do the same. We're gonna enfilade them from three sides. Wait for my signal then give them their lead injections. Captain, you and me are going to take Gerald's pit truck and ram that car to the left, right into the whole nest of them. Then we'll bail out firing. Ms. Loonch, you slip around the bank there and tell those boys that the cavalry has showed up. When they hear me rev the pit truck they should open up with all the firepower they've got. I'll give Ms. Loonch— "

"Call me Rad, please."

"We'll give Rad ten minutes to make contact with her friends, then we'll open the gates of hell for these bastards. We will have the element of surprise. I think we can do this with no one getting hurt."

It was for a long ten minutes that they waited. Rad got around to her friends and allies, telling them the part of the plan each needed to know. They waited, sweat running down their faces, down their backs, sweat bees and gnats crawling on them. Then they heard Polo rev the engine and the two sets of twins opened up with a steady pop pop pop of semi-automatic fire. The Spencer boomed and Gerald's truck came roaring through the notch with that wooden bumper aimed dead-on for the taillights of one of the Volvoes. The Russians were flanked, nearly surrounded, and none of them could decide what to shoot at. One opened up with an AK-47 at the speeding pick-up but the Volvo was between them and he didn't score one hit. At thirty-five miles per hour, the truck smacked that Volvo, propelling it toward the crouching Russians and sending them running in all directions. The sky opened up with a pelting rain, lightning, and immediate thunder. The first man to come out from behind the trailer, running for the trees, was dropped by Sperling with a head shot from his twenty-two. The second one, coming right behind him in that direction, made it just to the trees when Moses Snow stepped from behind a black locust and crushed out his life with one blow from his cypress knee war club. Darrell and Merrill, with the better angle, shot up three more Russians so many times that they danced like mad cloggers. Polo and the Captain, who'd been crouching behind the dashboard, piled out of the pick-up looking for action. It stopped suddenly. There were no bad guys moving at all.

The Captain looked over a near-vertical slide and saw one man tumbling and sliding down in a spray of gravel. He aimed his big handgun, fired, hit loose rocks, fired again, and saw the Russian plow into the trees at the bottom and move out of range. Gerald, who'd sprinted over to the trailer, took aim with his thirty-ought-six, fired once, and aimed to fire again.

"Gerald, that's enough. Let him go, he can tell his masters not ever to mess with Stoneburner, Ohio." Polo looked around at the devastation. The rain stopped abruptly, moving over the hill in a rush like an express train. It had ended with silence. One minute: shouting, thunder, running gunfire, chaos, and confusion. Moments later: the birds singing, the sweat bees back buzzing around eyes and ears, the bright sun scrunching up everyone's eyes.

The two men killed early in the morning lay where they had fallen, drawing flies and bees to their wounds and the pooled blood. The fresher bodies were unmoving lumps of flesh. The trailer was completely shot up with huge jagged holes where the slugs from the Spencer had ripped through the backside. The Volvo that had been rammed had also been shot to pieces. Gerald's pit truck had survived unscathed.

Those involved in the fight assembled around the trailer. Marv and Randi came around one side of the spoil bank with Sperling and Joe. Snoot, Crash, and Rad came around the other side. Gerald and Harold were disappointed, "All we got to shoot up was the trailer. I never even drew a bead on a Rooshian."

Darrell and Merrill walked forward reloading as they came, "Anymore bastards around?" asked Darrell.

"That's all of them, counting that one running over there." Joe pointed to a wave of breaking branches moving through the bushes a thousand yards away and far below their position.

"That looks like a moose going through the willows. Noisy ain't he?" They all had a good laugh at Sperling's comment.

"We've got a mess to clean up and we've got to move on, 'cause there's more of these guys after Randi," Joe said.

Rad made the introductions as far as she knew them. Then she asked, "You guys want these guns?" She indicated the weapons scattered around the deceased gangsters.

"Sure, we'll divide them up."

"Our trailer's junk, so's that one Volvo." As she said that, people started picking up the scattered weapons. Mo walked into the circle dragging a dead Russian whose head was a smashed mess. He dropped him on top of another body.

"I know a guy who will get rid of the trailer, Dale Rand. He's got a holler on his place where he dumps old cars and stuff. He's also got a dozen half-wild hogs that'll take care of these bodies. It's where the county dumps road kill." Gerald looked at the ruined Volvo. "JR will take that car apart and sell what parts he can on eBay and scrap out the rest."

"Since there's five of us, I suppose we could use the other Volvo." Joe suggested.

Polo took charge. "Strip all the bodies and dump them in the trailer, go through their pockets first. Darrell, you've got that flatbed, go get it and run this trailer out to Rand's place. Stay off the main roads. You can tell Dale what happened. He'll talk, but nobody believes anything he says. Gerald, get ahold of JR; have him come out and tow this junk-heap Volvo away. He can part it out. Harold, you and Merrill guard this site. We'll scrape some stones over this blood and leave this place to the bugs."

When all the weapons had been recovered from the ground and the trunks of the Volvoes, every one of the boys had a souvenir. Meanwhile, Marv tossed the electronic device the Russian leader had been carrying into the good Volvo's trunk.

"I'd have sworn that they were tracking the Caddy, but they homed in on the trailer. Maybe we'll be able to shake them now." Marv was optimistic.

"I don't see what chances they had to bug either the car or the trailer." Joe said. Then he moved on to other things. "Here's the second map that Mel Loonch gave us, we'll move on to the Peter Power Recreation Area and spend tonight. Rad, you and Marv and Randi take the Cadillac, I'll drive the Volvo with Mo."

"You sure that Volvo ain't bugged?"

"No Marv, I'm not sure. If I was ever sure of anything, I forgot it."

The climax of the battle had lasted less than ten minutes, the clean-up only forty-five. With thanks and high-fives all around, the parties departed.

Chapter 17
Noble County Ohio

—June 19th—

Now that they had gotten rid of the trailer, Joe and Mo agreed that they would have left a cold trail for the Russians. The rescue team moved across the Muskingum River into Noble County and went into camp at the Peter Power Recreation Area. This was a more recent reclamation project than the Buckeye Power area that they had just left. At Buckeye Power the company had spared the bulldozers, planted a few scrub pine trees on one side of the hardpan hills and a few black locust trees on the other side and gone on their way. Consequently, there were ponds that after forty years were still hot. Here in the Peter Power Recreation Area the power company figured out that with a few picnic tables and a little work they could reclaim the public's good will. The hot ponds had been drained and filled in; three-season roads had been built; new, clean water ponds, stocked with fish, had been arranged around the several campsites; and an open public hunting, camping, and fishing area had been declared.

Forty years of neglect augmented by the work of beavers and Mother Nature had reclaimed about a third of the total land at Buckeye Power. The camp at Peter Power Area Number Seven was less secluded for the rescue team, and their bullet-riddled tent drew looks and muttered asides from those who saw it. Rad had argued that Randi needed time in fresh air, long nights of sleep, and a simple life away from artificial stimuli like TV, radio, computers, and such. They would stay there for two nights and then move back to Tony Gill's hunting cabin on the edge of the Allegheny National Forest. After a stay in the remote cabin, Rad hoped that Randi's mom could handle the remainder of what rehab was required.

Marv had gone to the nearest village, with Randi in the Volvo, to get some food and supplies for the next portion of the road trip. They were to go by back roads to an area on the Ohio River below Pittsburgh to meet George Jankovich, another member of Joe's network of musky industry people. Joe and Marv would fish their way upriver past the city and onto the Allegheny River. Mo and Rad and Randi would drive by back roads to a small town above Pittsburgh called Jake City and meet a guide who would take them by country roads to Tony Gill's camp. He would also take over Joe's movement up the Allegheny River on his jet boat. Since a jet boat can skim over very shallow water and go where no outboard-equipped boat can, it would have no problem going up the Allegheny. Joe and Marv would be able to fish their way back to Tony Gill's cabin. Joe was sure that the Russian's no longer knew where they were. He needed to get in some fishing with his partners, cousins, and those good men of Pennsylvania who were in his network. That was what he thought anyway until Marv came flying back from the grocery store with another Volvo and a Toyota Tundra in pursuit.

Mo, Rad, and Joe stood in the bright sunshine enjoying the warmth. It would be too hot and too humid in an hour or two, but right now the sun radiated all of life's goodness on their upturned faces. Into one end of the campsite came the captured Volvo with Marv driving like a maniac. He leaned out the window, "They've found us. They're right behind. A car and a truck. We gotta go!"

"You know where to go from here?" Joe asked this as he handed Marv the two handguns he'd been holding while Marv was in town.

"Hell no, but we gotta get out of here." Joe raced for the Caddy and jumped in. Rad was revving the engine and Mo got in the back seat setting out his weapons. Rad peeled out of the back entrance to the campground with Marv right behind.

An elderly man stepped out of his camper to see what the noise was about. He and his wife were the only other occupants of the campsite. The Caddy and Volvo raced out the east end of the campsite just as a pickup and another Volvo rooster-tailed into the west entrance, spraying gravel as they passed the camper. They raced after the escaping cars.

"Kids these days," the man said as he shook his head.

The rescue team had been caught un-prepared by not having planned an escape route beforehand. The roads through the Peter Power area were designed for slow traffic with many switchbacks and loops around ponds and campsites. There was no direct way out to normal roadways where the speed of Daddy's Caddy could obtain an advantage. Marv who was driving the Volvo, couldn't keep up with the Cadillac, and Randi was with him. Rad slammed and screeched around curves and up hills, smoking the tires and fishtailing wide on the corners. She handled the sliding rear end without thinking about what she was doing. Danger focused her mind. Joe tried to make sense of the map — a map designed for people to find the next campsite or fishing spot — not for evasion of pursuing murderers.

"Uh, area 9," Joe said as a campsite zipped behind them. "There should be a state route around the next bend. Rad pulled a trooper turn to the right and saw a cattle gate standing open with a man ready to close it. She punched the pedal. The car rocked back and forth then straightened out.

"Hey," the gate keeper yelled at the retreating Cadillac. Then the first Volvo flew by with Marv at the wheel. He had the window down as he was alternately laughing and screaming. "Hey!" the worker said, still holding the gate.

He started to close the gate again when two more vehicles came along, a pickup flew past and a different Volvo went in the gate and stopped.

"You can't go in there," he said as he grabbed for his cell phone in a clip at his belt. "I'm calling this in."

"Nyet," said a slight man with a Slavic face, high cheekbones slanted eyes, hair the color of dead grass. He pulled out an Uzi, riddled the workman with bullets, walked over, and closed the gate. Another man, hulking in an ill-fitting suit, with a mullet haircut, a face that was young but hard as iron, and eyes as dead as dinosaur bones, dragged the worker to his company truck, threw him into the bed, and drove the truck around a corner behind a few trees. The Volvo moved ahead.

"Did you see that sign?" Mo asked.

"What sign?" Joe was trying to see the map. The rough haul road they were on was interrupting the Caddy's normal smooth ride and the map was jumping in his hands so badly that he could not read it.

"It said. 'Mining ahead. No private vehicles! Go back' "

"Too late now."

Rad slammed on the brakes and a cloud of dust, dirt, and gravel flew past them. They were at the edge of a huge open-pit strip mine. The mining was being done by two medium-sized draglines at the bottom of the pit, one hundred twenty feet down below the rim they were on. A haul road went down through a series of switchbacks and crossed the bottom of the pit and went up the other side switching back and forth to a rim on the other side. That rim was two or three football fields away and at roughly the same height as where the cars now stood.

"Nowhere to go but across the pit," Rad said. It was Sunday. None of the machinery was moving. On the rim on the other side of the pit was a huge Terex dump truck with tires as tall as a basketball rim. Rad headed down into the pit with the Caddy sashaying left and right. Each one hundred eighty-degree turn threw up a cloud of dust and gravel. Marv followed in the Volvo. The Volvo now had the better of the going as it was the more maneuverable vehicle. Rad got to the bottom and headed across the pit, under the draglines. Mo watched out the back window through the following dust cloud.

The Toyota pickup had stopped at the rim. A man with a rifle was aiming, and occasionally firing, a few ranging shots, but Mo thought they were waiting for their Volvo to continue pursuit. The Volvo came up beside the truck, the rifleman jumping into the cab of the truck, and the man in the bed threw a cover aside.

"Here they come," Mo said and looked up at the forest of booms and cables overhead. They were beneath the two draglines that sat in the bottom of the pit. One shovel faced north and one faced south. Neither of these huge power shovels was anywhere near as large as the famed, now retired, Big Muskie, but they were big. The hydraulic power was provided by a monstrous tracked vehicle, with an aerie attached to its side that would inch along so slowly it took twenty hours to move a hundred yards. Attached to the powerhouse was a boom two-hundred feet long that handled cables as big around as a man's arm. At the end of these cables was a huge shovel that scooped a big load of coal, pivoted the entire mechanism and dropped the load in Terex dump tucks that carried the material away. The overburden was dumped back down the pit and the coal went to a railroad siding where it was loaded into Gondola cars. It was then taken to a crushing facility to be pulverized into pea-size pieces for fuel.

The Russians couldn't get an accurate shot at either car through the maze of booms and cables when they were on the rim. When the Russians reached the bottom, they couldn't shoot up hill to the climbing cars for the same reason.

Rad worked the Caddy like a stunt driver as they began the assent. Joe remarked through the fear and tension, "Damn, girl, you are a driver!"

Rad, brow wrinkled, eyes squinted, and shoulders tensed, turned and said, "Yes, I am."

The Caddy was going south one level above Marv and the Volvo going north. Marv had to ease off a little to wait, since the Cadillac slowed for switchback turns, when all hell broke loose.

Mo yelled, "Incoming." Joe looked down to his side and saw a man with an RPG fire his missile from the bed of the Toyota.

"Oh my God." Joe watched the smoke trail headed their way. Mo keened his Mohawk death song.

Firing uphill or downhill in steep terrain with any weapon is ineffective, most shots go too low and hit the ground or too high and fly harmlessly overhead. The RPG missile flew high and went past the front windshield of both Marv's Volvo and the Cadillac with an extremely bright flash. It blinded Joe, who had watched, but not Rad, who'd closed her eyes. It didn't miss everything though, two levels above the Caddy the grenade blew out one of the ten-foot diameter tires on the Terex dump truck. It hit the tire low and a fireball instantaneously appeared and disappeared into a smoke cloud. Behind the fireball the truck, too big to be blown to bits, reared up like a stallion, hovered on its rear end for a second and dropped down on its front wheels. Then the body of the monster truck, right front corner mangled, rolled over, dropped down one level, bounced high, fell past Rad as it turned in the air, and, upside down now, hit the front of Marv's car with a protruding lance of steel that stuck out like an elephant's tusk.

Marv's vehicle's front end was flattened into the haul road. The windscreen glass was broken and knocked inward by the steel tusk. The monster dump truck hit a bench above the road, again went airborne, flipped over onto its side, and came down squarely with a metallic roar on the pickup that had killed it. The scream of metal on metal was sickening. Screeching grating noises echoed through the pit. When the dust cleared the dump truck had flattened the pickup entirely, rolled over and pushed the Russian's Volvo and itself into a pool of water.

The dump truck was half in the water. Of the Volvo, nothing could be seen but bubbles. After the gravel and metal bits stopped falling, the silence was deafening.

The Cadillac was unharmed. By the looks of their Volvo, Marv and Randi should have been hurt. Rad, who had opened her eyes after the rocket passed, had seen everything. Joe, who had been blinded by the flash, had seen nothing. Mo was out of the back door and sliding on his seat down one level of road to the smashed Volvo.

The back door opened and Mo climbed in past the groceries in the back seat. He looked over at Randi in the passenger's seat. She was screaming, covered with pebblized glass from the windshield, but able to move and, though terrified, unharmed. She'd saved herself by ducking down when the rocket passed, Marv's condition was another matter. He'd been sitting up when the truck's steel tusk cleaned out the windshield and had managed to put his forearms in front of his face. The glass bits propelled into the car were imbedded in his arms and the areas of his face that he couldn't cover, both shoulders and his neck. He was bloody and semi-conscious.

Mo grabbed Randi by the shoulders and lifted her over the seat and said, "Daughter! Listen to me. Take some of these groceries to Rad's car, get her and Joe and come back for more. I'm going to open the trunk. We will strip this Volvo. Move fast, we must leave this place."

"What about Marv?" Her question showed concern but she was already grabbing some groceries.

"I'll get him out. Send Joe to me." Mo said this as he climbed into the front seat and got beside Marv. Mo leaned across his body and hit the button that popped the trunk open.

"How do you feel? Is anything broken?" Mo was reaching across Marv's legs now on the driver's side between steering wheel and Marv. He was trying to locate the lever that would move the seat back. Though the crash had stalled the car, the ignition was still on. The accessories worked and the radio played a country song at a low volume.

"Unh. Wha happened?" Marv groaned and spoke at the same time.

The seat was moving and Mo sat up and reached forward to see if Marv's legs were pinned. With his right hand, he opened the glove compartment.

"Marvin I'm going to pull you back over into the back seat then if you can't walk, we'll carry you to the other car. We're going to strip this car and get out of here. We need to find a doctor. But we have to get gone before anybody else shows up." Marv groaned in response but didn't resist as Mo tried to find the lever to lay the seat back. Marv was not pinned in the front seat but, being only semi-conscious, was unable to help extricate himself.

Neither front door would open, they were both crinkled too much. Mo moved into the back seat, removed the groceries, and set them on the ground nearby. He looked up the hill and Rad, Randi, and Joe were coming down the switchback road. Joe was being assisted by Rad and Mo saw no limp. He wondered what was wrong. Around at the driver's side rear door he easily reached the seat control and laid it back the maximum amount. He said, "All we're going to do is pull you back far enough to get your legs free, then Joe and I will help you to the other car."

"I can walk, I think."

"Joe, come over here." The others had arrived.

"Joe was blinded by the flash." Rad proclaimed.

"I'm gonna be okay Mo, I'm starting to see a little already. Tell me what to do."

"Daughters, strip this car of everything we can use. Clothes, food, weapons, anything. Joe, grab Marvin's shoulder, I will move to the other side; when I count to three pull him back." Mo returned to the back seat. It turned out to be easy to pull Marv into the back seat, and he swung out next to Joe who supported him with an arm around his shoulder.

As Marv was turned toward the back of the car, Rad saw his new injuries for the first time. She gasped and dropped the electronic wand they'd taken from the Russian commissar back at the shooting range. The device hit a rock in the road and with a beep turned itself on. Marv looked like he'd taken a double shotgun blast in the upper body. His shirt was shredded on both shoulders. His face and the sides of his head and both ears were covered in blood though the blood was not flowing steadily. Rad couldn't see the undersides of his forearms but they were shot to rags too. It looked bad. Arms around each other's shoulder, Joe and Marv started back up the road. Joe could walk and Marv could see a little. Walking wounded, off they went. Randi had her left hand on the edge of the trunk as she fished into the recesses for the car's first-aid kit. Rad picked up the electronic wand and moved to toss it into one of their backpacks.

EEEEEEEeeeeeeeEEEEEEEeeeee. It went crazy as it moved across Randi's left hand. Rad moved it away and back. The beeping intensified and an LCD display indicated direction and distance. Rad looked at Randi who moved her hand away and looked guilty. Mo, loaded down with guns and gear, reached out, took the wand, and looked at the display. He moved it to Randi's hand. There, under the tattooed red star, was the center of the attraction for this wand. He pulled out his Arkansas toothpick flicked it on the web of Randi's left hand and a spurt of blood came out.

"Sorry."

"Ow!" Randi tried to pull back but Mo held her, made a tiny dig with the point of the knife, and sitting in a drop of blood on the blade was a capsule, slender as a grain of rice. He shook the capsule off onto the roof of the car and the wand indicated that this was the target. Rad pulled a gauze pad from the first aid kit, pressed it to Randi's hand, and turned to Mo. "Now we know why they were able to find us so easily."

"Let us get on the trail." Mo said. They left the transmitter on the roof of the Volvo.

Olivia Shanio

Chapter 18
Shippingport Pennsylvania

—June 20th—

Joe Gaspe had friends all over the eastern reaches of the fishing world. He knew musky specialists from his membership in fishing/conservation clubs. He knew many within the cadre of small manufacturers of lures and rods. He knew guys he'd made friends with at shows and sales. He knew a number of his own customers on a personal basis. It was one of those customers-friends that he was looking for now. Marv needed a doctor, not desperately, but just to be safe. His face would be scarred, that was certain. Someone to clean and disinfect the cuts in his face, arms, shoulder, and hands, in a sterile setting, would improve the outlook. Joe had been to George Jankovich's house once but he had been inebriated, someone else had been driving, and now was having trouble relocating the correct road.

George lived in Shippingport, Pennsylvania, and worked in East Liverpool, Ohio. His wife was a physician in general practice at a hospital in Weirton, West Virginia. A true Tri-State family they were situated around the big bend of the Ohio River.

Rad was driving and Joe was directing, but his eyes were still affected by the rocket contrail he'd watched. No one else had any idea where the house was, so it was cut and try all the way. They were going along a road parallel to the south side of the Ohio and taking various loops that swung closer to some shoreline homes and cabins then swung back to join the main road. These loops all looked the same and Joe was working hard to see. He had a screaming headache, was squinting constantly, and needed help reading the signs.

He wanted to find George's place for two reasons: George had a small summer house on the wooded edge of his property, where the crew could stay, and George's wife had a laboratory in their house that doubled as a clinic for house calls by the neighbors. Marv and Joe could get some medical attention while Randi, Rad, and Mo could relax and evade the Russians. Since Mo had removed the transmitter from Randi's hand, they felt safer.

Finally on loop five along the river they found the lane that slipped down toward George's compound. The trees shaded the driveway until, on a slight rise, the house sat with a majestic view across the brownish-gray waters of the Ohio. It was Sunday so both cars were there, George's Red F-150 and his wife's Lexus. Rad parked beside the truck and got out. George's wife, Rene Howard who went by her maiden name, came down from her front porch and looked at her visitors. A German shepherd barked a single warning beside her. She looked everyone over, not recognizing them, because Joe had his head down and was shading his sore eyes with his right hand. She noticed the crude wrappings on Marv's face, was intrigued by Mo's fearsome visage, and glanced at the two young women with a question apparent on her open face.

"May I help you?" Rene said this to the group but she faced Rad.

"Rene, it's Joe Gaspe, George's friend from the muskie club. Is George here?"

"It's Sunday during fishing season, where do you think George is?" she said this with a smile. "I remember you, Joe, you build custom rods. How are you? What happened to your eyes?"

Before Joe could answer, Rad piped in, "It's a long story but we need some medical help as you can see. I'm Radleigh Loonch, this is Marv Ankara, Randi DesChutes, and Moses Snow. Can you help us?"

A look of concern came across Rene's face as she saw the peaked look of Randi, got close enough to see the blood all over Marv and scanned the squinty eyes of Joe. "Yes. Come up to the house please. Tell me all about it."

Mo walked down to the dock and sat with the dog that came right up to him as if he was a long lost friend. He sat on a bench with the dog curled so close that its tail covered Mo's feet. "There was a time when a Mohawk would consider you to be two days worth of meat." He scratched behind the ear as he said this. The shepherd's tail thumped on the wooden dock.

It took some time, with Rad helping, to get the three walking wounded sorted out. Joe was given some eye drops, a sleeping mask, and a sleep-inducing tea. "Your eyes will clear themselves if you rest them until to-morrow morning. No bright lights, no reading or detail work, no strain." Rene instructed Rad to bundle him into a dark, cool spare bed-room.

Randi was given a different herbal tea and told to sit at the kitchen table with an orange to peel. She was in her own world: silent, unsee-ing, occasionally giving a little keening sound, and shuddering all over for a few seconds.

Marv took a lot of work. With tweezers and a magnifying light Rene pulled pieces of glass from his face, neck, and the underside of his forearms. Some of this glass was as small as a pinhead, some as large as a chunk of rock salt, and the doctor began to accumulate quite a pile on a metal plate beside her. "There's another layer of black dirt under this glass."

"That's coal slag. A ricochet sprayed it into me. The big cut was from a chunk of my sunglasses. Pulling that out is what caused all the bleeding." Marv was bored but tried to sit still.

"These Russians attacked you twice? Why didn't you call the police?"

"Did you ever wait for the police? They are never there for the first shots. We couldn't be sure about them, the Russians have compromised a lot of cops. Besides, we were sure each time that we had lost them. But they kept finding us until Mo removed that transmitter from Randi's hand."

The doctor sat up straight to stretch out and rest her neck and shoulders, went into the kitchen, reached out, and looked at Randi's hand. "The incision here is so clean. It won't even need a stitch. Who did this?"

"It was Mo. He dabbed it with Super Glue and put pressure on for a few seconds." Rad couldn't help sounding proud of Mo.

"That man's got a good hand with a blade."

After an hour and a half of work, Marv was cleaned, disinfected, slathered with antiseptic, and liberally bandaged. "Except for the one under your left eye, none of these will leave noticeable scars. You are lucky." Working together, Rad and Rene had developed the kind of camaraderie that close co-workers achieve, and they relaxed with beer and nibbled on a vegetable platter while Rad went through the adventure a second time. Rene did not ask questions or interrupt and, by the end of the story, had been convinced to record these visits as first-aid cases. As such no official report was necessary.

George pulled his Triton bass boat into the dock surprised to see a stranger sitting peacefully with his dog.

"Some watch dog you are, " he said. He looked at Mo and said, "Hello."

"Hello, brother. I am Moses X Snow, cousin of Joseph Gaspe: we have come here for refuge and your wife has given medical assistance to members of our party. Joe has spoken of your virtues, George." Mo grabbed the boat's painter and tied it to a cleat. As George exited the boat, the men shook hands.

Later in the darkened guest room, Joe told George the story of Randi's rescue and it was arranged that, on Monday, everyone would rest during the day. Toward evening Mo, Randi, and Rad would move on to Jake City and get help from Jack Richardson in finding a back-roads way to get to Tony Gill's hunting camp near the Allegheny National Forest. Marv and Joe would fish their way up the Ohio with George where they would meet Harold Weber and Jack, in the jet boat, for some more fishing up the Allegheny River.

Jack Richardson, another musky fisherman, partner of Harold Weber and friend of Joe Gaspe, had guided Rad and the Cadillac on a back-roads journey through the hills of western Pennsylvania into the New York side of the Allegheny National Forest. Rad, Randi, and Mo had settled in at Tony Gill's hunting cabin and Jack had returned to take Marv and Joe on a fishing trip up the Allegheny River.

Rad thought about Randi and her recovery on the ride to the airport. She thought about seeing Olivia and how practical she'd become in the year since graduation from college. Rad was sure that Olivia, with her newfound mastery of southern comfort food, her keen ability to judge situations, her ironic but joyful turn on life, would improve the situation. It had been difficult for the last day and a half. Joe and Marv were fishing with Harold and Jack. No matter what the situation was, they had to take a crack at catching their muskies. Mo, Randi, and Rad had been at the hunting camp just outside the national forest. It was remote and beautiful. But Mo needed to get back to his business. Randi was jumpy around anyone but Marv, and Rad was worried. They were moving one step back for each step forward in their "treatment" of Randi's addictions, along with her malnutrition, depression, and anxiety driven fear. They were in the remote cabin because they didn't trust any no institution or hospital to protect Randi from the overreaching grasp of the Russians.

Joe had made a call to his wife's friend, Dr. Marie Bramton, for medical advice, but she was at an overseas conference and would not return for two more days. Rad was a determined young woman. She would carry on and, with the exception of Olivia, no one would know her worries. Still, though Rad knew Mo to be a reliable man, she knew he scared Randi. Stern, abrupt, fierce; he cultivated that scary "big Indian" image. Rad knew she could count on him, but Randi might try to run away. She was not only afraid that she might get hurt or killed but that she'd lead Marv into danger.

Before Rad left to drive to the airport, Mo had said to her, "Radleigh, I must see to my business. I left it in the hands of my nephews. Trustworthy they are. They will not rob me. But young Mohawks might look into a beautiful sunrise and decide to go fishing for a week, leaving the bait to die in the reefer trucks. Those boys can be distracted by a frog hopping across the road, and if offered a drink, look out. It is worrisome."

Rad squinted at him. "Moses X Snow," her voice was scolding, "you're not a person I'd expect to traffic in racial stereotypes." Exaggerating her body language, she placed her hands on her hips and stared him down.

"Stereotypes, little sister, are based on realities." Mo had a way of holding his face stiff and only letting his humor show in the way the light glinted through his eyes, "I will wait until your friend is here, then I must attend to business for a few days. I will return as soon as I can."

"Can't you phone your nephew? Ease your mind a little?"

"No cell phone, but perhaps I'll send up some smoke." He grinned and walked into the woods to do his thing. Rad shook her head at his receding form and returned to getting the Cadillac ready for the trip to the Pittsburgh airport.

On the ride back Rad was beaming, happy and excited as only Olivia could make her. Her face was flushed and there was a little stutter in her speech as she related her adventures to her old college roommate. They had saved each other's college careers by connecting emotionally after meeting in a registration line and discovering that, though from diverse backgrounds, they could be true friends. Olivia, a traditional southern girl in many ways despite her Italian last name, which she'd taken from one of her three stepfathers, came to Saltillo University from a Connecticut prep school.

Olivia had money but was completely down to earth. She had been sent away to prep school because her mother worried about what would become of her hanging about with idle rich friends in the Big Easy. Like many high school students of the day, she found school stultifying and as mind numbing as a heavy sedative.

Radleigh, the product of an intact but challenged family, had changed her outlook toward education in her sophomore year in high school and, with the help of her parents, had transcended her educational environment. She admitted years later that, although she went to a good public high school in a well-to-do suburb, she'd only ever had two inspiring teachers that weren't time-servers.

Rooming three years together, the two girls endured the politically correct and intellectually rigid college years and received bachelor's degrees that were their entre into the world of work.

They stopped on the way to the cabin and picked up some groceries. Olivia's cure for drug addiction and malnutrition included plenty of comfort food. Disappointed by the canned collard greens and frozen okra, Liv came out of Farmer Bob's Super Store with three sacks of groceries and said, "At least we've got butter and ice cream. Is there anything at the cabin?"

"Joe's cousin, Mo, will have caught some fish and probably a turkey or a couple of rabbits. There's bacon and lunchmeat and a few hamburger patties. There's stuff there."

"Mo? Is he the big Indian you told me about on the phone?"

"Sure is, don't let him scare you. He's on our side, and he is very competent." She made a throat-slitting motion.

"Scare? Girl when did you ever know me to scare?"

"Moses X Snow can be very formidable. He is stoic, silent, abrupt, and very very competent."

"He sounds cool. Do you like him?" Olivia's eyes crinkled in a smile.

"Not in that way! But I admire him and respect him, and he's been a real leader on these adventures we've been on."

"Tell me about the truckers helping you get away again. Was it this car you were driving?"

"Yeah, you wanna see her scoot? She's got a Corvette motor and she can really get going."

On one of the rare straight-aways in Northwest Pennsylvania, Rad let the Caddy fly.

✧✦✧

Mo came along a path from the woods with a tom turkey over his shoulder and stopped at the edge of the trail to watch. There was the backside of a woman bending over to pull a bag of groceries from the back seat of the Cadillac. He could see Rad and Randi chatting on the porch so he deduced that this must be Rad's friend.

Olivia straightened up, knowing someone was watching, looked over at the girls on the porch and then turned to Mo. "Were you looking at my butt?"

"Absolutely, positively, yes." He let his lips form the wry smile that barely creased his stone face. He looked into her eyes with a look of soul searching that he seldom attempted but used to good effect.

Mo's dreams of the egret and his present eyeful of a handsome white woman came together in his mind, He realized that he was destined to talk to this white woman, walk the wooded trails with her, endure the cold of winter, and, though feeling guilty about her race, bring her totally into his life.

Liv looked at him. Her eyes lit up, her cheeks pinked up quickly, she scanned him up and down lingering on his coppery, wedge-shaped, tattooed, bare chest and six-pack abs. She raised her eyes to his and said, "Well, all right."

Olivia Shanio was of average height for an American woman, she had an hourglass shape, with a few extra hours on the lower side of the glass, and she had an open, yet skeptical face. She was sophisticated but not jaded. Rad, the anthropologist, would call her hyper-feminine, with cranial bossing, small hands and feet, and a small straight nose. A hint of rosacea in her face gave her a blushing look, exaggerated now since she was actually blushing.

Mo and Liv looked at each other with their eyes boring in. Rad stepped to the car, took the bag of groceries from Liv and said, "Moses X Snow, this is my best friend in the world, Olivia Shanio."

Liv held out her hand to shake and said, "Hi."

"Radleigh did not tell me you were a goddess," Mo took her hand and held it, gently but firmly, so that she did not want him to stop.

"What does the X stand for, Mr. Snow?" Olivia asked. Rad had always wanted to know this but had been too shy to ask.

"The Real People often could not sign their names to treaties, so they used the X. Now, many humorous parents give the middle name X. It stands for nothing except the entire history of relations between our people and yours." He delivered a sly wink, their eyes still locked.

Rad turned with the groceries and said, "Mo, would you like me to brew up some tea while you dress that bird? Liv is here to help Randi gain weight. She's an expert at southern cooking."

Mo pulled his eyes from Olivia and said, "Tea would be pleasant, and I have left four fine trout in the refrigerator for dinner." He said this to Rad's retreating back; his eyes jumped right back to Olivia.

"I bought some avocados and some sliced almonds, I'll fix those fish up real nice. Are you married, Mister X?" she was surprised at her boldness.

Rad, who had her leg raised to step onto the porch step, halted, turned, and looked back.

"My sleeping mat is lonely these sixteen years." A sad look crossed Mo's stoic face for just a second. Olivia beamed.

Rad turned back to the house and said, "Wow."

Chapter 19
Near the Allegheny National Forest

—June 21st—

Mo rose above the forests of New York and soared over the abandoned farms and hilltop cabins of the southern tier. He was on his way to the shores of Lake Ontario trying to find his two nephews. He had dreamed that there was a collision of his reefer truck with a flying horned owl. The nephews had wondered what they had hit in the dark of night. It sounded as big as a turkey when it slammed into the truck's grill. They stopped at an all-night trucker's café and looked at the front end of the truck. The sight of an owl plastered into the grill, had unnerved them both. Though they were modern Indians and did not put any faith in the old ways, they had grown up listening to tribal stories. Their grandmother had told them that the owl was the harbinger of death and disaster. After coffee at the restaurant they came back to the truck and looked again at the dead owl wedged into the grill of the vehicle. Neither would touch it to remove it. Instead, they had locked the keys inside and cadged a ride back to the northeast leaving a truck filled with live bait to await the summer sun.

Mo had seen this and knew he must use his dream to find the truck stop and his merchandise. He knew he must act right away to save his business.

Before he returned to his truck full of bait, Mo brought a gift to Olivia. He gave her a small beaded bag. It was old and beautiful, and she felt its power when it went into her hands. It contained some jerky he'd dried over an apple wood fire. He also gave her a small skillet of cornbread he'd made that morning. He didn't say much to her except with his eyes.

"I have much of the American in me. It is always business, business, business with them. It interrupts the dreaming. I shall go and take care of my shipments — every two weeks — they must be done. My nephews are drinking, the truck sits in Clayton, and the product is overheating. I will be back before the final battle takes place. Joe and Marvin will be back in two days." He said this to all three women. He turned his eyes back to Olivia. "We will be together in the dreaming." Their eyes locked for half a minute.

Mo turned and left. A man of contrasts, driving a Jetta, a car that none would expect him to drive, he smiled with satisfaction. He had left this car at Tony Gill's when he went with Joe for their rescue adventure. Mo was worried, an emotion he was not used to. He was tingled all over when he looked upon Olivia Shanio; he could not concentrate and he had struggled to remember his dreams that morning. To not honor the dreaming was upsetting to his concept of himself. To balance his Mohawk side (the warrior) with his business side (the man of the world) was always tricky. He must get away from this woman for a little while and create a plan of action toward her. He must decide. He knew where the decision would lead, he just didn't know when and how to proceed. He would be back on Tuesday. Then, he and Olivia could reach an understanding.

"That crazy Indian just proposed to you," Randi hadn't been saying much and most of it had been jibberish, but this was prescient.

"Don't call him crazy," Liv scolded Randi, who accepted the rebuke. As soon as she'd arrived to take over the detox treatment, Liv took charge and Randi accepted the bossiness from Liv that she had resisted from Radleigh all along. Olivia knew Randi was right about the proposal. Liv had studied cultural and physical anthropology. Mo had given her food, a symbol of his desire to provide for her. He'd given her the traditional beadwork of the Mohawks, a symbol of his desire to bring her into the traditions of his people. She could never misinterpret those eyes and what they said to her. Olivia smiled broadly and poured more tea.

"I told you about him, didn't I? Quite a man." Rad spoke but Olivia seemed unaware of her words.

"He brought me cornbread. Cornbread for a southern girl!"

"But he just left; why are men so stupid?" Randi spoke generally to the table. She was taken aback when both women turned on her with scowls.

"Randi, you need to wear more clothes when Mo is here." Randi looked down at her pajama bottoms and tight tee shirt. She wore nothing under these. "I need you to peel some oranges." Olivia pushed a bowl toward her. Peeling one orange for each person had become a morning ritual for Randi, something to bring her mind down to a routine task that required some dexterity. She was not allowed to use a knife.

At the counter Rad was preparing dishes for breakfast. Liv stood beside her, melting a stick of butter. Under her breath Rad said, "He's only got eyes for you, Ollie."

Olivia smiled and nodded, "Randi needs to regain some of her modesty. I'll bet she flaunts it in front of any man, doesn't she?"

Rad said, "We've got to clean this place up before they get back and get some more food. I'll go get some groceries and cleaning supplies after we eat."

"Be sure to get more oranges, and ice cream and of course…"

They both said, "butter," at the same time.

Jack Richardson was a teacher by trade and thus possessed a firm grasp of the obvious. Able to say the most common things as if they had great weight, he said, "If muskies were easy to catch every time you tried, without all the work, there would be no value in musky fishing. How sporting is that?"

Marv grunted, neither agreeing nor encouraging Jack to continue. Marv's face looked like he'd been in a razor fight without a razor of his own. He was in Jack Richardson's boat while Joe was fishing in another boat with Harold Weber. They were trolling up and drifting down while casting on opposite sides of the Kinzua Reservoir. There was a bet on and Joe knew that Harold was the more accomplished fisherman making his chances to win the case of Yuengling Lager better than Marv's. Marv had begun to worry about Randi whenever he was apart from her. He thought her progress in getting back to normal was too slow. He could not concentrate on his casting and Jack was not one to prod him.

When casting for muskies, one must cast well and cast often. When the lure is in the boat or in the air it has zero effectiveness. An angler must move fast to keep the lure in the water and maximize opportunities to catch fish. When the fish are neutral towards potential food, or negative because they just ate, they will not pursue lures for long distances. This means the sloppy caster, or the one with his mind elsewhere, is at a disadvantage. The person who can precisely drop his baits on the likeliest spot to hold a fish will do better over time. In addition, since Marv was in the front of the boat and he casts left-handed and Jack was in the back of the boat and he casts right-handed, they crowded each other when fishing the left shore of the reservoir. Jack didn't know Marv very well and he was frustrated by his lack of concentration.

Joe and Marv were fishing their way through Pennsylvania because Joe was convinced that, since Mo had removed the RF transmitter from Randi's hand, the Russians couldn't find her if she stayed away from populated areas. Joe's network of friends and informants consisted largely of people who were related to musky fishing in some way, and he needed fishing as one of the ways to stay current with his boys. Rad and her friend had Randi at the cabin for rehabilitation, and nourishment. Joe couldn't help with any of that. The Kinzua Reservoir had been clear-cut and had all the logs removed before it was flooded. This created a lake with no structure. No underwater structure made for hard, frustrating fishing. That, and the nagging feeling he had at the edge of his consciousness, convinced Joe that something may be going wrong. Mo was with the women and he could protect them or warn them in any event. Still, there had been that dream last night.

Joe had tossed and turned for a long time in the cot at the rental cabin. In his dream he saw Mo busy searching — not for the women at the hunting camp but for his nephews who'd left a reefer truck on a roadside rest and disappeared leaving the bait to die. Joe was annoyed because Mo was supposed to be prowling the woods near the hunting camp protecting and warning the girls.

Joe was on his fishing trip with Harold Weber. Mo was resting his eyes in his refrigerated truck at a rest stop on the highway. Both were sleeping the deep sleep of dreamers. In those dreams they saw Amy lead them onto a cabin porch. Amy didn't speak. She communicated to both men through gestures. She swept her arm to the north and there sat The Old One. Each had seen the old man before in his dreaming. He was seated on a log with a wolf skin draped across his shoulders. The fierce head of the gray wolf sat atop his head, slightly askew. The look in his eyes bored into each dreamer's awareness. He turned to his right, the northwest, and there stood a black bear growling a warning.

Amy swept her arm back to The Old One. He turned to his left, drawing attention to the northeast quadrant. There, coming through the woods on the creep were warriors, clad in black and armed slipping through the shadows.

Amy diverted attention to the southwest. In dreams they could see behind the cabin. Wolves appeared in a tight pack. These were helpers that would be coming. Amy's last gesture showed The Old One smiling into the trees to the southeast. There perched in the many trees were ravens: watching, nodding, calling, warning of danger, assistance, and mischief. These visions showed what was ahead and what would happen soon.

Chapter 20
Fish Mountain

—June 24th—

Agent Andre had a bad feeling about things. He was ticked off at Joe for his cowboy tactics, though the snail's pace of government action peeved him as often as not. Officially, he had to make a show of disciplining Joe, but in his heart he knew the effect of government raids on these white slavers was usually to give the girls right back to the Russians. They couldn't speak English and didn't trust anyone, any Russian émigrés who they contacted would turn them back to the human traffickers for self-preservation.

He had gotten a pay-phone call from Joe, who was fishing again, somewhere in Pennsylvania, unreachable by phone. Joe was convinced that Radleigh and Randi were in danger from the Russian mob at the isolated hunting camp of Tony Gill. Joe would not say how he had come to this conclusion. Andre didn't know why, but he believed him.

Mo returned from recovering his reefer truck full of bait late Monday night. Mo and Olivia left the cabin before first light, forty-five minutes prior to dawn, in order to be at the rock formation known to the Iroquois as the Eagle's Nest, to watch sunrise in the eastern sky together. As a night person, Olivia had had to stay awake all night to be with Mo at that early hour. Mo, able by long practice to control his sleep cycle, woke from a dream of destruction, concerned by the prospect of violence, but took Liv, two slices of jerked venison, two squares of cornbread, and, his favorite, hot clear tea, and hiked down through a saddle and up the next mountainside with the woman of his dreams.

Unlike those who say they like long hikes but lose enthusiasm when the going gets sticky, Liv did not falter in the dark. She used the toes-in rolling gait that Mo had shown her. She moved swiftly with him and wasn't short of breath, despite being out of shape and having the lungs of a cigarette smoker.

Olivia Shanio had given her heart, too quickly, to young men in her life only to be hurt and dissatisfied in due course. Men of her generation expected sexual relations to be only a short step beyond shaking hands. They considered it a debt owed, by the woman, just for hanging out together. An older man, such as Mo, seemed to have no such immediate expectation. She felt that he was interested in her as a person as well as a prospective lover. She understood that she was falling for this wild Indian and she was falling hard. It was a difficult task to hold back emotionally and she didn't. The hardest thing for her to comprehend was how he had become so quickly set on making her his partner. Liv was convinced that Mo would get what he wanted.

Sitting on a rock ledge on the eastern side of the Eagle's Nest, looking down at low hills before them, Mo laid out a skin, tanned side up, and arranged his ceremonial items. In the front he placed the iridescent preserved head of a great blue heron, a blue crest feather pointed toward them, and a beak pointing toward a notch across the valley below them. He poured scalding clear tea into two small sturdy teacups. He unwrapped two small pieces of cornbread and laid a strip of jerked meat over each. From his pouch he took a pinch of native blend tobacco and tossed it toward the east and then, after words were spoken that Liv did not understand, he tossed a pinch to each of the other compass points. The sky lightened as he did this. "Come, drink," he said as he picked up his cup, smiled serenely at Olivia, and sipped the brew. She followed suit.

The sun had risen over low eastern clouds bathing the horizon in pink and red hues that changed minute by minute. Liv watched and listened to Mo's ceremonial incantations. Then leaned against him, smelling his masculine scent, a mixture of sweat, musk, gasoline, and tobacco with a faint hint of something disgusting. She sampled the simple breakfast he offered and felt a tingling sensation she had never before experienced. Her conscious mind said one phrase, over and over, "This is the man for me." Unconsciously her mind swam through a reel of images, and she felt as if she were floating above this stunning morning and a future that dazzled her.

Below them the Allegheny River curved around a cut bank, carving a scour on its western side and leaving a sand bar on its eastern side. The dawn light had not penetrated this low area. It came to gradual life with movement in the shoreline bushes. Mo pointed his right arm to a floating mat of weeds to the right in the stream. A great blue heron facing them turned its head in profile. Leaving that arm extended, Mo lifted his left arm toward a snowy egret standing in the shallows. Its profile faced the heron. Neither bird was in visual contact with the other because of the intervening curve of the stream. Olivia looked where he had pointed, then looked at Mo. He was beaming in a broad smile.

The glimmer of day inched along and unrolled its light down the hill to the curving stream. Mo made a twisting upward motion with his right and then his left hand. The heron rose and began a slow flapping flight to the north. The egret rose and flew likewise to the south. Mo's arms closed and his hands met as each bird landed on the sand beach below Olivia and Mo. She looked from the birds, standing together facing north in profile, to Mo who now lowered his clasped hands and closed his eyes. He said a word in Mohawk. Liv did not know the word but she understood the meaning.

She imagined herself with Mo floating above the cattails on the Ottawa River, where it met the St Lawrence. In green spring, hazy summer, golden autumn, she soared above the water with her man. When she imagined the frozen ice sheets of winter, it made her shiver. Mo draped his heavy shirt across her shoulders and gave her a gentle squeeze. She sipped her tea and slipped into a reverie that made her as happy as she had ever been.

By the time the sun was fully above the far mountains, the red gone from the sky, she understood that Mo had proposed to her without saying any words at all.

"I'm going to have to go south and talk to my parents. They aren't going to like your age or probably your being an Indian either. But, I'll be back. You can count on that."

As he packed his otter skin bag, Mo said, "We must return to the camp now. Radleigh and the others are in danger and I must help." Mo set off downhill at a brisk pace. "We will be together until the next hunger moon."

"Hunger moon? That's March isn't it?" Liv struggled to keep up as she found out that hiking downhill was harder on the knees than going uphill.

"Yes. Hurry. I am needed."

Igor Nesterenko was in the lead Volvo. Back in charge because of his successful recovery of eleven assets, Igor was leading the expedition to erase the problem once and for all. A second car contained five well-armed operatives as did the first. Since her RF seed had been located in Ohio, Jimmy Maxwell's brain trust had needed other means to locate the last of the thirteen strippers that had been stolen from his club at the Cincinnati airport. Igor didn't know how Judah got the information but he had been directed to this mountain by a Mapquest.com search and his handheld GPS.

Jimmy Maxwell was so unused to being foiled in his efforts that he had activated a mole in Homeland Security. Unwise though it would be, Maxwell was ready to take out everyone frustrating him, up to and including Thomas Andre.

What Igor couldn't figure out in the fog was how to get up the mountain. The base of the hill was ringed with driveways that went to modest hunting camps and cabins, none at the top of the mountain. The best English speaker of his team was reading the Mapquest printout by flashlight. They pulled up next to a road with a sign. Iggie was already annoyed with Americans' penchant calling their driveways "Williams Avenue" or "Battaglia Boulevard." He thought that the government ought to put a stop to this confusing practice.

"What's that sign say?" asked Igor of the driver who was the only one close enough to read it through the fog. "What road are we looking for, Alex?"

"You Nanama Road." The voice from the backseat was a little tentative when he said, "Uh, I'm not sure about this."

"Give the paper and the light to me." Igor took the instructions and read them. The last line said, Turn onto unnamed road. The line above that said, turn onto unnamed road, as did the line above that. "Jesus," Igor crumpled the paper and threw the sheet down. Despite being an avowed atheist, Igor used the name of Jesus as a catchall imprecation.

"We're lost, you idiot." He turned to glare at the backseat, looked out into the fog and said, "We've got a GPS waypoint on our left. We will go up every driveway we come to until we find that green Cadillac. There is no one else about. Proceed."

Joe and Marv had been dropped off at the cabin late at night by Whitey Charles, the charter captain with whom they'd spent the previous day. The bunkhouse area of the cabin was occupied by Rad, Randi, and Olivia, so Marv and Joe crashed on the two old couches and were snoring and wheezing in the slow breathing of sleep in a few minutes. Mo, sleeping outside under the stars, had watched them enter the cabin and returned to his rest. All were snug in their beds except Mo and Joe, who were made restless by the dreaming. Olivia heard the late arrivals come in, listened to the whispered conversation with Mo and remained awake, listening to music on her Ipod.

The fishing with Harold and Jack, and then the charter with Whitey, had been bad. Only one small musky was caught in three days and Marv had raised that on the last hour of daylight with his secret casting lure, a huge black and white Daredevle spoon. They had fished hard and were exhausted. Joe had gone through the motions but had been unable to concentrate due to an unshakeable feeling of dread that weighed on his mind.

Joe's hawk circled the mountain through and above a wooly blanket of fog. He glimpsed the cars in patches of light and saw the bronze Volvos favored by his enemies. There had been two in Cincinnati, one on the road, two in Stoneburner, and another in the Peter Power Recreation Area. These two must *hold more Russians. He saw Radleigh on her cell phone, talking to Randi's mother pacing, trying to be calm, hoping to reassure the poor woman. He also saw a second call with Rad talking on her phone, in an assertive manner, letting Agent Andre know that she would report for work on Thursday as planned. The hawk continued to circle, hearing car doors slam, guns being shot…Joe was unable to see what was happening, but was sure trouble was coming.*

Joe was awakened by numbness in the arm upon which he had been sleeping awkwardly, just at the time that Mo slipped into the house to meet Olivia for their pre-dawn date. Mo was quiet but introduced Joe and Liv in a whisper. When those two left, Joe stepped over to the kitchen area and began clanking around making coffee. Marv stirred, Joe was aware that his partner would be ticked off, but he was heedless of that. Maybe they would get a chance to nap when the excitement that he was convinced was coming was over.

The Russians were at the end of a long series of driveways when they entered one that was doubly wide. The left one curved away and stopped in front of a one-room cabin. The right one continued around a stand of birch trees with their four-inch diameter trunks standing like a picket fence in the fog.

"There must be many rich Americans around here, so many dachas," This came from a bored operative in the back seat.

Iggie, who had been frustrated up until now, felt like the road they were looking for was ahead of them. He considered informing the stupid man in the back seat that many ordinary Americans owned vacation camps, cabins, and cottages. Instead he said, "I think this is the one. GPS points straight ahead seven hundred meters. Check your loads." He turned to the driver. "When I signal to stop at 150 meters distance, we will consult with the car behind, and finalize our plan."

"Da," said the driver. Several minutes later Igor dropped his left hand and the driver stopped. With a cracking of plastic and crunch of metal, the following Volvo hit them, jolting everyone forward, pushing the lead car ahead and causing Igor to string together a dozen Russian curses. He got out and looked at the damage, glared at the driver of the car behind his and shook his head when the driver shrugged and looked sorry. The damage was minor and Igor ignored it while talking to the other nine associates in a huddle shrouded by the morning fog. One man was smoking a cigarette. Igor grabbed the butt from his mouth, threw it down, and stomped on it. They made their final preparations.

The screech and clunk of the two Volvos colliding echoed through the heavy morning air. Mo heard it and the softer sound of closing car doors. He was headed directly west while these noises were slightly northwest. It was trouble he was sure of that. Olivia, panting heavily from her exertion, heard nothing but her rasping breath and pounding heart. Mo had stopped moving and turned. She came up short before him. "There is going to be gunfire. Do not try to keep up with me. Make your way slowly to the cabin. Keep yourself concealed. When you come up behind the woodpile, stop and wait for me to fetch you." Olivia didn't normally like taking orders but felt confidence in Mo. She was panting too hard to reply. He took off into the fog at a double-time pace in his loping gait. She saw that he carried his war hammer in his hand. Everyone she knew carried a gun in New Orleans. She shook her head wondering about the man she thought she loved carrying a club to a gunfight. After a short rest to settle her breathing, she moved ahead.

Joe heard the car crash, faint and mechanical, muffled by the fog, and lower down the mountain. He looked at Marv whose head had risen above the back of the couch. "Wake up Rad and Randi. I think they've found us and it's time for the big dance." Joe calmed himself, sipped his coffee and formulated a plan. A deadly seriousness rippled through him. Weapons, positions, and plans occupied his mind. Marv knocked on the bunkhouse door, called to Randi, and stumbled into the bathroom.

The Volvos were reloaded and, guns at the ready, the Russians drove up to the turnout below Tony Gill's camp. As quietly as possible, they got out of the vehicles and eased the doors closed. They moved to flank the cabin on both sides, thankful for the cover of the fog. There were medium-sized scrubby pines on both sides of the house, with a massive pile of cordwood on the eastern side, poor fields of fire for defenders. Two thugs, in a half crouch, crept forward toward the front porch. Igor had chosen his least capable associates for the frontal assault.

At the bottom of the hill five vehicles had assembled. Special Agent Thomas Andre was the nominal leader of a multi-jurisdictional task force. He positioned three state police cruisers around the base of the hill, one in the driveway to Tony Gill's camp, one a quarter mile down the road and one a quarter mile up the road. They were to prevent re-inforcements and escape of the gangsters who had gone up to the top. The SWAT team from Jimmytown under their own leader, a swarthy, olive-skinned lieutenant named Ramone, insisted on deployment based on their own tactical doctrine. Andre shrugged and said Okay. The eight-man-and-one-woman team, heavily armed and armored, trudged up the mountain from the north, spread across the road, moving at a crawl. Agent Andre and his assistant, Vic, and bodyguard/driver Bill, began walking uphill through the fog on an oblique approach to the cabin from the east. The three men had windbreakers with FBI in large letters on the back. It was hoped no friendlies would shoot each other.

Each person disappeared up the mountain into the fog. As the morning wore on, a puffy breeze swept away patches of fog occasionally improving visibility from ten to twenty five feet.

Joe and Marv were posted at the two front corner windows of the cabin. They had shotguns with buckshot loads that they had borrowed from Tony's gun safe. Rad was in the widow's watch, a small room raised above the roof with windows on all four sides. She was armed with her service pistol. The glass-enclosed turret was too small to turn in with a long gun and bring it to bear. She had her cell phone in intercom mode and could tell Joe what she was seeing through an earpiece. Marv had settled Randi in a position of safety between the stone fieldstone fireplace and a gun safe that was as big as a refrigerator.

Rad spoke into the phone to tell Joe what she was seeing. "It's a white-out up here, I'm looking down onto cotton balls. Maybe it'll clear up but I see nothing."

"Okay, keep watching. We've got two bad guys at the edge of the driveway. If they move our way Marv's gonna let 'em know we're awake." Joe was signaling to Marv that he was welcome to take his turn with the pump gun.

The main body of the Russians split into two groups of four each heading around the sides of the house. They hoped to force their way in through a back door or windows. Igor had assigned the driver of the second car to be one of the two decoys at the front of the building. That driver fingered his remote control in his pocket and, inexplicably, pressed the button to lock the doors. The Volvo's horn beeped and it flashed the lights. When that happened, Marv's finger squeezed his shotgun's trigger and a blast of shot peppered the front of the car breaking the headlights and setting off an ear-splitting car alarm. That noise brought on shooting from several semi-auto and fully-automatic weapons. The Russians were shooting without targets at the log building. With everyone blinded by the fog, many shots went wild into the morning. Joe held his fire. He could see nothing. Rad saw muzzle flashes from both side and pumped three bullets from her Sig-Sauer at one of them. Abruptly the firing stopped. The car alarm drowned out the groans of someone who had been hit. Without visual clues, it was hard to locate the sources of most sounds.

The leader of the SWAT team, all members equipped with radios, ordered the group to double time their march up the hill. They were in line of battle and headed up the road toward the blaring car alarm.

The car's driver had dropped his remote when Marv's shotgun went off, and he could not find it in the pine needles near him. He hoped that pressing the remote would silence the racket. He wasn't sure that the alarm could be shut off with the car as damaged as it was.

Special Agent Thomas Andre and his two assistants picked up their pace through the woods after the first blast of firing. Ignoring doctrine, Andre quickly outpaced the other two. Bill deliberately dropped back to keep an eye on Vic whom he considered to be suspect for no specific reason beyond jealousy.

Joe called over to Marv, "Don't hit that car again, let's keep the alarm going. Maybe someone local will call the cops!" Marv nodded. Rad listened from her perch.

"I think they are trying to flank us and get around back," said Rad. "No way in back there but, they don't know that. The trees come up so close that I won't be able to see them."

"Just make sure that they don't see you. We can hold them off for quite a while. Shotguns scare people. Even a bad shot can hit targets with a shot gun." Joe worried that Rad was too exposed but they had few choices in what to do for defense.

"I'm a little scared up here, Joe."

"Me too."

"What'll we do?"
"We'll fight."

Olivia followed Mo at a pace that she judged to be slow enough to be out of the line of fire. But what did she know, alone in a fog that was silent and muffling? From time to time, a little fold of a breeze dropped down from the hilltop and cleared a pocket of air around or ahead of her.

She and Mo were approaching from directly east with the sun rising behind them. Andre and his two men were coming from the northeast to the side of the snaky driveway. The members of the SWAT team were approaching in assault formation, dashing forward, covering each other's advance. The two men on the outermost end of line were using night vision scopes that could see a thermal outline of an enemy through the fog. They talked through their radios to the boss and each other. They were well drilled in their rules of engagement and the shooting protocol for SWAT teams.

Olivia thought she had picked up Mo's scent from ahead but stared into the thickest white blanket she had encountered so far. She was squinting hard when a puff of air came down the mountain and unzipped a layer of fog. There, ahead of her and slightly to the right, she saw the back of an FBI windbreaker as a man moved swiftly across a fallen tree.

Andre hadn't heard firing in a few minutes but he was driven forward by a sense of dread that this unplanned but impending gun battle could cost him two agents and blow open the whole Special Projects program. He wasn't sure what he could do but he could try to help.

Olivia looked again when a puff of fog rolled down past her. There was a man crouching behind a rock outcropping. The mica in the granite sparkled as she watched him pull a black hoodie from his small bag and slip it on after discarding his FBI windbreaker. He laid his bag by the rock and stood up, braced his feet, and held a handgun aimed at the FBI person in a windbreaker ahead of him. "What the hell," thought Liv. The guy in the hoodie moved past the granite outcrop and sidled to his left a little.

✧✦✧

Rad saw through the fog first because she was fifteen feet higher in elevation. She whispered, "Joe! Marv! They are coming around front on both sides of the house. They'll be right on top of you when they get there. They are too close to the house for me to get a shot at them."

Andre had reached the flat top of the mountain and was between a tool shed and a huge pile of firewood when he peered over the top. The fog was swirling, now encasing him in its blanket, now dropping away to give him a clearer view.

The blaring car alarm was permanent and grated on everyone's nerves though it had become background noise having gone on so long, its regular bursts were like whip cracks. The Russian closest to the remote reached for it and when Marv saw his arm and shoulder poked out from cover, he fired two rounds from his pistol. The first made the man draw his arm back and the second must have hit the remote because the car alarm abruptly quit. There was an awful second of silence, then gunfire erupted on all sides. Everyone was shooting and it would take a long time poring over the after-action reports to sort out what happened that morning in the fog.

At the sound of Marv's pistol, Andre assumed a fighting stance and began to look for something to draw a bead on.

Olivia saw the FBI man in the hoodie take aim at Andre's back, draw a long breath and appear to wait for a chance.

The Russians came four and four around the two sides, guns at the ready, intent on storming the double front doors.

The SWAT members with night sights simultaneously called out, "Target identified, permission to engage."

The two Russians, pinned down in front of the building, heard the static from the SWAT team's radio and turned to fire at the noise.

"Engage targets!"

There was a lot of shooting now. The Russians waved automatics and sprayed the woods near the driveway with bullets. Joe and Marv shot at the backs of the men who ran past the corners of the building blasting away. The SWAT team methodically dumped the charging and cowering Russians on their backsides: one, two, three, four, five, six, until the last three were cowering, hands on their necks.

Andre never took a shot. He had identified no known target. The man in the hoodie rest his arm on a tree branch and aimed at Andre's back. Olivia was about to yell a warning when Mo, silent as a shadow emerging from the fog, moved in from hoodie's left, smashed his left arm with a death blow from his cypress knee war club and the gun fired twice into the ground close enough behind Andre that the back of his trousers were sprayed with pine needles from the forest floor. Mo twirled his club and brought it sideways into the man's face. He crumpled with a groan and fell back down hill a few feet. Andre turned and looked at Mo, saw the man at his feet and lowered his gun to his side. Was this man a friend or foe?

Materializing from the fog beside Olivia, a man in an FBI windbreaker took up a firing position. He appeared to be going to shoot at Mo, who he must have thought was going to shoot Andre. Liv shouted, "Oh no you don't!" and slammed into him with a hip check hard enough for him to slide to his knees on some slippery pine needles. She pounced on him and gripped his right wrist with both of her tiny, but powerful, hands.

Andre peered back down the hill catching glimpses through the swirling fog receding as the sun lit up the top of the mountain. A man stood waiting beside a black lump on top of a granite outcropping. Neither made a sound. A woman sat on his driver Bill, and held Bill's gun hand tightly in both of her hands. These two were yelling at each other. The shooting on top of Fish Mountain had stopped. Andre looked over his shoulder and saw that the SWAT team was rounding up a few men. The camp was quiet. He walked swiftly down the hill and came to Moses X Snow who nodded but made no threatening gestures. He looked down and his assistant rolled over bringing his left hand to his crushed face. He wiped some blood away and cast a defiant stare at Andre. Mo spoke. "His kit is just there," he said as he nodded to the cutout downhill from where they were.

"You stay where you are. Ma'am! Let that man up he won't hurt you or anyone else. I'm in charge here and I guarantee everyone's safety. Bill, you can holster your weapon. Grab that duffel bag and we'll all go up to the top and sort this out. When they got up near the woodpile Andre shouted and identified himself to the SWAT team. He came onto the flat to join Lieutenant Ramone and his team with their prisoners.

Assistant Special Agent in Charge Thomas Andre walked to the parking area in front of Tony Gill's camp and shouted, "Hello the cabin! Joe, this is Andre. It's all over. Please come out here."

Epilogue
Pantherville

—July 5th—

Joe was tucking in to his Souvlaki and eyeing Rad's french fries while Andre explained it all, over lunch, a week later. The SWAT team, from Jimmytown, had killed six Russian thugs and captured three. All were illegal immigrants. One member of the group had escaped. Unfortunately he had been the leader of the expedition. The man Mo stopped from shooting Andre had been a mole — it had been he who tipped the Russians to Randi's presence on Fish Mountain. He had listened in on the call from Radleigh to Andre.

"How'd you know they were going to attack us? You have a mole in with them?" Joe asked between bites.

Andre merely raised his eyebrows. "The tactical officers used their night vision equipment to good effect when the bad guys came boiling around both sides of the cabin. The fellows with the night sights, on each end of the battle line, dropped them two by two until the last few dropped to the ground with their hands behind their necks." Andre sipped his coffee.

"My cousin, Mo, he saved your life, huh?" Joe washed down half his sandwich with a great slug of Pepsi.

"And Olivia saved Mo from your driver. He thought it was Mo who'd shot at you. It was pretty foggy out there." Rad said this to Andre with a french fry poised before her mouth. Instead of popping it in, she put it down on her plate.

"It was certainly foggy," Andre said.

Joe nodded his head and said, "Mmm hmm."

"What about the Sweet Cherries clubs? Anything going to happen to them?" Joe turned to Rad, "You want those fries?" She pushed the plate his way.

"ICE raided two-dozen of those clubs the next day and dozens of Eastern European women and some few American women were released. At least the Euros are free temporarily. The ones from the old Soviet bloc have nowhere to go and many will end up in similar circumstances. At least the American kids have a chance to go home. It will all be in court for a long time. No way of knowing the eventual outcome."

"You're telling me, without saying it, that these jerks are going to go right back into business aren't you?" Joe stared at Andre who again arched his eyebrows. "Is there someone in the government protecting them?"

Andre turned to face Rad and asked, "How did your friend fare? Is she back in The Big Easy? I must say that she has quite the grip. Bill still winces when he turns his right wrist just so."

"Relatively tiny hands and feet on a full-bodied woman is a hyper-feminine trait. There is a lot of power in those hands, they're like a lobster's crusher claw. I called it the grip of death in college. She has gone to the Akwesasne Rez with Mr. Snow. I believe they are an item." Rad smiled at her memory of the happiness Liv had shown when she headed off with Mo.

Joe moved Rad's plate on top of his own, he held three fries in his left hand, "Marv delivered Randi back to her mom, who now lives with a new husband in Manchester. He tells me that he asked her new step-father for permission to court Randi. The man said, no!" Joe let out a big belly laugh and said, "At least I didn't lose the old fool as my fishing partner."

Turn the page to order additional copies of this or other books from All Esox Publications.

ALL ESOX
PUBLICATIONS

Handy Order Form

Postal orders:
All Esox Publications
P.O. Box 493
East Aurora, New York 14052
Fax orders: 716-655-2621 Phone Orders: 716-655-2621
Email orders: info@allesoxpublications.com
Website: AllEsoxPublications.com

Please send more information on Publications: Yes______ No _______

Name:____

Address: ____

City:__________________State/Prov:_____ ZIP/Postal Code_______

Please send the following materials. I understand that I may return any of them for a full refund, for any reason, no questions asked.

Quantity	Title	Price	Total
_______	*Girls Before Swine*	$37.50 US	__________
_______	*Fireships & Brimstone*	$37.50 US	__________
_______	*The Accidental Musky*	$ 6.95 US	__________
_______	*The Quest for Girthra*	$16.95 US	__________
_______	*Becoming a Musky Hunter*	$14.95 US	__________
_______	Understanding River Muskellunge DVD:	$15.95 US	__________

Sales Tax: NYS residents add 8.25%..................__________
Shipping: U.S $4 (Can $5) for first item
$1 (Can $1.50) each add'l item ....__________
Total ....__________

Payment: Check____ Credit Card_____Visa___ Mastercard____

Card Number ____

Name (print)________________________Exp. Date _____________

Signature____